That Demon Life

That Demon Life

Lowell Mick White

ALAMO BAY PRESS
SEADRIFT·AUSTIN

Copyright © 2024 by Lowell Mick White

All rights reserved. No part of this book may be reproduced in any form without permission in writing from the publisher, except by a reviewer who may quote brief passages in a review.

Cover Design: ABP
Author Photograph: LMW
Book Design: ABP

For orders and information:

Alamo Bay Press
Pamela Booton, Director
825 W 11th Ste 114
Austin, Texas 78701
pam@alamobaypress.com
www.alamobaypress.com

Names: White, Lowell Mick, 1958- author.

Title: That demon life / Lowell Mick White.

Description: Second edition. | Seadrift, [Texas] ; Austin : Alamo Bay Press, [2024] | Previously published: Arlington, Va. : Gival Press, 2009.

Identifiers: ISBN: 978-1-943306-26-8 (paperback) | 978-1-943306-29-9 (ebook) | LCCN: 2024943057

Subjects: LCSH: Women lawyers--Texas--Austin--Fiction. | Criminals--Texas--Austin--Fiction. | Man-woman relationships--Fiction. | Extortion--Fiction. | Employees--Dismissal of--Fiction. | LCGFT: Humorous fiction. | Legal fiction (Literature) | Black humor. | BISAC: FICTION / Humorous / Dark Humor. | FICTION / Legal. | FICTION / Absurdist.

Classification: LCC: PS3623.H57865 T47 2024 | DDC: 813/.6--dc23

For
Pamela Booton

It's just that demon life
has got me in its sway
    —The Rolling Stones

All these people do is drink and drink and drink to boredom...and screw and screw and screw to death.
    —J. Frank Dobie

That Demon Life

1. The Crisis	1
2. Criminals	16
3. Personal Messes	26
4. Happiness	39
5. The Little Wagon	50
6. Law and Order	64
7. Grackles	77
8. Pave it All	89
9. Almost Relaxed	99
10. Too Much Trouble	106
11. Fitting	118
12. Brains	130
13. Down to the Limestone	140
14. Really Good Air Conditioning	151
15. Defenders of Civilization	172
16. Reasonable Accommodations	186
17. Poisoned	197
18. A Group Thing	206
19. Dad Always Knew You'd Do Good	224
20. I Will Help You	245
Epilogue	255
About That Demon Life	257
Acknowledgments	261
About Lowell Mick White	263

That Demon Life

Chapter One

The Crisis

AFTER A DULL NIGHT OF CRISIS—A LONELY NIGHT OF pacing, of fretting, of drinking and smoking, of making telephone calls to so-called friends who all seemed to be either drunk or sleeping or "busy"—Linda Smallwood stepped into her bedroom and found that one of her two monk parakeets had died.

Linda felt slightly ill. Not so much from the sight of the dead bird, a sad crumpled fluff of green and white feathers in the corner of the brass birdcage, as from the beginnings of a hangover. The drinking was starting to catch up with her—the fretting, too. She just couldn't seem to get a handle on her life: an image, a hazy idea of what had gone wrong would appear, but before Linda could bring herself to examine it, the idea would sort of—flutter away. It was the damndest thing. Frustrating! All night long Linda felt empty-headed and confused—vexed, tormented, tortured. She would have another glass of wine, make another fruitless phone call or two, and wait for another wispy, ill-formed idea to appear—and disappear. It was frustrating.

Now there was this dead parakeet—a small crisis compared to the larger crisis of her apparently wasted and ruined life, but a crisis nonetheless, and disturbing. The birds had been a gift of her ex-fiancé, and she had, over the years, become attached to them, though she never got around to naming them, and, indeed, had trouble telling them apart, referring to them vaguely as "That One Bird," and "That Other Bird." Right now, That One Bird was alive, rocking on its little swing. Linda thought it was the male, which would mean that That Other Bird was the female—dead.

"Well," Linda said aloud. She obviously couldn't go to sleep with a dead parakeet in the room. "*This* sucks."

Linda lifted the cage from its hook—That One Bird thrashing around to keep its balance—and carried it down the stairs, through the messy, cluttered living room to the front steps of her condo. Outside the morning was quiet and bright and hot—

Hot, she realized. Texas was hot in the summer. Hot. Those fluffy pink-tinted clouds that floated up to Austin from the Gulf in the early mornings would burn away by mid-day and the hard white sun would beat down, reflecting off the city's glass buildings, off the cars and SUVs on the expressways, heat radiating up from the concrete and asphalt. The day would be hot. Linda spent as much time as possible in dim, air-conditioned rooms, and she had tried to forget the sun, the outdoors, the Texas summer heat. Now she wondered if That Other Bird, the dead one, would start to stink.

Linda had a notion to call up her ex-fiancé, Gilbert Hardison, and tell him to get busy and dispose of the poor dead thing, except that Gilbert was too often unresponsive and difficult to motivate, not to mention lazy and argumentative and deliberately incompetent, and the dead bird really *would* stink by the time he to work.

Also, Linda had a blurry memory of calling Gilbert in the middle of the night and getting his fat new wife, who had sounded cranky.

Bitch.

That One Bird squawked and fluttered around the cage.

"What a mess," Linda said. "*Life*."

Part of the problem, Linda knew, was her job: she was a criminal defense attorney. What a stupid career choice *that* had been! She wanted a legal career like on television, where an attorney might get motivated enough to file a motion or something but would still have enough time to go to Happy Hour and have adventures. What had happened, though, was that she had been hired by a firm whose senior partners took the law seriously. For them it was a *calling*. They believed in justice, in the rule of law—and they expected her to believe in those things as well. She had heard all the stories about easy-going, relaxed Texas lawyers who blew cases or fell asleep in court or showed up drunk, only to find that in real life her bosses frowned on incompetence. Even worse, she had to get up in the goddamn *mornings* and try to be competent; she had to stagger around through the day half-asleep, unfocused, ill-tempered, quarrelsome, depressed. Mornings, Linda thought. Mornings. When am I supposed to sleep?

Maybe my life would be better if I just *quit*.

Linda tightened her grip on the cage and walked across the courtyard and banged on the door of her friend, Paige Davenport. Live oak and pecan trees shaded Paige's side of the complex, and wild birds, mostly great-tailed grackles, were happily croaking and hissing in the branches above. She banged on the door again, and it opened.

"Linda!" Paige said. She looked awfully bright and chipper for a Saturday morning—after what had probably been a long Friday night. Linda looked past Paige into the house and saw not only Paige's boyfriend's bicycle parked in the hallway, but also a large, naked black man stretched out on the couch, snoring.

"Oh, I guess you really *were* busy," Linda said. Paige led an—active—life.

"Are you feeling better?" Paige asked.

Linda shook her head. "One of these little birds died."

Paige stepped aside and Linda went past her and set the cage on the coffee table by the couch.

"Oh, that's too bad." Paige knelt down to look at the birds. "What happened?"

"Oh, I don't know," Linda said. "Maybe they have avian flu. Do you think?" She stared at the cage. It would be like Gilbert Hardison to give her sickly birds. "Maybe they're contagious—maybe we'll all get sick."

"You've had these birds for years," Paige said.

"So? Maybe it's a slow-acting flu."

"I doubt it." Paige shook her head and went back to the kitchen and picked up a mop. Linda watched her, marveling, as she usually did, that Paige, with her busy life—Paige, who worked, worked out, studied, tutored, drank, drugged, and had an unseemly if not totally absurd sex life—could find the time to keep her townhouse so utterly immaculate. Paige was manic, though. Maybe that helped.

"So you're not feeling better?" Paige asked.

"It's just one damn thing after another," Linda said. She lit a cigarette and blew smoke toward the ceiling. Paige went back to her mopping. That One Bird hopped around the cage, apparently untroubled by his dead mate. The black man sighed in his sleep, a deep sigh just this side of a moan. Linda felt another hollow wave of depression wash through her body. Really, it *was* just one damn thing after another. What a life. What a mess.

"I guess I need to find another job or something," Linda said. "I can't take this legal thing much longer." She thought for a moment, and sighed. "It's too much trouble to get up in the morning, and then when I do people are rude to me."

"You spent all that time in law school," Paige said.

"I *liked* law school," Linda said. Maybe I can go back, somehow, she thought. Well, no. Maybe not.

"There's other kinds of law you can do."

Linda shook her head. Mornings lurked everywhere. Rude people, too. She said, "I guess I need to get rid of That Other Bird."

"*I'm* not going to touch it," Paige said. "Poor little bird." Paige straightened up and stretched, immodest almost to the point of exhibitionism, wearing a black thong and a black t-shirt cropped so high on her flat belly that the bottoms of her breasts were showing. Paige was an athlete—track and field, body-building, tennis—and was in perfect shape.

"I didn't *ask* you," Linda said. "What about your boyfriend?"

Paige looked up the stairs to the bedroom and shrugged. She said, "*You* ask him."

The strange black man on the couch rolled to his side and mumbled something in his sleep. With an effort, Linda got out of her chair and trudged up the stairs. Maybe it was all a matter of *competence,* she thought. Maybe I'm—how goddamn embarrassing—*incompetent.* It could be, though. Probably. Maybe I was just born inept. Or maybe it was a matter of experience—maybe lack of experience could lead to incompetence and ineptitude. Linda had never had a real job before this stupid legal thing, and this stupid legal thing certainly wasn't working out. Always before in her life she'd gotten other people—mostly men—to do basic things for her: pay the cable bill, wash the car, dispose of dead parakeets—

Linda pushed open the bedroom door. Raul Ledesma was sleeping with his mouth open, boyish-looking and tranquil. Linda touched him on the shoulder.

"Raul, wake up."

Raul jerked awake, wild-eyed.

"I need some help."

Raul sat up and swung his legs off the bed, looking puzzled. Raul was soap opera-star handsome bordering on beautiful: late-twenties, dark hair, dark eyes, fine features. Linda thought he was an idiot.

"There's a dead bird out there you need to deal with."

"What?" Raul pulled a sheet across his lap to cover his

nakedness; he was unusually modest, for someone involved with Paige. "Deal with a dead bird?"

"*Dispose* of it," Linda said. "Come on." She turned and headed back down the stairs, assuming Raul would follow. Paige was scrubbing the already-gleaming sink. Linda leaned against the kitchen counter and sighed.

"I'm not even sure what's wrong," Linda said.

"Just try to isolate one problem," Paige suggested. "Then you can concentrate on fixing that one thing."

"One thing?" Linda shook her head. "Every goddamn thing."

Raul came out of the bedroom and started down the stairs, the sheet wrapped around his waist, but then he stopped—staring in surprise at the naked black man on the couch.

"Paige? Who's this—this *guy*?"

Linda lit another cigarette and watched Paige.

"Oh, I don't know," Paige said. She looked at Linda and winked. "He just sort of showed up this morning. It's not important."

"What?"

"What do you mean—what?" Paige was suddenly furious—violet blue eyes bulging, lip curled. "Who the hell are you to ask who I have for a guest in *my* home? Fuck you!"

Raul glared down at Linda as if she were somehow responsible for the strange man on the couch. Linda wasn't afraid of Raul but she took a step back just the same—and another step, and another, out the still-open door. Raul stomped down the stairs and slammed it shut in her face.

Linda heard Paige yell "Fuck you!" again, followed by the thump and crash of something—a lamp, maybe, or an ashtray—hitting the wall. The then door opened and Paige set the birdcage on the step. She looked at Linda and rolled her eyes. Then she ducked back inside and the door slammed again and Linda heard "*Motherfucker!*" followed by another heavy thump.

That One Bird in the cage—the living bird, the survivor—

flapped its wings and screeched. Linda suddenly decided that it was all Gilbert Hardison's fault. What the hell kind of engagement present were a pair of parakeets, anyway? Why hadn't he given her some pearls or something—diamonds, emeralds, a watch—something normal? Chocolate, even. Roses! Goddamn birds. It was crazy.

Gilbert Hardison was a big man, dark and powerful, yet he stepped lightly, cheerfully, coming down the stairs of his home, fumbling at his necktie. When he stopped at the mirror at the foot of the staircase to knot it properly, he could see around the corner into the living room, where his wife, Delia, was eating and watching television.

"You hear that phone ringing last night?" Delia asked.

"The phone? What phone?"

"You didn't hear it?"

"My cell phone?" Gilbert asked. The knot was wrong, the tie lopsided. Gilbert undid it and started over.

"It was ringing all night."

"Did you answer?" Gilbert was so big—his chest and his belly stuck out so far—that the tie looked too short. He wondered if they made especially long ties, somewhere.

"You need to turn that thing *off* when you go to bed."

"Who was it?"

"You need to stop giving your number out to people."

"Who was it?" Gilbert asked again. There was a long silence. Gilbert knotted the tie more or less adequately and went on into the kitchen. The remains of a huge breakfast cluttered the counters—broken eggshells, the crudely slashed rind of a grapefruit, slices of half-melted cheese in pools of congealing bacon grease. Gilbert frowned. "Hey, didn't you fix nothing for me?"

"Now, why would I fix something for you?" Delia asked. "I told you, that *phone* was ringing all *night*."

"Well, I'm hungry." Gilbert poured what coffee was left

in the pot, about half a cup. Half empty, he wondered, or half full. Or just half.

"I never did get back to sleep."

Gilbert looked around the corner at his wife. Delia was about to take a bite of a piece of crisp bacon. Gilbert lowered his gaze: he couldn't bear to watch his wife eat. Too often stray bits of food missed her mouth and tumbled down between her great, soft breasts. Popcorn was especially bad.

Delia noticed him and popped the bacon—most of it, at least—into her mouth. She slapped at the crumbs on her chest. "I said, I never *did* get back to sleep."

Gilbert said, "So take a damn pill."

"I have to work today!"

"So fucking work."

Delia turned and looked at him with cold, flat brown eyes. She was proud—ridiculously proud, Gilbert thought—of her job as a "dating consultant."

Gilbert asked, "What're you so pissed about?"

"I never said I was pissed."

"Well, you're *acting* pissed."

"You're not very observant."

"Well," Gilbert said, "something's going on, or else you wouldn't be acting this way."

"I said, you're not very observant."

"Maybe not," Gilbert said. He considered hurling the now fully empty coffee mug at the back of Delia's bitching, didn't get a wink of sleep skull, but he restrained himself. *I am restraining myself*, he thought. *I can do this.* Aloud, he said, "I got a murderer to go see."

"A murderer," Delia said. "On Saturday morning?"

"It's important."

"Important. Well, good for you."

"Yeah, it is," Gilbert said. "It's very good for me." He picked up his jacket and briefcase and went out into the garage, shutting the door behind him.

There was a brown-gray haze of smog lingering over the hills to the north and west, but the morning itself was sunny and traffic was, thankfully, light. Gilbert eased up Escarpment Boulevard, cheerful—a little more cheerful, at least—to be out of the house and away from Delia's griping. His neighborhood was brand new and fiercely suburban, and as he drove slowly along Gilbert read the passing street names. Many had Old West themes: Convict Hill Road, Abilene Trail, Open Range Trail, Wheel Rim Circle. Other streets were named after famous Texas cattlemen, like Richard King Trail, Issac Pryor Drive, or Robert Kleburg Lane. People liked the Western images, after all these citified years they still sold, they were still useful, they still somehow meant something to people. Gilbert in the past had sometimes even worn a cowboy hat to court until Delia told him he looked like a fool and made him stop.

Gilbert merged onto the expressway and zipped along to his exit, at Manchaca Road. Hungry, thinking of Delia and her selfish big breakfast, he drove through Taco Cabana for tacos and enchiladas and coffee. To get back around to Lamar Boulevard and his office, Gilbert cut through another neighborhood behind a strip mall, a somewhat older neighborhood but still with the Western street names: Frontier Trail, Roundup Trail, Western Trails Boulevard, Arapaho Pass. Those names, Gilbert thought, those Western names, they were something important—something he could maybe use.

Gilbert liked to brag that The Justice Store was the city's largest discount legal firm: starting with nothing, he had managed to build a minor empire with three locations—another on North Lamar, and one on East Seventh—employing a half-dozen paralegals and clerks. Tucked away in the dark, sunless corner of a red-brick strip-mall, the South Lamar location had been his favorite—*had* been, until Delia claimed half the space for her stupid dating service.

It was still kind of a shock. Delia had taken three offices on the left side of the hallway and had knocked out the walls, making one long, narrow room. She painted the walls purple and pink, and there were ferns and ivies and bright balloons hanging from the blue ceiling, with televisions and computers and jamboxes cluttering the desks and tables. There were giant fans in the corners blowing constantly, causing the plants and balloons to bob and toss around, and pieces of confetti to billow, and too often Dr. Dee's DateLine promotional material came sailing out into the hallway. Gilbert's clients, most of them poor, grim people in the middle of some serious crisis or other, would peek into the DateLine room—amazed, confused—as they passed down the hallway to the conference room or to Gilbert's personal office.

The office was at the back of the building, and Gilbert felt comfortable there, and safe—at least, when Delia wasn't around. There was a wide, sturdy sofa for napping between clients, and a television, a desk, and the usual diplomas on the walls—no one in Gilbert's family had been to college, much less law school—and photographs from his days as a linebacker for Baylor University. Gilbert had never been a star at Baylor, but he worked hard and was determined—he *had* played, just as he had graduated, had gone on to law school, and had made The Justice Store a successful business. Yet when he passed Delia's DateLine office and looked inside, it wasn't enough. Seeing the bobbing balloons, the swinging ivies, seeing Delia wrapped up in an apparently intense conversation with some rich young lonely computer professional, he felt amazed, too, and confused—and, somehow, mocked.

Now, though, Delia was safe at home, probably finishing off her second pound of bacon, and Gilbert felt secure. He dumped the bags of food onto his desk, tossed his jacket onto the couch, and sat down to eat his breakfast. He punched a button on the speakerphone to listen to his voicemail.

"Gilbert!" a familiar voice hissed. Gilbert was about to open the styrofoam box of enchiladas. He stopped and stared at the phone. A familiar voice—still familiar, though he had not heard it, had indeed been avoiding it, for something like over a year.

"I need to talk to you, goddammit! *Call* me!"

Gilbert reached over and punched the 3 button on the phone—delete.

"Message deleted," a flat computer voice said. "Save, delete, or next message."

Gilbert punched 6—Next Message.

"Goddammit, Gilbert, your wife answered the *cell* phone! Why'd you let her do that for? I mean—"

"Why're you whispering for?" Gilbert asked the phone. "Jesus."

"—I need help, you know? So call me—call me!"

"Crazy bitch," Gilbert said. He hit the 6 button.

"Message deleted. Save, Delete, or Next Message."

Gilbert hit the button for the next message.

"There are no more messages."

"Good," Gilbert said aloud. He looked down at his food and smiled. "Crazy bitch."

🍺 🍷 🥃 🍸

After her engagement with Gilbert collapsed, Linda had other men in her life, but they were about as distinct as the parakeets: there was That One Guy, That Other Guy, That Last Guy, That Little Guy, That Stupid Guy, and so forth. Linda was a demanding girlfriend, and tended to exhaust her guys with endless, tedious errands, most having to do with some form of cleaning, cooking, or car-repair. Some guys ran away, and some were dismissed because of performance problems, but Linda always seemed able to find another guy.

"It's amazing," Paige said once. "You treat these guys like shit, and they still do whatever you say."

"Yeah," Linda said, and a smile broke slowly across her face. "Yeah, and I don't look so good, either."

Which was not true, really. Linda was a tall, rangy woman, with sandy hair and warm brown eyes, and a decent figure that was beginning to sag a little in strategic areas as she slid into middle-age. She was, however, unusually indifferent to her appearance—her makeup was applied haphazardly, her hair stuck out at odd angles, and her clothes were rumpled even when she had a guy to do her ironing.

Now, though, Linda was between guys. The last one, a housepainter named Harold—was very good with a vacuum cleaner—had taken a load of trash out to the dumpster and had never returned. Since Paige wouldn't help, and Raul wouldn't help, and since she obviously couldn't touch the poor dead bird herself, the only thing to do was to get a new guy. Linda picked up the cage and crossed the courtyard and knocked on Tim Newlin's door. It opened immediately.

"I've got a problem here," Linda said.

"Yeah, I was watching," Tim said. He had sort of a dazed smile on his face—dazed, and sort of nervous. "Out the window. I like to sort of watch what goes on out here, you know?"

Linda looked at Tim's window: the bottom blades of the window blinds were broken back, and the glass was smudged, where Tim's face had apparently been pressed against it.

"Oh, you're a spy, too. I like that." Linda had known Tim for a couple of years but had never taken him seriously as a—guy. He was ten or twelve or maybe even fifteen years younger than she was, and seemed to lack focus—he spent all his time smoking pot and managing a couple of pornographic web sites. Still, he was convenient and available. "You've got to help me with this bird."

"Oh." Tim looked at the cage for a moment, blinking. "Uh, which one?"

"The goddamn dead one! Jesus!"

The door to Paige's townhouse opened and Linda and Tim turned to look. The large black man stepped out, looking sleepy in the harsh morning sunlight, fully clothed but rumpled in a Dallas Cowboys jersey and a pair of striped shorts that hung down below his knees—they looked like kilts, Linda thought. When he noticed Linda and Tim staring at him, he straightened up and walked off, almost swaggering.

"Help me with the bird," Linda said again.

"Oh, right." Tim disappeared into his apartment and came out with a plastic grocery bag. He knelt down by the cage. "Just throw her away?"

"Yes!" Great, Linda thought, another stupid guy.

Tim stuck his hand inside the cage. That One Bird was hopping around, getting in the way. Tim tried to nudge it aside with his wrist, but just as he picked up the dead bird, the living bird panicked or something and scraped up past his forearm toward the door.

"Hey!" Linda yelled. "Watch it!"

Tim tried to block the parakeet—he pinned its little wing to the cage for a moment—but it got past him and fluttered up into the trees.

"Well, goddamn," Linda said. "I didn't want you to let That One Bird *loose!*"

"I'm sorry," Tim said. He stood with That Other Bird dead in his hand. "I'm sorry. I just—"

"Screwed up," Linda finished. "Yeah, I saw. Damn."

Tim didn't say anything. He put the dead bird in the plastic bag. Linda was staring anxiously up into the trees. After a moment he asked, "You want me to—throw her away?"

"Yes—and be quick about it."

Tim trotted off to the dumpster with the bag—with That Other Bird. Linda lit another cigarette. Grackles fluttered in the branches above her but there was no sign of That One Bird. She heard a door open and turned to see Raul, shirtless but wearing a pair of red gym shorts, wheeling his bicycle out of Paige's townhouse. "Don't come back!" Paige shouted. The door slammed shut. My life has changed, Linda thought, looking back up into the trees for the lost parakeet. All that old stuff is—over. Flown away. She watched Raul mount his bike and ride off, passing Tim coming back from the dumpster. Over.

"Well, that's done," Tim said.

"Yeah, it is," Linda said. "Listen, you think That One

Bird can live outside?"

"Sure, I guess," Tim said. "I read in the paper there's like this whole flock of feral parakeets living south of the river."

"Feral parakeets," Linda repeated. What an ominous sounding phrase. Linda looked up into the trees again, but now even the grackles seemed to have flown away. The sun-dappled branches were empty. Her eyes teared. It was all over. "God*damn*."

"I'm really sorry," Tim said. "Wasn't he—they—a gift?"

"Some goddamn gift," Linda said bitterly. "Where're my pearls?"

"Yeah," Tim said, though he didn't know what she was talking about.

"Maybe if we set some food out, he'll come back," Linda said. "Sort of set a trap."

"Sure," Tim said. "It's worth a try."

"Good," Linda said. "You can get to work on that later."

"Oh, okay," Tim said slowly. He thought, Later?

Linda threw her cigarette to the ground and stepped on it. "Listen, are you busy now?"

"I—I guess not."

"Good. I need some more help. C'mon."

Linda walked away, leaving the birdcage on its side in front of Tim's door. Tim hesitated—what he really wanted to do was smoke some more pot and update his gay porn site and maybe think about how he was supposed to trap That One Bird—but after a moment he followed her up the stairs to her townhouse. Linda was in the kitchen, opening a bottle of merlot.

"Okay," Linda said, "first, I need you to take these empty bottles down to the dumpster." She pointed at a box full of empty wine bottles. "And I want you to make sure that people don't *see* the bottles—I know how people talk."

"Right," Tim said. "Sure."

"Then you can wash the dishes and do the vacuuming. I'm going to bed."

"Okay," Tim said, looking around the kitchen, the living

room, noticing a half-dozen or so dirty wine glasses and coffee mugs, at least four overflowing ashtrays, a bowl's worth of spilled popcorn stomped into the carpet, and odd clumps of clothing Linda had shed during the night as she paced and worried. A pile of newspapers, a beer can or two, stale pizza crusts, a stack of junk mail. Messy, messy, Tim thought. Messy. The room of a depressed person. But I guess I maybe owe her for the bird. Plus maybe I can get laid.

"Take those pizza boxes out, too." Linda poured another glass of wine.

"What about all these folders?" Tim pointed to a box of multicolored file folders—red, blue, yellow, green—that had overturned on the couch and spilled to the floor. Various legal-looking papers were sticking out of the folders—many of the papers had footprints on them, or soggy splotches of spilled wine.

"Just stack 'em somewhere," Linda said.

"Aren't they important?" Tim bent over and picked up a green folder that had been mangled or bent or something. Not only was there a footprint on it—there was a tire track, too. He frowned. "Aren't these your client folders?"

"My clients are just a bunch of goddamn criminals," Linda said. She slowly started up the stairs to her bedroom. "To hell with 'em."

Chapter Two

Criminals

CRIMINALS, SHE THOUGHT. CRIMINALS. *THEM.*

Linda slowly undressed to shower before sleeping, frowning, frowning. The parakeet crisis had distracted her from her Life crisis, but the little slacker, Tim, with his question, "Aren't these your *client* folders?," had brought her right back to where she had been all night—worried, worried, burdened with worry about her life, her job, her life, her job—her aptitude, her ineptitude—and all the damn *criminals* that seemed to surround her.

They were everywhere. They filled Linda's life; it seemed like there was no escape. Every miserable morning when she dragged herself out of bed and stumbled down to the office, haggard and hungover and worn-out, there they were—more criminals, more stupid people with stupid problems. And they all wanted something—from her! Sometimes they even called her at night! It was more than she could deal with. Lately, Linda had been thinking that she would be happiest if all the criminals could just be *executed*—gassed, electrocuted, shot, hanged—killed, somehow, all of them. Even if they were her clients—maybe especially if they were her clients and had tried calling her in the morning. She was not blind to the fact that her clients were all guilty—of something. Hell, everyone she knew was guilty of *something*, and only rarely was anyone punished for anything. And the criminals were also mostly uncouth and ill-educated, with crazy chaotic lives, the kinds of people she did not want to associate with. They were irritating—they were annoying. Something had to be done.

Linda had been pondering this one evening at Happy Hour, sitting with Paige and some other people, when her cell phone rang. Another criminal, she assumed—it seemed like the idiots always called either during Happy Hour or when she was trying to sleep.

"Law office," she barked into her phone.

But this time it wasn't a criminal, it was a guy named Wes Leonard, a columnist for the local newspaper. He usually wrote folksy columns about colorful Texas stuff, but now he was doing a more serious piece about capital punishment. He wanted the opinion of a defense attorney—a *female* defense attorney, at that—who might be sympathetic to—

"Oh, hell, just line the sons-of-bitches up against a wall and shoot 'em," Linda said, interrupting him.

"What?"

"You heard me," Linda said. "Line 'em up against a wall and shoot 'em. Or gas 'em, or whatever. Just kill 'em all."

Linda remembered that Paige and the other people at the table all fell silent—listening, very amused.

"Are you serious?" the columnist asked.

"Hell, yes, I'm serious! We need to rid the streets of all that scum out there—we need to be like in those Muslim countries where they chop off their hands, they chop off their heads—they just kill 'em all. You think some guy with no hands and no head is gonna steal my stereo? I mean, get serious."

The columnist asked a few more questions. Linda couldn't remember what they talked about, she remembered only the amusement on the faces of Paige and the others. Then the columnist got off the phone, and Linda went on to get drunk, as she usually did at Happy Hour. The incident didn't cross her mind for over two weeks, until—yesterday.

Linda stepped out of the shower and listened for a moment. She could hear the vacuum running downstairs—a friendly sound. For a pornographer, Tim seemed to be very loyal. He might not turn out to be house-husband material, but at least he wouldn't just disappear on the way back from the dumpster. Paige was loyal, too, and always had been, always, though she made it clear that she thought the whole thing was a tremendous joke. No doubt for her it was, but to be *involved* in it all—my God! What a burden—and it was all the criminals' fault!

Linda dried off and put on a white t-shirt and blue gym shorts and crawled into bed. The room was dim and cool, and quiet now that the birds were gone. Goddamn criminals, she thought. Goddamn Gilbert! Birds—*dead* birds. Flyaway birds. Feral parakeets. Linda listened to the vacuum cleaner, listened and fretted, back on the endless circular carking worry-track she'd been on all night.

Linda seldom took the time to read the morning newspaper, of course. It seemed like she never had time to do anything except hang out at night and rush around during the day half-comatose from getting up too early, ill and cranky, trying to arrange probation for her criminals. But still, when she showed up Friday morning at Travis County Court-at-Law 6-B, she did notice—despite a slight hangover—that all the regulars sort of *stared* at her. Even her criminal of the day, a young, wild-haired thug named Love, eyed her warily as they sat on a bench in the hallway.

"Say," Love said, after a few minutes.

Linda was searching through her client folders, trying to find something about this Love character. Originally there had been some sort of order to the colored file folders—different colors for different kinds of criminals—but Linda had quickly forgotten which color she had chosen for what crime, and now it was all just a confusing jumble.

"*Say!*"

Linda looked up. "What?"

"Say, what's this about you wantin' to lynch me?"

"What?" Linda asked. "Don't be absurd."

"Linda!" someone called. Linda looked around and saw Angie Hunter, a secretary, standing in an office doorway holding a newspaper. She was smiling. "This article's hilarious!"

"What article?" Linda glanced at Love.

"This." Angie came over and spread the newspaper over the colored folders. "You're famous!"

At first all Linda saw was the photograph—a black-and-white shot of a severe-looking young blond woman in a ball gown. She looked familiar. Some time passed—several heartbeats, each harder than the preceding one—and then Linda realized, *Oh, that's me.*

Linda read the headline.

Debutante Justice: 'Let's Kill 'em All'

"I don't get it," Linda said, though a vague memory of talking to some reporter guy was fluttering around in the back of her mind.

"It's about how you want me dead!" Love said.

Linda read:

> Friends, we have reached a turning point in Texas, if not in the nation as a whole. Forget all that high-falutin' talk about a public backlash against capital punishment. What we seem to have here is a backlash against the capital punishment backlash.
>
> "Oh, hell, we might as well kill 'em all," says Austin defense attorney Linda Smallwood.
>
> That's right. Austin defense attorney. Defense attorney, as in charged with saving criminals from

> execution; and Austin, as in the former "liberal oasis" of Texas. What we have here is a defense attorney in favor of lynching her own clients.
>
> "Why not?" asks Smallwood. "We ought to be like in those Arab countries where they chop off [the criminals'] heads or whatever. You think some guy's going to rob me after his head's been chopped off?"
>
> Smallwood, 39, is a former San Antonio debutante—

"What has *that* got to do with anything?" Linda asked. She looked again at the photo at the top of the column. She looked mad—she remembered *being* mad. The whole debutante process had been tortuous and infuriating. She'd had endless fights with her mother over her hair, over her makeup, over the damn dress—and the damn dress itself was tortuous and infuriating: heavy, constricting, sweaty, uncomfortable. Linda's father was drinking a lot in those days, and he got a great deal of pleasure from all the arguing, all the messy family drama, pleasure that Linda did not share. And her date was a dolt—the whole thing was a disaster. Linda ended up fleeing the ball and hooking up with Paige, and they drove up to Austin to see one of Paige's boyfriends, a musician named Sweeny. Then off to a beer joint out by Lake Travis, drinking beer, playing pool, dancing to an amateurish blues band in the stupid hot dress. Sweeny had a dog that drank beer, too, a dachshund named Larry. Linda remembered dancing with Larry, the little dog tucked under her arm. But what did all that have to do with the death penalty? Linda said, "That was a long *time* ago."

> —and an associate at the Austin law firm Foster & Moomaw. Though she's never had the opportunity to "defend" someone charged with a capital crime, she's ready.
>
> "Heck, I'd strap 'em to the gurney myself,"

Smallwood says. "I'd even stick the I-V in their arms—wouldn't that be sexy?"

Hmm. Well, no, not really.

"I mean, I was at a football game a few years ago, and there were like 80,000 people or so there, and it occurred to me that someday those 80,000 people would all be dead. So now when I see some criminal sitting my office, I think, 'Why not kill this idiot now and get it over with so I can make it to Happy Hour on time?'"

What about charges that the death penalty is applied unfairly to minorities?

"Not a problem," Smallwood says. "We'll just round up some white people and execute *them*. It's been my experience that white people instigate all the trouble around here, anyway. We'll just empty out some trailer parks—we'll clean up this country in a hurry!"

Indeed. And lawyer Linda Smallwood could pull the guillotine lever herself.

Justice for All! Let the Terror Begin!

"What a bunch of shit!" Linda tossed the newspaper to the floor. "I never said *any* of that—not exactly."

"But it's in the paper," Angie pointed out.

"Yeah," Love said. "All that lynchin' shit."

"Lies," Linda said. "I never once mentioned lynching."

Another clerk stuck her head out of the courtroom. "Linda? Aren't you handling that McNeil case?"

Linda looked back at her folders. "I think so—"

Love said, "That's me."

Linda looked at him, frowning. "Your name's *McNeil*? You must be in the wrong folder."

Love shrugged.

"The judge wants you now." The clerk went back inside.

"Oh, well, come on," Linda said to Love. She led the way into the courtroom.

🍷🍶🍸🍺

"Ah, so they found you," Judge Richard A. Cantu said when Linda and Love took their places in front of him. A newspaper was spread out across his bench. "You were out in the hallway, what, planning some execution or something?"

"*No*," Linda said sharply. Linda did not know Judge Cantu very well, but he had always seemed like one of the bouncy, aggressive little guys she found so very annoying—a little on the chubby side, though, and roundish: round body, round balding head, round brown eyes behind round glasses. Today Linda thought he looked worn-out, tired, and hungover. She repeated, "No."

"But the newspaper says you're big for these executions, right?"

"Yeah," Love nodded.

"I don't know what the newspaper says."

"But you was just readin' it," Love said.

The prosecutor laughed. Linda had him figured out, too: he was one of those wussy white guys who grew bushy, bandito-style moustaches in an attempt to look fierce. But when Linda glared at him he looked away.

"No?" Judge Cantu looked at her flatly, with his tired round eyes. "From what I read here, we need to fit you with one of those black hoods like those guys in the cartoons wear—"

Black hoods like those guys in the cartoons wear. Goddamn. Linda looked down, red with embarrassment and growing irritation. I could be home in bed, she thought. I should be home in bed. I could wake up when I wanted to, watch TV....

"—so you can kill these people in style, you know, the old-fashioned way. I think you might look pretty good in one of those, huh? With a black bag over your head?"

"I don't think so," Linda said. "Judge."

"No? Well, that's good," Cantu said. "'Cause I'm the

judge, right? That's *my* job."

"To wear a—a bag over your head?"

"To decide who gets executed!"

Linda looked warily at Richard Cantu. He had only been a judge for three months, appointed by the County Commissioners to fill out the elected term of the previous judge, who had dropped dead of a heart attack while shopping at Wal-Mart. Even so, Cantu should have known that low-level County Court-at-Law Judges did not handle capital murder cases—District Judges did. Linda considered reminding him of that, but thought better of it.

"Oh," she said. "Okay. Whatever."

"Well, all right, then." Cantu folded the newspaper and set it aside, and then looked through some other papers in front of him. After a moment he asked, "Is this Mr. McNeil?"

"Yeah, Judge—I think so." Linda started searching through her folders again. "Maybe."

"You *think* so? Maybe?"

"They call me Love," Love said. He was staring at the floor.

"Yeah, I think that's his name—McNair, or something. If you can just give me a second so I can find his folder...."

The prosecutor snickered again, and when Linda looked up to glare at him she somehow lost her grip on the folders, and they scattered to the floor.

"They call me Love."

"Shut up," Linda said. She was looking at the floor trying to find the folder.

"Ms. Smallwood..." Cantu began.

"There it is!" A yellow folder. Linda bent over and picked it up. "Yeah," she said, "James McNair is his name, right?"

"Ms. Smallwood," Cantu began again. He closed his eyes and took a deep breath, his face gray and puffy. He looked sick. "I'm not exactly a bleeding heart, but I *do* think an attorney really should know his client's name."

"*His* clients?" Linda asked.

"*Your* client," Cantu said. He took another deep breath

and finally opened his eyes to squint at Linda. "You don't even know your client's *name*."

"Well, come on, memorizing all that shit—all that—it's a lot of trouble." Linda shrugged. This goddamn sick judge—he obviously had a hangover. He must still be impaired. Drunk, or crazy. He probably liked to get *up* in the mornings, the fool. "I mean, what difference does it make? The kid's obviously guilty. I think he even admits it in here somewhere."

"Admits what?" Cantu asked. "No, Ms. Smallwood, don't look in your folder. Do you know what your client's even charged with?"

Linda looked at McNair—or McNeil, or whatever his name was. Love. He wasn't very large, so he probably wasn't a bully, or an armed robber. He probably wasn't a burglar, either: the first burglar Linda defended had had an immense, fetus-like head, and Linda now associated burglars with that strange scary look.

"Listen," Linda said. "I've been *really* busy, okay?"

Cantu didn't say anything. He slowly closed his eyes and sighed.

Linda glanced again at her client. Love was young, black, nervous—somewhat thuggish, but otherwise normal-looking. *Normal*. She guessed, "Drugs?"

Cantu opened his eyes and squinted at the prosecutor. "Mr. Andersen? What's Mr. McNeil charged with?"

Andersen looked in his own folder. "Possession of drug paraphernalia."

"Well, all right, then!" Linda was pleased. But then she looked down into the yellow folder and frowned. "Hey, wait a minute—this guy's McNair, right? Driving while intoxicated?"

Cantu ignored her. "Is this the defendant's first offense?"

Andersen nodded. "On this charge, yeah."

"I'm going to dismiss." Cantu looked at Love. "You don't want to come back here, Mr. McNeil, do you?"

Linda said, "McNair, right?"

Love shook his head. "Huh-uh, sir."

"McNair?"

"I think you've been punished enough." Cantu smacked his gavel. "Dismissed. Ms. Smallwood, I suggest you go home and give some serious thought to your career." Before Linda could say anything Cantu stood up and rapped the gavel again. He said, "I need a break."

Give some serious thought to your career. The son-of-a-bitch. Serious thought! For a whole day, for an entire awful night, Linda had done nothing else except think seriously about her career, about her *life*—and she had gotten nowhere. Nowhere. Now, stretched out uneasily in the dim, silent bedroom, exhausted, on the cusp of sleep, Linda suddenly realized that the criminals weren't the problem, and neither was her aptitude—the goddamn *system* was the problem. The system—the tyranny, the oppressiveness of authority, the incredible rudeness of Judge Cantu—*that* was the problem. Judge Richard A. Cantu, that asshole. Everything was all his goddamn fault.

Chapter Three

Personal Messes

A STIFF, HOT WIND WAS BLOWING, AND THE HAIR ON top of Richard Cantu's head blew back, exposing his bare skull. He wished he had a baseball cap to wear. But there were no caps—his wife, Kelly, had nagged him for years about baseball caps and how *stupid* he looked when he wore them, nagged him and nagged him until finally he gave in and the caps went to Goodwill, and now he had to stand outside on a hot, windy, Saturday afternoon, mowing his yard bareheaded.

It was the damndest thing. What was it women had against baseball caps? Richard had a friend in law school—a big, rugged, handsome guy—who'd said that his fiancée would not let him wear a baseball cap. Richard had lost respect for his friend right then, the poor, pussy-whipped fool—no woman was going to tell *him* what to wear on his head! And, in fact, it had taken Kelly almost 15 years to break him of caps—but she *had* done it. "Go ahead," Kelly would always say, "wear what you want. But you have no idea how utterly *stupid* you look." After almost 15 years her determined, unending nagging worked. After almost 15 years Richard realized that he was as spineless and hen-pecked as any other man.

He shut off the mower and looked back over the yard. Not too bad. A little edging and it would look fine. He pushed the mower back to the garage, leaving a little wheeled trail in the grass—Richard noticed the trail and wished for a moment that his son, Davy, would come out and join him in the yard work—to rake the clippings or just joke around a little. Maybe they could toss a baseball around. But Davy was a strange, quiet boy who did not like to go outside; he was up in his room, reading, or playing on his computer, or something. Richard knew that if he asked Davy to come out, he would likely be met by a refusal and maybe even tears—how embarrassing, his own boy crying like that, over nothing, and Davy would surely tell his mother, and Kelly would get mad, too, and her anger would spread to their daughter, Amy, and the whole household would be clouded in anger and resentment—and tears—and Richard would be left outside, alone in the yard, the sun beating down on his bald head—mad, too, if nothing else mad at himself for finally giving in about the baseball caps, mad at himself for being such a damn pussy.

Richard parked the mower in the front of the garage and went inside the house. The kitchen was dim, and cool, and he went over to the phone and dialed a number. Instead of a person, he got a voicemail message. At the beep, he said, "Hey! It's me! I'll see you at Caesar's at 8:30 or so," and hung up.

Outside, Richard untangled the long cord of the electric weed-whacker and plugged it in. He tested it—the machine whirred deeply—and waded into the weeds along the side of the house. Oh, hell, he thought. I am so tired, tired, *tired*.

He looked up in time to see his wife's minivan come round the corner and pull into the driveway. He shut the whacker off and walked over to the car. His daughter, Amy, got out first.

"Hey there, girl!" Richard said, smiling. "You get me something good to eat?"

"Nothing *I* wanted," Amy said sullenly. She went into the garage and through the kitchen door.

Kelly got out of the car. She was tall, slender, blond, with ancient acne scars along her cheeks.

"I'm about done!" Richard pointed at the yard.

"Yeah," Kelly said. "Help me with these bags."

Richard helped his wife carry in the groceries. The supermarkets were all using plastic bags now, and when the bags plopped down on the table or countertop, they would collapse and the contents of the bag—cans, bottles, whatever—would flop to the floor. Richard—gracefully, he thought, like a cat—caught a package of pork chops as they fell. He held them up to show Kelly.

"Dinner," she said.

"Good." Richard put his arm around Kelly and kissed her neck.

"You're all hot and sweaty," Kelly said.

"Yeah, I've been working in the yard."

"That's no reason why you can't take a shower." Kelly pulled away and returned to putting up groceries. "Besides, I didn't ask you *how* you got all hot and sweaty—I just said that you *were*."

"I need to finish the trimming," Richard said. He waited a moment, but Kelly didn't answer him: she was peering intently into a cupboard. He trudged back outside and slowly picked up the weed-whacker. Really, it was the damndest thing. He was just so tired—so *tired* of being *married*. He never thought it would happen to him.

🍺 🍸 🍻 🍷

After a long, refreshing nap and another quick swing through Taco Cabana, Gilbert Hardison went up to the new criminal justice building to see his murderer. Billy Johnston, a skinny little sad white man, was a chronic amphetamine user who didn't quite understand why he was charged with capital murder—the killing and robbing of a cab driver.

"You *shot* the man," Gilbert said. He wanted to keep the meeting short, but Johnston was so depressed that he wanted to go over the crime again and again—as if in the retelling the event itself might somehow actually change. "You shot the man, and then you took his wallet, right? And then you rolled his body in the creek and drove the cab on home to your house, right?"

"Yeah, well, but I didn't really *rob* the guy," Johnston said. He shook his head slowly. "I just sort of...."

"You just sort of stole his wallet once he was already dead," Gilbert finished, smiling—amused. That had been a stroke of luck, Johnston's taking the wallet: for some reason, the cab driver had been carrying a business card from The Justice Store. When Johnston woke up the next afternoon, wrung out and worried, aware that he had made a big mistake, he'd come across the card and had called Gilbert seeking legal representation.

"But I'm not a *robber*," Johnston insisted.

Gilbert leaned back in his chair and shrugged. It didn't matter anymore. Gilbert had helped Johnston turn himself in, and was confident that they could get the charges knocked down from capital murder—carrying the death penalty—to second degree murder or maybe even manslaughter. The only thing pending was the fee. Gilbert's usual practice when he had a client in serious trouble was to demand everything they owned. Since most of these criminals were poor people—small-time chiselers, drunks, drug addicts, scofflaws—Gilbert didn't get too much for his work: cheap jewelry, television sets, stereos, and DVD players, mostly, which he had a secretary carry over to the nearest pawnshop. But Billy Johnston—William *Beitleman* Johnston—was different. This murderer, pathetic and grungy and depressed, was the sole and unencumbered owner of Beitleman Ranch, 825 reasonably pristine acres southwest of town, straight in the path of the city's growth corridor.

Gilbert took some papers from his briefcase and slid them across the table to Johnston. "I drew up this deed," he said. "Sign it, and I'll take it by the courthouse on Monday."

Johnston shook his head and shivered. "Man, oh, man," he said quietly.

"You need to sign this," Gilbert said. "Otherwise they're going to kill you. I'm saving your life, right?"

Johnston kept shaking his head. "This was my *family's* place."

"This was your family's place," Gilbert repeated. "But it's not going to do you any good dead. The Governor's gonna stick a goddamn needle in your arm unless you let me help you, you know?"

"Shit," Johnston said. But he signed the deed.

🍸🍺🍷

Bright light flooded the room, and Linda cracked open an eye to see Paige standing in front of her bedroom window. It was early evening but the summer sun was still very bright—too damn bright. Linda rolled over and pulled a sheet up close to her face.

"Close the blinds," she said.

"It's depressing in here," Paige said. "You need some sunlight."

"People are looking in at us."

"There's nobody out there to look in at us."

"Paige, there are goddamned serial killers out there looking in at us right now—so close the damn blinds!"

Paige didn't see any serial killers outside perched in the trees peering in, but she lowered the blinds anyway, leaving the flaps mostly open. The room dimmed but was still too bright for sleep. Linda rolled back over to face Paige.

"Thank you," she said softly.

"I hate to see you wallowing in depression," Paige said.

"I'm not wallowing," Linda said. She thought, *depressed*. Depression—maybe that's my problem. Maybe. She said, "I'm not wallowing, I'm—*lounging*."

Paige frowned. "Well, you can lounge later. I made an appointment for you to see Madame Bustos. She'll come up with a solution."

"Oh, great," Linda said. Madame Bustos was her favorite

psychic, but Linda wasn't in a mood to see anyone, much less someone with psychic powers. "I don't have anything to wear," Linda said. "Besides, I bet she saw that—thing—in the newspaper, and she hates me."

"Madame Bustos has the power to see very deeply," Paige said. "I'm sure she knows the truth about you. So get up—we're late."

Paige left the room and Linda heard her talking to someone downstairs—Tim, probably. Linda lay on her back, staring at the ceiling. She was quite fond of Madame Bustos, who had been one of her very first clients. Linda had defended her after she had been arrested on a charge of fortune-telling—you could read the past in Texas, or the present, but not the future. Madame Bustos had arrived at the law office without an appointment, and the receptionist had dumped her off onto Linda, bringing her to the door and gravely announcing "Madame Bustos" as if they were at a formal state dinner. Linda had been flummoxed—here was no ordinary poverty-ridden, scummy, ignorant crook but a beautiful woman with black hair and thin features and clear brown skin, sitting impeccable and straight in a well-tailored suit. They stared at each other for several moments—Linda, sleepy, trying not to yawn.

Finally, Madame Bustos said, "I believe that you are in your first incarnation as a woman."

Linda said, "What?"

"I'm getting the feeling that this is your first incarnation as a woman."

Linda thought about that. She asked, "Are you saying I'm a lesbian?"

"No, no—only always before you have been a man. This is your first incarnation as a woman. You're just not used to it yet."

Linda smiled, touched, her life finally defined. From then on, whenever someone would make a snarky comment about her housekeeping or appearance or attitude, she'd snap, "This is my first incarnation as a woman—give me a goddamn break."

Now, though, the truth of her incarnation did not cheer Linda. Making a fool of yourself in the newspaper didn't really depend on home many times you had been incarnated as a man or as a woman—or as a dog, or as a fruit fly, for that matter—only on how many times you opened your stupid mouth, or, really, only on making a poor career choice, on having to get up in the mornings, on how long you had been compelled to get up way way *way* too early, pushed to the brink of madness by lack of sleep and a bunch of goddamn needy criminals and cocky lawyers and rude arrogant judges. What a world. One goddamn thing after another. Linda sighed and stretched, lounging, lolling, wallowing, staring at her ceiling: shadows moved slowly across the plaster. She didn't want to move.

"Linda!" Paige yelled from downstairs. "We're late!"

"Well, goddamn," Linda said to herself. She rolled out of bed and slowly dressed. A bra was far too much trouble, as was makeup. Linda crawled into an oversized University of Texas sweatshirt and a pair of jeans. After a few minutes of hunting around she was able to find a pair of sneakers that matched, and she put those on. She had gone to bed straight from the shower, with her hair still wet; it had dried and tangled as she slept and was sticking out in various directions. She tried running a comb through it a time or two, then a brush, then gave up. "To hell with it," she sighed. It was only Madame Bustos. If she really did see very deeply, she'd quickly see how desperate—how depressed—Linda was.

🍶 🍸 🍺 🍷

Though her name implied that she was Hispanic, Linda knew that Madame Bustos was really from Mumbai, by way of Houston. On first seeing her, noticing her deep brown eyes and dark complexion, most people in Texas assumed that she was Mexican. It had happened so often that Madame Bustos took the professional name Bustos, a good Spanish name—though, not speaking Spanish, she referred to herself as "Madame" rather than "Señora." She did a very good business, meeting with clients in the spacious but dimly-lit dining room of her old house, reading palms and tarot cards and crystals. Linda, though, relied on Madame Bustos' reading of what she called "the wild stones"—a blue-tinted glass jar filled with pebbles "from the rivers of the world."

"All rivers feed into one," Madame Bustos said. "The waters of the world know many secrets, and they share their secrets with the stones."

Though Linda was always tempted to ask why the hell they didn't just gaze into a goddamn bucket of water and cut out the middleman, she refrained. She'd once read an article about a forensic geologist who'd solved a murder with a handful of gravel, or something—she couldn't remember the details, exactly, but based on the blurry memory she was inclined to accept that the stones might know a secret or two.

Linda reached into the jar and pulled out a handful of stones—eight, when they counted them, tan, brown, reddish, round, smooth, jagged. They made little clicking sounds as Madame Bustos moved them around the table.

"So what's the word?" Linda asked.

"I don't know yet," Madame Bustos said. She reached out and touched one of the smooth brown stones—then drew her hand back as if it were hot.

"I think I've made a lot of bad decisions," Linda said. "My life is a mess."

"Wait—" Madame Bustos began.

"Messes are the fun part," Paige said. "Messes make life interesting."

"Not really," Linda said. *Other* people's messes were sometimes interesting, from a distance. That was why it was fun to watch *COPS*, or read the *National Enquirer*. Personal messes, though, were—messy. And personal. "I think maybe I should just—retire."

"No," Madame Bustos said. "Wait. This—situation—could turn out okay for you, I think."

"If you make the right decisions," Paige said. Linda shot her a dark look.

"Certainly." Madame Bustos pursed her lips.

"That's not terribly reassuring."

"Well, look, you have a lot going on here, there are many factors at—"

"Play," Paige said.

"—*work*," Madam Bustos said, glancing at Paige. "And if things go well, they will be fine."

"Certainly," Linda said tartly. She slumped back in her chair. "Boy, *that* tells me a whole hell of a lot."

Madame Bustos looked at the stones for a long time. "Linda, there are many possible paths here that you can choose, though every path has its own mess, you know? And all the paths have the same end."

"Death," Paige said, nodding.

"Well, goddamn," Linda said. "If that's the case I might as well retire. I could stay home and watch TV, if people would just leave me the hell alone. You know?"

"That is a possible path," Madame Bustos said. "But if you take it, you will miss out on some possibly good things."

"Messes," Linda said.

Madame Bustos shook her head, gazing again at the stones. "You *do* have an enemy—that's always good to know."

Of course, Linda thought. Judge Cantu, the prick. He's an enemy. She leaned over the table, trying to read the stones.

Madame Bustos closed her eyes. "I'm getting, I don't know—a dark man, sort of fat, kind of bald."

Linda nodded. "Richard Cantu. He was rude to me."

"Not an enemy, really, more of a bad influence."

"He was rude," Linda said. She told Madame Bustos what had happened in court on Friday. Paige, who had heard the story eight or nine times, listened to it again, shaking her head. Linda said, "He told me to think about my career! The little shit—as if I *cared* about my goddamn career."

"I'm not sure," Madame Bustos said. She sighed. "The stones indicate that soon you will make decisions—make the right ones, and your situation will improve. Make the wrong ones—"

"And you're screwed," Paige finished. "And you need to look out for that enemy."

"The bad influence," Madame Bustos said. "Your decisions are linked to the bad influence. It will be best if you just try to avoid the bad influence. You know?"

🍸 🍹 🍺 🍷

Ceasar's was a dark little beer joint set into the west side of a parking garage, and every time someone opened the door a shaft of the setting sun would shoot in, blinding the customers along the bar. Everyone would squint for a moment or two while their eyes readjusted; generally the regulars avoided looking at the door. Richard Cantu, though, watched the door intently, sitting alone, sipping a beer. He knew it was foolish to feel like a teenager, but there it was—every time the door opened and the light shot in, his heart took a couple of extra heavy beats, just on the chance that it might be Giselle. A television behind the bar was showing a baseball game, the Rangers and the White Sox, and a few of the other customers were drinking and watching. Richard pretended to watch the game—he glanced at it every now and then—but his attention was really focused on the door. Giselle was a barmaid at the Hyatt, and Ceasar's was an easy two-block walk away.

Richard always thought it was strange—a shock—how suddenly, how easily, the concept of adultery had come to him. For the first fourteen years of their marriage Richard had not even fantasized about a woman other than Kelly—she had that much of a hold over him. But then, about a week after he'd been appointed judge, a young woman came before him, a perfect, doll-like girl wearing a torn t-shirt and jeans. Her hair was shoulder-length and honey-colored, eyes blue, teeth flashing white, and the neck of her t-shirt was torn so that he could see well down between her round breasts. And on her left breast was a tattoo: *Property of Animal.*

Property of Animal! Richard couldn't keep his eyes off the girl's chest. His penis stiffened suddenly, and he shifted in his chair. Animal—who the hell was Animal? How had he convinced the beautiful girl—*wooed* her—into getting the tattoo? Richard had a swift fantasy, right there in court: He came out from behind the bench and walked up to the girl and pulled her t-shirt off, right up over her head, slowly, careful not to snag on her dangling earrings, and then, the blond girl topless in front of him, he took her left breast in his hand, Property of Animal. That was it. The whole fantasy. They didn't have sex or anything, they just stood there in front of everyone, Richard holding the girl's tit in his hand.

And then—something happened. The boring prosecutor finished speaking and Richard jerked back from his fantasy and sentenced the girl to community service, or probation, or something—he wasn't paying much attention—and the perfect blond girl with the tattooed breast was gone.

Richard kept thinking about her, though. When he got home that night he waited impatiently until he could get Kelly alone, and then he did her twice, quickly. Kelly put up with his attentions for three nights—there was something about that tattoo, Property of Animal, he couldn't stop thinking about it—until Kelly crankily pushed him away. "Leave me alone!" she said. "Go watch TV or something!"

But Richard was stuck with the fantasy—the shock—of the girl with the tattooed breast. When Kelly wouldn't have him, Richard turned to masturbating in the shower, alone, scared that Kelly would discover him, scared like a little schoolboy. The girl with the breast—Property of Animal, what did they *do* together?—was always with him, a slutty mirage, a sleazy centerfold come to life, a dirty dirty dirty movie. And she had stayed there, the focus of his fantasies, right up until the day Giselle Fernández flounced into his courtroom.

Linda said, "I'm *tired* of being a lawyer. I'm tired of all those damn criminals." She looked at the stones again, trying to see what Madame Bustos saw—if she really saw anything. "I'm tired of getting up in the mornings."

Paige said, "It's only been six or seven months since you passed the bar."

"So what? I'm tired." Linda frowned. It was something else she could blame on Gilbert Hardison—the stupid legal career. When she met Gilbert she was recently divorced and was—drifting. Drinking a lot, hanging out, watching television, sleeping whenever she felt like it—a relaxed, mess-free way of life that now, in retrospect, seemed very attractive. But Gilbert changed all that: He was big, black, successful, and interesting in ways her ex-husband had never been. Before long Gilbert had persuaded her to go to law school. They talked of having a joint practice. He gave her those damn birds. Then something happened. Linda had never bothered to figure it out herself, but she had become *tired*, or something. The engagement was off. Gilbert quickly rebounded and married that fat woman. That Other Bird died. That One Bird escaped. And now Linda was stuck being a lawyer, tired and sleepy, burdened with messes, an associate of criminals, a victim of judicial oppression, a laughingstock.

"You know," she said, "none of this is my fault."

Madame Bustos shrugged. "You have to do something," she said. "You can't just lounge—"

"Wallow," Paige said.

"—around, you have to take action. You have to make choices, you have to make decisions, you have to do something about this bad influence. You have to follow the path with heart."

"That sounds like an awful lot of trouble," Linda said. She looked at the stones scattered across the table. How much easier it would be to just go home and turn on the TV and goddamn *lounge* around! Home much easier it would be to crawl into bed and wait for everyone to go the hell away!

There was a harsh buzzing sound—Linda's cell phone.

She hauled it out of her bag: the phone was huge, almost the size of a World War II-era walkie-talkie. Linda was afraid that she'd lose one of the sexy little smart models everyone else had, and had put in a special order for the giant. Every time she talked on it she looked like she was calling in an artillery strike.

"Law office!" Paige and Madame Bustos pretended not to listen, but Linda knew they were—it was annoying, even if she was just talking to some stupid criminal. "Who's there? What do you want?"

Linda listened for a moment, then said, "Oh," then listened some more. She said, "Yeah, later, whatever," and punched a button on the phone. She dropped it twice trying to get it into her bag. Paige and Madame Bustos were still studying the stones and pretending to ignore her.

"I'm turning the damn phone off," Linda announced. "I'm tired of people calling me—they always want things."

Paige looked at Madame Bustos and rolled her eyes.

Linda stood up. "That was Charlie Bessent," she said to Paige. "Your friend Raul is over there and Charlie wants us to come take him off his hands."

Chapter Four

Happiness

CHARLIE BESSENT WAS A WEALTHY AND INFLUENTIAL older attorney, semi-retired, mostly gay, who, for reasons Linda had never understood, was quite fond of Raul Ledesma. Paige not only didn't mind Raul's relationship with Charlie, she encouraged it, hoping that contact with Charlie would smooth some of Raul's rougher edges. So far Linda had not noticed any improvement.

"I'm *so* glad to see you," Charlie said, letting them in. He was wearing a long red vicuna bathrobe and sandals. "Our friend Raul is depressed, I'm afraid."

"How unfortunate," Linda said.

"Hello, Raul!" Paige called.

Raul was sitting on a couch in front of the television. When he saw Paige he lifted the remote and turned up the TV's sound.

"We're here," Paige said.

"I see you." Raul turned up the sound even more.

Charlie had built his house back in the 1960s, a period when he was heavily influenced by James Bond movies and quaaludes. He liked to imagine himself as an evil lord in his bluff-top lair: supreme in real estate law, a top lobbyist, friend and drinking (and sometimes drugging and screwing) companion of governors and legislators and judges. The central part of the house, the living room and kitchen, was covered with an immense red stucco dome. There were statues of nude men and boys all over the place, some of them quite lewd, and scented candles flickered everywhere. Linda thought it was like visiting a very strange church.

"Fix yourselves drinks and let's go out on the deck," Charlie said. "It must be cooling off some now."

Linda and Paige crossed the domed room to the sliding glass doors that overlooked the lake.

"Raul, would you like to join us?" Charlie asked.

"I'm watching the news," Raul said.

"Raul, be polite," Paige said.

"This is important—people are *dying*." Raul did not look up from the television. The screen showed some raggedy, sad-looking people standing around in the mud. Apparently there had been a disaster.

🍸 🍺 🍷 🍶

Linda found an open bottle of wine and a glass and went out on the deck. It was still warm—she was rather *too* warm in her baggy sweatshirt—but there was a breeze blowing, and far below she could see the running lights of speedboats cutting across the lake in the dark. She liked Charlie a great deal but coming out here to pick up Raul was a waste of time. As far as she could tell, Raul himself was a waste of time. Paige had always chosen her boyfriends—always, always— based on their looks, and far too often ended up with beautiful men who were also creeps, drunks, psychos, or dummies. Paige—and Charlie—maintained that Raul was actually very intelligent, that the dumb act was just that, an act, but Linda had never noticed any particular brilliance on his part and remained unconvinced. At any rate, she wanted *her* men to be useful—she wanted men who could take orders, men who could wash dishes, or vacuum, or iron, or fix her car—or, even better, Linda wanted a man wealthy enough to *hire* someone to do the chores—wealthy, yes, but still willing to take orders. Raul was beautiful, but he was also stubborn, and poor, and seemed to be fit for nothing more challenging than puttering around in the garden, or fucking.

Charlie and Paige came out on the deck carrying drinks.

"He rode his bicycle out here this morning," Charlie said, "and he's been just like *that*—just terribly depressed and withdrawn. I mean, I like the boy, but I like him better when he's amusing."

Linda turned and looked in through the glass doors at Raul. He was still staring at the television. Amusing, she thought. Goddamn. She looked over at Paige and Charlie.

"What about me?" she asked. "Isn't anyone concerned about *my* feelings?"

"You saw that thing in the newspaper?" Paige asked Charlie.

"Oh, indeed," Charlie said cheerfully. "You most certainly struck a blow for the legal profession. You spoke the hidden truth! Kill all the brutes!"

"Don't tease me," Linda said.

"I wouldn't tease you." Charlie sat easily, his knobby legs crossed, and though he sat in the shadows, a dark silhouette, Linda could sense him smiling. It made her mad. "No," he said, "really, having a reputation like this might actually be a boost for your career."

"I don't think I want a career any more—I just want to watch TV."

"And catch up on your sleep," Paige said.

"Exactly!"

"No, really," Charlie said, "I had some business over at the County Commissioners Court yesterday afternoon, and the commissioners were all talking about you. They were impressed—very favorably impressed."

Paige smiled. "Were they all drunk?"

"Oh, one or two were drunk, I suppose, coming back tipsy from lunch," Charlie said, "but, you know, you don't see that as much as that as you used to. I suppose it's because they televise all the meetings now. People don't want to appear on TV drunk."

"Not like the old days, huh?" Paige asked.

"I could tell you stories—I could tell you many, many stories." Charlie paused, thinking of one.

"About me," Linda said.

"Oh—they were very impressed! Don't worry, honey, you have important friends you don't even know about."

Paige asked Charlie, "Do you know a judge named Richard—Cantu?" She looked at Linda. "Is that it? Cantu?"

"Ah, him." Charlie smiled and took a long drink. "I've seen him around. Richard Cantu's not too impressive, he just got that job because nobody else wanted it. He does have this little girlfriend with a tattoo, she's a barmaid somewhere, I think. Word is he bangs her about every chance he gets. I wonder what she sees in him? Maybe he fixed a ticket for her or something. At any rate, people are talking."

"She's got a tattoo?" Linda asked.

"Oh, indeed," Charlie said. "This girl, she's got a complete mynah bird on her back, takes up her whole back, and the beak pops up over her shoulder. Big yellow beak, runs right down between her titties." Charlie thumped his bony chest to show where the beak ran. "I hear it's pretty amazing."

"Sounds grotesque," Linda said.

Charlie shrugged. "I once knew a man who had a snake's head tattooed on his penis."

Paige nodded. "Yeah, I think I knew that guy, too."

The bar's door opened and Giselle was there. Richard smiled and shifted—squirmed—again. It was just like that first day in court. He got hard just looking at her standing in the doorway—heavy breasts, wide hips, wild thick hair—and then Giselle came down the bar, beads, bangles, bracelets jangling, breasts swaying, heavy sweet perfume trailing behind, the men at the bar all squinting, taking their eyes off the baseball game, trying to give her a look.

"Hi, Richie," she said, smiling, sliding onto a bar stool beside him.

"Hey there." Richard waved at the bartender. "How's your day been?"

"Slow," Giselle said. "It was a slow afternoon."

"That's too bad," Richard said. He ordered her a margarita and glanced over at her. Giselle had changed out of the starched white shirt she wore at work and was wearing a sheer, lacy black blouse—sheer, and it was hard to tell where the lacy things ended and her tattoos began. He could see the tip of the bird's bill coming over her shoulder, and traces of feathers around the tops of her breasts. "You look great."

Giselle smiled. "Thank you." Her drink came and she took a sip. "I'm so hungry."

"We had a big dinner tonight," Richard said. "Pork chops." As soon as he spoke, though, he knew it was a mistake. He couldn't stop himself. Damn.

Giselle stopped smiling. "Well, I'm hungry *now*, Richie," she said harshly. "I didn't get to eat any nice big dinner with the fucking *family*."

"We'll get you something to eat," Richard said nervously. "Don't worry."

"Jesus," Giselle said. She looked away. "*Pork* chops."

Richard sighed. Giselle was hard to please—but, then, every woman he had ever known had been hard to please. He wanted to be accommodating but women always seemed to be hard to please, and moody. Giselle was different only in that her moods shifted so rapidly—that crazy exciting fickleness, and those tattoos.

"We'll get you some fried chicken, babe," Richard said. Fried chicken would sooth her. "Don't worry."

Linda was telling Charlie about her day in court—about that damn article, about the incredible incivility of her new-found enemy—and all Paige could do was shake her head and sigh. She stared off into space, looking at lights—red and green lights of ski-boats on the lake below them, glimmering porch lights from houses on the far shore, the landing lights of a distant airliner making its approach. Everything was remote and twinkly, and Paige felt the urge for some—fun. Some activity—some *trouble*. Linda wasn't any help; she just wouldn't shut up about that damn newspaper column, about that stupid judge. Paige had hoped that the visit to Madame Bustos would point to the absurdity of the whole thing, but poor Linda was apparently blind to any sort of absurdity—at least, blind to the absurdity of her own life. Charlie seemed to see how it truly was, but his gentle laugher only seemed to make Linda more defensive. She took things too seriously. Paige got up and went back into the house to fix another drink.

From the kitchen she could see Raul staring at the television.

"Hey, Raul, do you want a drink?"

"No, thank you." Raul's lower lip pouted out—29 years old and he still pouted like a little boy. Paige knew he was still mad about the naked man on the couch that morning.

Paige placed her drink on a table next to the sofa and crossed the room to the cabinet where Charlie stored his videos. She could feel Raul glaring at her, and she glanced over her shoulder and smiled at him. Raul glared harder. Charlie had the videos neatly sorted by category—musicals, war movies, porn—lots and lots of porn, most of it gay porn. Paige pulled out a random disk—"Oriental Anal, Part III"—popped it into the DVD player, and pushed the play button on the remote. CNN disappeared and a pair of slender Asian men were on the screen.

"Paige, c'mon—they were talking about civil war and terrorism in Yemen."

"This is more important," Paige said.

"Yemen is crucial to the security of the Red Sea." Raul was looking around for the remote but Paige had left it on top of the television.

Paige swung onto the couch, sitting very close to Raul. He tried to scrunch away, but there wasn't anywhere for him to scrunch to. Paige tried to pull one of his arms around her—he yanked it back, but the second time she tried he let it rest on her shoulder.

The Asian men on the TV were making grunty, moaning noises, and then there was an Asian woman with them, the three of them squirming around to form a sort of anal chain.

"I'm really sorry you got mad at me this morning," Paige said.

"Yeah, well, I'm really sorry you *made* me get mad at you," Raul said. "I'm really sorry you invited that black guy in while I was asleep."

"Oh, Raul, I told you, he's just an old friend."

"So why was he naked?"

"Raul, he got *hot*—he got hot, and I wouldn't let him turn up the air conditioning. I know how you get cold so easily."

Raul pouted. "I'll bet he got hot."

Paige tried to kiss Raul but he turned away. The second time, though, she connected, and on the third kiss Raul responded—enough of a response, at least, for Paige. She pushed Raul back, at the same time removing her shorts, her thong, and then somehow Raul's jeans were down—his dick was sticking up—Paige slipped it in—Raul was frowning—Paige said, "Oh, *baby*"—and then, one-two-three—just like that—it was over. Over. Paige said, "Yes!" She caught her breath, then kissed Raul on the cheek and was off him and over to the DVD player, looking for another video.

"Paige, I didn't even *come*," Raul whined.

He was pouting again.

"Paige is a remarkable woman," Charlie said. He was looking in from the deck. Paige was standing in front of his television, naked from the waist down, perfect, looking for videos. Raul was still sprawled back on the couch, angry, his heavy penis tilted at a crazy angle.

"I suppose," Linda said.

Charlie smiled at Linda. He had known Linda's father in San Antonio, and her uncle in Austin, when they had served in the legislature. In fact, Charlie and Uncle Bud had been lovers, though he never told Linda.

"You really are upset, aren't you?"

Linda sat up straight. "I've been trying to tell you how horrible this is—that stupid judge was rude to me, people are laughing at me, and Jeff and Karl are going to be pissed at me." Jeff Foster and Karl Moomaw were the senior partners in the small law firm where Linda worked. "They've already made some nasty comments about my work ethic."

Charlie nodded. "I suppose they want you to work in the mornings."

"Oh, my God! They *expect* me to go to court at eight in the goddamn morning—that's their word, expect. They *expect* me to meet with clients in the morning. They *expect* me to put in ten or so hours a day. Ten hours a day—doing *what*? It's crazy! What the hell are they thinking?"

Linda paused for a moment. The sound of speedboats came floating up from the darkness.

"I guess I never really thought this lawyer thing through." Linda sighed. "It's not like on TV. All I do is mess around with stupid, disgusting human beings."

"Well, it's good that you do at least see them as human," Charlie said.

"Stupid ones," Linda said.

"Surely you must meet *some* nice people."

"Oh, you'll get some educated people involved with drugs

or drunk driving or bad checks, but they're all stupid, too, or else they wouldn't have gotten caught."

Linda thought of the criminal she would take to court on Monday, a skinny little training technician for a software company. He'd flown into Austin from San Jose, and once off the plane decided that he just *had* to smoke a joint, so he went into the nearest restroom and lit up—and got caught, of course. Linda told him to his face that she thought he was stupid. The client was shocked: how could his own lawyer say such a thing? Because you *are*, Linda said. Still, she was going to get him off with probation.

"I think I've irrevocably messed up my life," Linda said.

🍸🍺🍷🥃

Outside after their drinks bats wheeled around the streetlights in the soft warm darkness, and Giselle cheered up and took Richard's arm as they walked to his car. He opened the car door for her, and she scooted over and unlocked the driver's side. When he got in, she grabbed his face and kissed him hard—deep and wet, and he could smell her heavy perfume, and, past that, traces of bar smoke and beer in her hair.

"I want some Popeye's," Giselle whispered, pulling away.

"You got it." Richard was afraid he'd come in his pants, and he slid backwards in his seat. Giselle put her head on his shoulder, and ran a hand along his thigh. "You got it."

"I'm so tired," Giselle whispered.

The first time they had been together—the first time they'd met at a motel—Richard had not been able to bring himself to have sex with her. He was okay with the *concept* of adultery, but when they arrived at the actual act—he couldn't do it. At the last moment he thought of Kelly and Davy and Amy—his *family*—and despite Giselle naked on the motel bed in front of him—tattoos, breasts, piercings, her big round butt—he couldn't do it. He looked away, thinking of his *family*. Giselle got pissed and bit him on the chest, hard, on his left breast, saying she was going to eat his heart, and the bruise had lasted for days, purple and tender, as big as the palm of his hand. Richard of course lied about it to Kelly, mumbling something crazy about closing the bathroom door on his man boob, and Kelly was so uninterested in him that she hadn't even bothered to ask again. Kelly—skinny, bony, acne-scarred. *Bitchy.* Now Richard could not believe that he had ever passed up a moment, a second, with Giselle because of the thought of—Kelly.

"Baby, I'm hungry," Giselle said.

"It's okay." Richard pulled the car into the Popeye's drive-through and got a ten-piece meal, and then stopped across the street at a gas station for a twelve-pack of beer. Then they were on their way to the highway, to a motel. Richard had gotten a room before going to Ceasar's. There were sleazier, cheaper—more exciting—places over on Congress Avenue, but Richard knew that the police were always getting calls to those motels, complaints about hookers and crack smokers, people arguing and fighting, crazy people running around naked, and so he relied instead on the comforting anonymity of the chain motels along the highway.

At the motel Richard parked in the front of the room door, and Giselle flounced out of the car and stood next to it, frowning.

"Hurry, baby," she said. "It's *hot.*"

Richard gathered up the bag of chicken, the box of beer, and the room key, and stumbled out of the car. Giselle took the key from him and opened the door—the air conditioning was already on and he felt good cold air spill from the room. He dumped the food next to the television and turned to find Giselle already on the bed, pulling off her filmy blouse. Richard kicked the door shut, struggling with his clothes, placing his pants and shirt onto the dresser as neatly as he could, then flopping onto the bed, pulling Giselle close, breathing, loving the smell of her hair: smoke, beer, forbidden fun. He pushed her away to look at the amazing designs on her body, the wings of the bird curling around her, swirls of red and green feathers leaving the tips of her breasts creamy white, then pulled her back and they were locked together, Giselle's strong legs trapping him—and then, later, then—they got to the chicken. They sat naked on the mussed bed eating greasy chicken and drinking warm beer, and Richard felt that nothing in his life—nothing, nothing, nothing, ever—had tasted better. He was just so damn *happy*.

Chapter Five

The Little Wagon

LINDA WAS SILENT ON THE DRIVE BACK FROM CHARLIE'S. Paige and Raul were still bickering—Raul wanted to watch the news, while Paige was in a mood to stir up trouble—but Linda filtered them out and drove quietly down out of the hills and across the low-water bridge. She didn't feel like going home, though—she wasn't in a mood to lounge around, and there wasn't anything else to do at her house except pace and fret. And she had tried that: pacing and fretting led nowhere.

"I need a drink," Linda suddenly said. She made a sudden looping turn into the parking lot of the Little Wagon, a tiny beer joint, more or less their neighborhood bar. "You people can wait out here and argue if you want."

The Little Wagon, a battered relic of an older Austin, was dark inside, and crowded, and very smoky. Linda made her way through a group of loud sorority girls to the bar and ordered a glass of cheap wine.

"Hey," someone said over her shoulder. "You're way wrong! I think you're way, *way* wrong!"

In the mirror behind the bar Linda saw a massive blond guy looming up behind her, angry and drunk, towering over the sorority girls, who moved out of his way, regarding him with distaste. With stringy long hair and a scraggly beard on the underside of his chin, the guy looked like a big drunk Viking.

"Hey! Counselor! Did you hear me? I said you're wrong!"

The barmaid brought the wine and Linda paid for it and turned around and looked at the Viking. She asked, "What?"

"I read that article—I think you're wrong. I think the death penalty is wrong and I think *you're* wrong."

"Oh, well, that's okay." Linda had sort of been expecting this: in addition to all the people who were laughing at her, there were going to be a few who wanted to argue with her. What a goddamn world.

"Yeah, really, you are!" The blond giant had blue eyes that were almost glowing. He waved his mug of beer in the air. "I mean, you don't get it—if even one innocent person is executed—just *one*—then the whole system is flawed!"

Linda nodded. "I think you're right. You convinced me." She patted the guy on the shoulder and made her way over to an empty table by the jukebox. Crazy people, she thought. Didn't they have anything better to do than read the newspaper? Didn't they have anything better to do than argue with people in bars about what they *read* in the newspaper?

When Linda looked up to light a cigarette she saw Gilbert Hardison standing in front of her.

"Sunshine!" Gilbert said. "I've been waiting for you—I was hoping you'd stop in."

Linda felt tired for a moment, and blank—a smallish wave of depression rolling through—but then she remembered the early-morning phone calls. The messages. Oh. Hell. *Gilbert*. Gilbert's wife, too. He was standing there, swaying slightly, grinning down at her—he looked good. His close-cropped beard was a little grizzled, and his jacket was a little too small for his belly, but he looked good. Then Linda remembered that she was mad at him, that all these messes were *his* fault—the career, the birds, the enemy, no pearls, no roses, no chocolate. Yet he had the gall to stand there and grin like he was pleased to see her!

"Oh," Linda said. She went ahead and lit her cigarette, puffing, adding a vast cloud of smoke to the Wagon's already thick air. "Those birds you gave me—they died."

"They what?" Gilbert stooped over a bit to hear her better.

"Gilbert!" Paige came up to the table, smiling.

Gilbert smiled and hugged her. "You're lookin' good!"

"Gilbert, one of those little birds you gave Linda died."

"One of them?" Gilbert looked at Linda.

"That One Bird got away," Linda said. "He might be dead." She looked across the bar: the sorority girls were leaving to head downtown. The Viking was haranguing a couple of nervous-looking older guys. "I hope not."

"Don't worry, I'll get you some more birds," Gilbert said.

"I don't *want* any more birds!" Linda snapped. "What happened to my goddamn pearls?"

"Pearls?" Gilbert sat down across from Linda looking puzzled. His expensive jacket was wrinkled and rumpled, as if he'd been sleeping in it, and his tie was loose and askew. Paige brought a pitcher of beer and mugs over from the bar and sat down. Raul wandered past them, pouting, headed toward the pinball machines.

Linda stared at Gilbert for a moment, smiling thinly. "So," she asked, "how's the wife?"

"The wife?" Gilbert was filling his mug. He looked carefully at Linda. "Delia? She's fine—she's at home."

"You sure?"

"'Course—she's at home."

"You talk to her?"

"I know where Delia is."

Paige moved around the table and whispered in Linda's ear. "*Never* ask married men about their wives—it makes them impotent."

"Good!" Linda said loudly. She smiled at Gilbert. "That's what I want in a man."

"I was down seeing a client," Gilbert said.

"All night?" Linda asked.

"—and then I came here, looking for you."

Linda ignored that last comment. "So," she said, "you don't really know what your wife's up to, do you? All these Dating Dos and Don'ts, all these ads in the newspaper, these singles mixers she runs, and you don't even know where she's at. She could be anywhere!"

"What the fuck you trying to do?" Gilbert asked. "You trying to stir up trouble?"

"That's Paige's job," Linda said. "Stirring up trouble. Never mind what I'm up to."

Gilbert sighed. Women had been picking on him all day—on what should have been a very *good* day. It wasn't fair. Though Linda was seldom fair. When she suddenly broke off their engagement, Linda had gone and just left her engagement ring with one of the secretaries at The Justice Store. No note, no nothing. The secretary, thinking that the ring was payment for a legal service of some sort, gave Linda a receipt and then carried it across the street and pawned it—it was almost two weeks before Gilbert figured out what the hell was going on. At least Delia would get in your face and let you know what was wrong, he thought—but, no, then he remembered Delia's mysterious bitching that morning about her lack of sleep and that phone call—that phone call from Linda. So maybe not. Damn. It was all so fucking confusing. Women.

"Never mind," Gilbert said.

"You wouldn't believe what a pain in the ass Raul's been," Paige said.

"Yeah, I might," Gilbert said. Years went by and nothing ever changed with Paige and Raul. He looked at Linda. "So what're *you* mad about?"

"Mad? I was born mad. Ask anybody—ask my father. I was an angry child."

"But now you're an adult," Gilbert said, filling his mug.

"Don't be absurd. Age only intensifies the anger process. You start to see the world as the stupid, crappy place it really is. Anger is wisdom."

"She's depressed," Paige said.

"It's that newspaper thing," Gilbert said. "Right?"

Linda shrugged and blew smoke from the side of her mouth. "Among other things."

The big blond guy—the anti-capital punishment guy—broke away from the bar and approached the table.

"The thing is, Counselors," he said. "Innocent people *are* being executed!"

"Who says?" Gilbert demanded.

Linda looked away. Raul was playing pinball, lost in his own world. Linda wished she had her own world to get lost in. She heard the blond guy say "innocent" and "not guilty of murder."

"Well, I just saved a guilty man's life today," Gilbert said. "What'd you think about that?"

"What did you get for it?" Paige asked. "A jambox?"

"Much better than a jambox, baby," Gilbert chuckled. "Much better."

"—state-sponsored murder!"

Linda stood up and stomped off toward the bathroom.

All the bartenders at the Little Wagon were women, and they kept the ladies' bathroom very clean—at least in comparison with the men's room, which was covered with foul graffiti and had an ancient leaking toilet that seeped beery urine onto the floor. The ladies' room had a sink with running water, a clean toilet, a mirror, plastic plants, and a photo of the Austrian Alps. Linda stood in front of the photo, trying to imagine what it would be like to be in the goddamn Alps—clean air, white wine, waking in the afternoons to maybe try a little of the German she sort of half-remembered from college.

"Is someone in there?" The door rattled.

"I'm busy!" Linda snapped. Thank God she'd remembered to lock the door.

There wouldn't be anyone to yell at her in the Alps—she'd be a foreigner, people would think she was creepy and strange, they'd leave her alone. She could stay in her room all day and watch TV—maybe they had *COPS* in Austria, or *Law & Order*. *COPS* dubbed into German would be pretty funny.

Linda sighed. Really, it was a lot of trouble to cross a goddamn ocean just to be left alone. It was a shame people couldn't leave her alone here.

There was a bang at the door. "Hey! Is anybody *in* there?"

Linda looked at the photo of the Alps and shook her head.

🍺 🍸 🍷 🍹

Gilbert looked at Paige. "What's she pissed about?" he asked. "She pissed at me?"

"No, I don't think so," Paige said. "But even if she is, she'll get over it—Linda's very easy-going."

"Easy-going," Gilbert repeated. "Yeah, I guess, except for all those criminals she wants to execute."

"And she's having problem with some judge," Paige said. "Cantu—I think that's his name. He was very rude to Linda."

"Oh, hell, Judge Richard Cantu can kiss my ass," Gilbert said. He scooted his chair a bit closer to Paige and leaned over the table. "Is that the problem? Is he messin' with her? That man's a moron."

"Apparently so," Paige said.

"If he picks a fight with my Sunshine, he's gonna have to pick a fight with me," Gilbert said grandly. "We'll kick him in the nuts."

The Viking plopped down into Linda's chair. He stared drunkenly off into space, apparently drained of argument. Paige considered him, then said to Gilbert, "I hear this Cantu's got a girlfriend or something."

"Some*thing*," Gilbert laughed. "That's about it. He's got this girl, she's got these crazy big-assed tattoos all over the place." Gilbert took a long drink of beer. "I was there the day he met her, I think—she came into court for writing a bunch of bad checks, and Cantu was just staring at her with his eyes popping out of his goddamn head and a hard-on like a baseball bat. He dismissed all the charges—wasn't even going to make her pay restitution, but the prosecutor got pissed, so I guess she at least had to make the checks good."

"And she tends bar somewhere?"

"Yeah," Gilbert said. "At some hotel downtown. The Driskill, I think."

Linda came back from the bathroom and stood looking blankly at the near-comatose blond man sitting slumped in her chair. She said, "Oh, great."

"Never mind," Paige said. "Gilbert's taking us for drinks at the Driskill—go round up Raul."

Gilbert never questioned Paige's interest in finding the tattooed barmaid; it just seemed like a normal Saturday night misadventure. When they couldn't find her at the Driskill, Gilbert decided that she worked at the Stephen F. Austin—except that they couldn't find her there, either, or at the Omni.

"I don't know," Gilbert said, looking around. "I know I saw her tending bar at *some* hotel—she had this big tattoo wrapped around her neck."

Gilbert was having fun, though, dragging them all from bar to bar. He kept draping his massive arm over Linda's shoulder, saying things like "Listen, Sunshine, I've got some big things coming up, big things—you might want a piece," or, "I'll be makin' a big move pretty soon—you might want to move, too, you know?" Linda couldn't tell if he was talking about business or sex. If it was sex—well, then.

"Gilbert," she said, "if anything is going to happen

between us tonight, I'm going to have to get *extremely* intoxicated."

"Well, shit, let's get you another drink, then," Gilbert said, grinning, gold teeth flashing. He waved at the tattoo-less barmaid with one hand while pulling Linda close with the other.

Linda shook her head. *Sex.* It was an uncomfortable mystery. Since their teen years Linda had marveled at Paige's relaxed physicality and lack of inhibition. For Paige, sex wasn't too different from throwing a javelin or leaping a hurdle. Linda, though, couldn't achieve that level of ease unless she was seriously drunk, with maybe a Quaalude or a Valium or a Xanax thrown in—and, even then, it wasn't exactly a whole lot of *fun.*

"Orgasms are a waste of time," Linda told Paige once. "You get breathless, and your heart beats fast, and you start to sweat, and you get all—*nasty.* They're stupid."

Paige said, "Oh, come on, orgasms must feel good—just a little bit."

"Listen," Linda said, "when I was a little girl I used to have a dog that'd go around licking my belly. I didn't like *that* much, either, but at least I knew she wouldn't get me pregnant or anything, and I didn't have to listen to her snore after it was all over—or *talk* to her, either."

"She?"

"Ginger. She must've been a lesbian dog. The mailman ran her over—I think he did it on purpose."

"I think you've just had the wrong boyfriends," Paige said. "If you had the right boyfriends, you'd like sex."

Linda shook her head. Besides Raul, Paige usually had a regular boyfriend or two, and she tried to keep her weekends free for more athletic endeavors—threesomes, foursomes, sixsomes, whatever. Linda had accompanied her to a few of these scrums, drunk enough to participate but sober enough to note that all the clumsy mewling and grunting around, the accidental collisions of elbows or knees with unprotected genitals, the rubbery slapping of belly against belly, all this eventually dwindled to the women making out between themselves while the men watched and reminisced about those youthful days when their dicks would stay hard all night long. It was ridiculous. Paige thought it was ridiculous, too, but she *liked* that sort of thing. Linda would rather watch television.

Now, though, sitting in the lobby bar at the Four Seasons while Gilbert was off getting them a suite of rooms, Linda was starting to feel—something—for him. Even though he was responsible for all her troubles, even though he was married to that rude fat bitch, even though he had given her those sickly birds instead of nice pearls—Linda surprised herself by feeling something approaching actual tenderness for Gilbert. She thought, I guess I can borrow a condom from Paige—after another drink.

"Why are we looking for this female?" Raul asked. He had been mad and pouty all evening—he wanted to stay home and watch the news, but had been tagging along to keep Paige out of trouble and away from strange men.

"Linda wants to find the judge's girlfriend," Paige said.

"I do?" Linda asked.

Raul frowned. "Why?"

"So she can—" Paige looked at Linda. "What? Blackmail him?"

"Oh, hell, I don't know," Linda said. *Blackmail*, she thought. Well! "It's an idea, I guess." She shrugged. Blackmail. Cantu was her enemy, after all. "Sure, blackmail. Why not?"

🍺🍷🥃🍸

Linda stood looking out the window at the lights on the far side of the river until Gilbert passed by and shut the drapes. She took a deep breath, and sighed. Raul settled back on the couch and turned on the television—CNN again, with new disasters, or new video of old disasters. Paige fixed herself a drink and sat close to Raul, chasing him once more across the couch.

Gilbert came back around, smiling, and put a big hand on Linda's neck. He clumsily tried to pull her close for a kiss, but she turned away.

"I'm hungry," she said. "I haven't eaten all day."

"We'll get you a big steak," Gilbert said. He got on the phone to room service. Linda thought—Gilbert, Gilbert. That jacket was too small for his shoulders—for his belly—but, really, he looked pretty good. When he got off the phone Linda was smiling at him.

"Aw," Gilbert said, "there's my Sunshine." He came over and put his arms around Linda. "I like to see you smile."

"I need another drink."

"I got what you need right here." He tried to guide her hand towards his crotch.

"Hmm," Linda murmured. "I doubt it."

Though she had little interest in sex, and needed to be drunk, Linda also liked things orderly and planned out. In her teens, sweet on an Army helicopter pilot from Ft. Sam Houston, she drew up detailed lists of things to do on a date, starting with waking up and showering and ending with a reminder to pick up a pregnancy testing kit.

Now, almost forty, with whatever guy she was with at the time, the list had dwindled to a few crucial items:

1. Drinks.
2. Sit on couch, watch Homicide.
3. Sex.
4. Brush teeth.
5. Escort to door. Mention tomorrow's ironing.
6. Go to bed

Homicide might sometimes be *COPS* or *NYPD Blue* or some version or other of *Law & Order*, and ironing might be vacuuming or dishwashing or changing her Suburban's oil, but the essence of the list remained the same, guy after guy.

Now, though, in an unplanned situation with Gilbert, drunk, Linda still tried to impose some sort of order.

"You can kiss me now," she said.

Gilbert felt a little wave of nostalgia sweep through his heart—after all, they had been engaged for almost four years when they broke up. Linda was crazy—there wasn't anyone else he could tolerate crazy like this.

"You can kiss me now," Linda said softly. "Then you can put your right hand on my hip."

"What about my left hand?"

"Wait—"

Gilbert kissed her and grabbed her butt with both hands. Linda pulled away.

"I'm serious—I said your right hand!"

Gilbert laughed. "Baby, I'm teasing, you know that."

"We have to do this right," Linda said, "if we're going to do it at all."

They stood kissing, swaying, Gilbert's right hand on Linda's hip, his left hand held up in the air as if to ask a question in class.

"Okay," Linda whispered, "now you can put your left hand at the small of my back."

They kissed again, Gilbert almost enveloping Linda in his great arms. He ran his hand under Linda's sweatshirt, pressing her soft moist back, and then, well, without instruction, forced his right hand down beneath her jeans.

"Oh, what the hell," Linda said. She was used to her plans collapsing. "We might as well get naked."

"That's my Sunshine—my girl."

Linda pulled off her sweatshirt and sat on the bed to untie her sneakers. Then Gilbert—he could move quickly—was naked, holding her face to his hard round belly.

"Baby, you don't know how I've *missed* you."

Linda shut her eyes, letting the short stiff curly hairs of Gilbert's belly rub against her face. It reminded her of something—of something not necessarily bad. In a way the belly—the tiny scratchy hairs, the faint smell of cologne and baby powder, the tacky softness of its skin—was safe, and comforting, and familiar. Linda put her hand on Gilbert's thigh and felt up to his groin.

"Ah, Gilbert," she said, "I've always loved your cock—it's so small."

"What?" Gilbert froze. "Hey, c'mon, my cock's fucking *huge*!"

"Don't be shy," Linda said. "I love a small penis—they fit so much better. C'mere." She reached for him but he stepped back.

"My cock's fucking huge," Gilbert said again, drunk, holding his dick in his hand. "How can you look at that and say it's small?"

Linda sat back on the bed. "Goddamn, I told you I *liked* it, okay? Big penises give me bladder infections—yours is perfect."

"Goddamn," Gilbert said. He let go of his penis and ran his hand up his belly, rubbing it, frowning down at Linda. "Why you pullin' this shit?"

"I said I liked it," Linda said. "What's the matter, your little wife doesn't?"

"My wife—" Gilbert looked hurt. He turned and went out the door. "Paige!"

Paige was sitting on the couch with Raul, her head on his shoulder, her hand on *his* crotch. The raggedy poor people on CNN were still standing around in the mud.

"Paige, look at this here." Gilbert stumbled out of the bedroom and stood in front of her. "Homegirl says my dick's too small—it's *not*! I got a good nine inches of man-meat hangin' here, right?"

Paige laughed and studied Gilbert closely. His erection was fading fast but could not have been very impressive at its peak.

"I don't know," Paige said. "What do you think, Raul?"

"I think you are all ridiculous."

"Nine inches of man-meat," Gilbert said drunkenly.

Paige said, "Raul, *life* is ridiculous."

"Maybe your life is ridiculous, but mine is rational."

"Raul, if you're hanging around with me, you're not

rational."

"My goal is to impose rationality upon you." Raul never took his eyes off the television.

"Whatever."

"My dick—" Gilbert began.

"Is fine," Paige said.

"Hey, I told him I *liked* it," Linda said from the doorway, finally naked, her pale breasts wobbling as she took a long drink from a bottle of red wine. She swallowed, wiped her mouth on her forearm, and took another drink. Finally, she was getting to the point where she felt—intoxicated—enough for sex. "Gilbert, c'mon over here and do me before I get a hangover."

"Don't worry," Paige said to Gilbert. "I think it just looks small compared to your belly."

"Yeah, I guess that makes sense." Gilbert rubbed his belly and nodded. "Sunshine's—what you call it?—her *perspective*, it's skewed, right?"

Paige smiled, "Her perspective is *very* skewed."

Linda took another long gulping pull from the bottle, her eyes closed. She swallowed, sniffed, and opened her eyes. "Gilbert? C'mon."

"My Sunshine."

Linda laughed and reached out for Gilbert's hand, leading him back to the bedroom, pulling him close, hugging, reaching down and squeezing his—what?—four or five or six inches of man-meat. A handful—a modest, just-right handful. Linda fell back onto the bed, still holding Gilbert, feeling him get hard again, and harder, and she flopped her legs apart and felt him in her—and *on* her, that heavy scratchy-haired belly pressing her down, his man-meat moving, his broad bald forehead smacking her in the eye as he bucked, smacking again on the nose, in the eye—*hard*, damn it! Jesus! *Cut it out*! Linda—trapped, pinned-down, squashed, desperate, drunk—suddenly realized to her horror that she was maybe a bit *too* intoxicated. A *bit*. Or more. Holy shit, she shouldn't have taken that last gulp of wine. God*damn*! She was going

to vomit. Now.
Now.
"Paige!" she managed to yell.

Chapter Six

Law and Order

COURT WAS SET TO CONVENE AT 8:00, BUT WHEN QUINCY Whittaker got there at 8:30 the courtroom was still almost empty. There were three Mexicans in the back row, all wearing cowboy hats, and a scared-looking white girl in the front row. Quincy sat at the far end of the third row, next to the window. There was some activity up by the bench: a deep-chested white woman pushed in a cart loaded with folders, and an older black woman helped her arrange the folders on a table next to the bench. Some well-dressed white men came into the room, very cheerful—lawyers, probably. More Mexicans. Some tough-looking white boys, and some older black men, also tough-looking. A timid-looking black girl, very skinny, very scared, sat in front of him. Quincy thought she looked familiar; perhaps she had ridden in his cab. One of the lawyers, young, well dressed, big gold watch on his wrist and some sort of stupid black bushy bandit moustache came over and bent down next to the girl.

"So, I understand you haven't been seeing your probation officer?"

"No, sir."

"And you haven't been making your payments?"

"No, sir."

"Don't worry, we'll get it all worked out." The lawyer straightened up and walked off.

Quincy thought, Yeah, you'll throw her ass in jail, that'll make you happy, ruin the poor girl's life, get it all worked out fine. Shit. He looked around for his own lawyer, Gilbert Hardison, but didn't see him. A door opened and ten prisoners dressed in orange pajamas filed in, all chained together. They sat in the jury box. What the fuck, maybe they *were* the damned jury—peers of all the crooks that had filled the courtroom. A cop stood up and said, "All rise. Travis County Court-at-Law 6-B is in session. Judge Richard A. Cantu presiding."

Quincy stood, along with almost everyone else. A few of the Mexicans in the back row were talking among themselves in Spanish and either didn't know what was going on or didn't care. A dark little man in a robe hurried into the room.

"You can sit down," Richard said. Everyone sat back down, and he looked out over the courtroom and noticed the Mexicans in cowboy hats. "Hey, in the back row—hats off! ¡Quitanse los gorros!"

The three Mexicans looked around and slowly slid their hats off, whispering to one another in Spanish.

"Okay," Richard said. "For people who have business here in court, I'm going to read a list of names, and if your name is *not* on this list, I want you to let me know. Okay? If you think you have business here, and your name is not on my list."

The judge began reading, and Quincy gazed out the window at the old courthouse across the way, not paying close attention until the judge stopped reading and he realized that his name had not been called. He looked around, and raised his hand like a kid in school.

"Hey, Judge! You didn't call my name!"

Richard said, "Okay, c'mon up here."

Quincy went up to the front of the room, flashing a gold-toothed smile at the chesty white woman, who looked away.

"What's your name?" Richard asked.

"Quincy Whittaker."

Richard ran his finger down a long computer printout. "Verbal assault?" he asked. "Your attorney is Mr. Hardison?"

"Yeah, that's right."

"Verbal *assault*," Cantu mused. He didn't look up from the printout. "Huh."

"Judge, listen, there's nothing right about this—nothing."

"Yeah, well, we need your attorney here to deal with this charge, whatever it is," Cantu said. "Mr. Hardison called in this morning—he's not feeling well. I agreed to postpone your appearance until September 23."

"What?" Quincy squinted. "Judge, I been down here two hours already—nobody told *me* about Hardison being sick."

Richard looked up at Quincy, looked at him for the first time, and Quincy noticed the bags under his eyes. The judge looked tired.

"Mr. Whittaker, I'm sorry. I'll see you September 23. Okay?"

Quincy stood there for a moment. "Yes, *sir*," he finally said. "Mercy and truth go before thy face." He turned and walked away without even glancing again at the big-titted white woman. Outside the courtroom, in the hall, he bent over a fountain to drink. All morning wasted. No money made. Motherfuckers. He felt like smashing something—someone—but there wasn't anything or anyone to smash.

"Hey—cab driver!"

Quincy stood up and looked around. A white woman with a bad black eye and a swollen nose was walking toward him, carrying a large cell phone—the crazy woman.

"Aren't you the guy that gave me a ride home yesterday?" Linda walked up to Quincy and glared at him with her good eye. "That cab driver?"

"Yeah, you're that crazy woman. How's your eye feel?"

"Like shit," Linda said. "What'd you think?"

"Well—"

"Listen," Linda said, "I need a ride—are you doing

anything right now?"

"Uh, no."

"My Suburban got towed—I need a ride to go pick it up. It's down south somewhere—some towing company on the south side. You know where it is?"

There were several towing companies on the south side. Quincy said, "I guess we can find it."

"Good," Linda said. "Well, good. Let's go."

○○○○

Linda and Quincy left the criminal justice building and walked around the old courthouse to the front.

"Man, my lawyer didn't show up in court today," Quincy said. "I'm *pissed*."

"I don't want to hear about it," Linda said. "Where're you parked?"

"Up the street about a block. Parking's for shit here. That's as close as I could get."

"I can't walk that far," Linda said. "My eye hurts. Go get your cab. I'll wait here."

Quincy looked at Linda for a moment. She was lighting a cigarette, huddling away from the hot breeze, sandy blond hair covering her face before she shook it free and took a long drag.

"Yes, *ma'am*," Quincy said. He thought, *Shit*. But there was money to be made and he went up the street to get his cab.

In a holdover from the days of segregation, Austin had three cab companies. Yellow had been the company for the Anglo community, Alamo Taxi for the Hispanic, and DeLuxe for the African American. Quincy drove for DeLuxe, in an old Chevy Caprice that had been shed by Yellow Cab years and miles earlier, the black paint of DeLuxe covering the yellow paint but not hiding the many dents and dings in the body.

The car started—always a blessing—and Quincy started the meter and pulled around the corner and down the street to where Linda stood in front of the courthouse. She came up to the cab and peered in through the heavy window tint, trying to see if she had the right car. After a moment she opened the door and got in.

"Thank God," Linda said. "Air conditioning!"

Quincy looked over his shoulder. "So where we supposed to go?"

"South," Linda said. "My truck got towed Saturday, or Sunday—sometime over the weekend. I've got the address here somewhere." She began digging around in her huge purse.

"That eye of yours came up pretty good," Quincy said.

"I don't want to talk about it." Linda shook her head. Actually, all she could really remember was puking her guts out while Gilbert kept banging his goddamn forehead into her face. Then waking up sometime in the afternoon and Paige hurrying her out of the room and into a cab—this cab.

"I didn't puke in your cab, did I?"

"Naw, you were just talking about some boyfriend—you wanted to go see him, wake him up, kick his wife's ass. You said he gave you some pearls or flowers or birds or some shit you didn't like."

"That son of a bitch." Linda leaned up against the front seat. "Why would I want to go see him?"

"Hell if I know."

"Hell if I know, either." Linda sat back and looked out the window. "He gave me these goddamn dead birds."

"Yeah, you said."

"And his wife is incredibly rude."

Quincy shrugged. "Yeah, they are, sometimes."

The cab crossed the First Street Bridge, and the water of the river reflected the sky—pale blue, hot, hard. The wind was from the southeast, and long lines of waves glinted under the sunlight.

"Okay," Quincy said. "Now we're south. So now where do we go?"

"Oh, I don't know," Linda said. "Just keep going."

"Shit." Quincy shook his head.

🍸🍷🍹🍺

Delia Huston Hardison—Dr. Dee—didn't know where her husband was. Every now and then she'd wander down the hall from her DateLine office to his private office, half-expecting—half-hoping—to find him snoring away on the couch, but he was never there. He might be in court, or at the North Lamar or East Seventh locations, but she certainly wasn't going to ask the clerks or secretaries where he was; every time there was trouble between her and her husband Delia could see the employees hunkering down, cringing like scared children, and she knew that they always took his side.

Goddamn Gilbert! It was all his fault, sneaking out in the morning, silent, angry, leaving everything between them all—unresolved. Hanging. Gilbert. Delia was supposed to be writing her weekly column for the Dr. Dee's DateLine advertisement but all she did was stare at her computer screen. Nothing would come. Her topic for the week was "Smile: It's Contagious!" but she couldn't think of a single damn thing to smile about—nothing.

The dog. Sunday morning Delia had gotten up, alone, to find Gilbert's clothes scattered across the floor of the bathroom—expensive clothes that she had selected for him, expensive clothes that smelled of beer and smoke and vomit—a reek that meant at the very least Bad Behavior and maybe even or probably even Another Woman. She had proof he was up to something—the smelly clothes. And that bitch calling in the middle of the night! What was that all about? What else *could* it be about? He was out with that crazy bitch—drinking, puking. Gilbert was a damn dog. And, on top of everything else, he'd come home and left the *oven* on all night—

From the bathroom Delia went downstairs and found Gilbert still asleep on the couch, a red-and-yellow afghan bunched up across his big belly. He looked like a pregnant whale. An *old* pregnant whale. For some reason Gilbert always looked younger when he wore his glasses, and of course now he was passed out with his glasses off, and he didn't look young or cute or sexy, he just looked like a middle-aged bald man sleeping off a drunk. Dog. Old pregnant whale.

"Gilbert," she said, "wake *up*."

Gilbert sighed, shaking his head, and he pulled the afghan up tight to his chest. What are you dreaming about? Delia wondered. Damn.

The first time Delia had noticed Gilbert he was on TV, in one of the ads he ran for The Justice Store. Delia had been with some friends watching *Saturday Night Live*, having a few drinks, and this ad came on, and everyone thought it was part of the show, a skit with a black man driving around in a vintage Cadillac, a giant red one, driving with a slow blues riff playing in the background. The black man was big and sexy—sort of like a pirate, with an ear stud and the hint of a gold tooth and a stubbly beard. Finally he took off his dark glasses and looked in the camera and said, very earnestly, "I will help you." I will help you! Everybody cracked up. I will help you. The Justice Store. "Se habla espanol." After that Delia noticed the ads everywhere, and she noticed people repeating the catch-phrase, too—store clerks, secretaries typing, stoner musicians, smart-assed college boys—"I will help you." I will *help* you. I *will* help you. I will help *you*. Later, when she knew Gilbert, she found that he had printed up vast truckloads of "I will help you" t-shirts, bumper-stickers and coffee mugs—typical Gilbert, running everything into the ground, taking a good idea three steps further than necessary, the line no longer useful or funny or even true, an embarrassing self-parody. Delia thought her own ads for the DateLine were much better: a tasteful page every week in the local alternative newspaper, with her photograph and an essay stressing positive outlooks on life and relationships. "Stop Procrastinating," was a recent title. "Listen More than You Speak," was another. "Give Honest Appreciation." "Don't Nag." This week, "Smile: It's Contagious!," but of course

Gilbert made that impossible.

It was Sunday afternoon when Delia bent over and shook Gilbert's shoulder. "Gilbert!" she said, louder. "I've had enough—wake up!"

Gilbert sighed in his sleep.

"I said, wake up! I saved your worthless life and you don't even know it."

Gilbert sighed again and slowly opened his eyes. "What?" he asked faintly.

"I saved your worthless life!" Delia stood up to her full height, hands on hips, pendulous breasts bobbing in a loose t-shirt. "You about killed us all."

"Leave me alone," Gilbert said softly. He sat up, rubbing his eyes.

"And let you burn the house down? Sure!"

Gilbert took a deep breath. After a moment he said, "What the fuck you talking about?"

"You left the oven on! All night!"

"Oh, yeah." Gilbert got up unsteadily. He remembered, sort of. Coming home. Hungry. Putting that room-service steak of Linda's in the oven to warm up. Taking a shower. That steak—

"Aw, shit." Gilbert stumbled toward the kitchen.

"That's right," Delia said, "you would've left the oven on forever—you would've burned the house down! You would've killed us all!"

There was a silver aluminum foil packet on top of the stove. Gilbert picked it apart—the remains of the big Porterhouse, blackened chunks of charcoaled, fossilized meat fused to a bone.

"Damn," Gilbert said.

Delia stood in the door. "Drunk," she said. "Could have killed us all!"

"Aw, shut up," Gilbert said. "I have a headache."

"Don't you tell me—"

"Shut *up*!" Gilbert turned and hurled the foil packet of steak at Delia. He had no intention of hitting her, and, despite

71

his hangover, didn't, quickly aiming for a spot over her shoulder. The steak sailed by her head and across the room to hit the white drapes. It fell to the floor, leaving a stain of grease and black char. Delia stared at him, open-mouthed.

"I'm sick of hearing your shit," Gilbert said. "I don't *feel* good." He turned and headed for the stairs. He was about halfway up when Delia recovered and followed him.

"I'm not cleaning that up!"

"Don't," Gilbert said over his shoulder.

Delia started up the stairs. "You said you were gonna see a murderer."

"I did."

"Yeah, then you're gone all day *and* all night, come home drunk—and that bitch called in the middle of the damn night at *our* house!"

Gilbert went into the bedroom and got some clothes— polo shirt, khaki shorts, underwear.

"Where're you going?" Delia demanded.

"Out."

"Out? You *were* out—*passed* out!"

Gilbert went into the bathroom and shut the door behind him. Delia heard him push the lock button. Then water was running.

"Good! You stay in there with those stinky clothes!" There was no answer. The house was almost silent: the air conditioner hummed, water ran in the bathroom. Delia stood outside the bathroom, catching her breath. Hiding in the bathroom, she thought. Scared little boy.

"Gilbert Hardison? You hear me? You're a coward, Gilbert! You're a damn phony, Gilbert, a liar and a coward and a phony and you don't help *anybody!*"

♀ 🍷 🍸 🍺

The important thing, Tim Newlin thought, was Linda. Thing—well, person. The important *person* was Linda: the important person in his life, the only one, the One. I guess

I—*love*—her, he thought. It was a *good* thought, a positive thought; it made Tim happy. He also wanted to fuck her, of course: he had thought of little else all weekend. He remembered her long legs and how they came together, her rounded butt, the slope of her belly—Lord, to put his head on her lap, her thighs more or less smooth against his cheeks—what a *comfort* that would be! Bliss! Then, maybe he could pull her shirt off, somehow, then kiss—

Tim rolled out of bed and washed his hands and put on clean boxers, then went over to his computer and stared at the screen. Linda! Damn, but he couldn't get her out of his mind. He had work to do, updating his porn websites with twenty new Thai fisting shots and ten new photos of hairy naked fat men, but he could only think about Linda.

Though he looked much younger, he was 24 years old, and he felt that he might be ready, at last, maybe, for a more-or-less *serious* sort of relationship. He had certainly always sort of been attracted to Linda—sort of. He first saw her when he was working at the front desk of the law school library, when Linda had been a student. She was a striking woman, older than the other students, blond and clumsy and kind of mussed-up. Her hair was usually all ahoo, and her clothes, while expensive-looking, were rumpled—a blouse half tucked-in to her skirt, and half out, or slacks that were ironed erratically. One night she wore shoes from different pairs, giving her an odd, lurching walk.

Sometimes Linda brought along her friend Paige, and on those nights they were usually half-drunk or more, sneaking in bottles of wine or six-packs of beer along with the law books. They'd stand around the copy machine, drinking and making copies, giggling like a couple of teenagers. They would stare across the room at Tim until he caught them staring—and then they'd giggle even harder. It made him—nervous.

After Tim moved into the apartment complex, he slept with Paige three times—three times being Paige's self-imposed limit on sleeping with men she didn't want "relationships" with—and now he was a little uncomfortable with it, a little worried that what had happened might somehow complicate or impede his possible potential future relationship with Linda. But Paige continued to treat him with the same cheerful friendliness she always had, as if nothing had ever happened between them, and that worried Tim even more: maybe nothing *had* happened between them. He had spent many evenings drinking and hanging out with Paige and Linda and had heard them talk, and their talk invariably turned to penises—especially *large* penises. They seemed fascinated and repulsed by them—fascinated, yes, repulsed, yes, always interested, yes, yes, yes. Tim tried to put it out of his mind, but he was well aware that his own penis was white and reasonably normal-sized, whatever that was—and that's *just* the way it was. Though he had looked at a couple of internet sites that promoted penile extension, he didn't take it seriously. He was—natural. Paige had never been unkind about it—had never even mentioned it—but Tim was aware that he couldn't match the legendary guys of pornography.

Still, Paige had given him one wonderful gift: she had turned him on to internet porn. Paige took a cheerful delight in pornography, especially porn photos of men with absurdly long penises, and Tim, always eager to please, had gotten to the point where he scanned the web every day for new photos to e-mail her. The strange thing was, he had gotten interested in large penises himself. He wasn't gay—at least, he didn't *think* so, not that there was anything wrong with being gay, of course—but he had come to find something fascinating and awesome in the sight of a brutally huge whanger. Nature could be so strange and cruel! There was just something about those big penises—they were compelling, they were frightening, they were addictive.

His search for penises led him to the webcams. They were digital cameras attached to computers that took photos and sent them back onto the web. Some of them were boring—a camera that showed 90-second updates of traffic going across a bridge, or whatever. A Coke machine, a coffee pot. Some people's webcams just sent out photos of them watching television, or close-ups of them messing around with the computer. But some people—the smart ones, Tim thought—were using their webcams to make money with pornography.

Tim's favorite was a topless dancer in Houston named Willow. She was a big grim blond woman, and if you sent her your credit card number, you got a password that allowed you access to her "private" area. For a measly twelve bucks a month you could watch live webcam video of Willow masturbating. She posted her schedule, and was usually online a couple of times a day. She never seemed to be having fun—she never smiled—but Tim admired the workmanlike way she approached her frigging.

After a few months of sending porn to Paige, Tim decided to go into business himself. He started by buying 500-photo packages of internet-ready porn and started two sites—austin_timgay.com, and austin_timstraight.com. Within weeks he was making enough money to quit his stupid job at the law library. He expanded the sites, with more and different kinds of photos, and video, and he had decided that the next step should be his own webcam—a way to turn his shortcoming, that unassuming white penis of his—into an asset that Paige and Linda would be proud of. There must be—at least several—people out there in the world who wanted to watch a white man with an average-sized penis masturbate.

Which brought him—again—back to Linda. Maybe if he was a porn tycoon, Linda would find him more—attractive. More of a househusband. It was obvious that she needed him; she couldn't seem to do anything for herself, and he was willing and able to do things for her, and convenient, and he really was sort of in love with her, or at least obsessed. I'm 24, Tim thought—it's time I had a girlfriend. A *real* girlfriend—Linda.

Still, he knew that he did a poor job of presenting himself. His apartment was dark and cluttered, with dirty dishes piled up in the sink and beer cans peeping out from under the furniture. Porn printouts were taped to the wall, along with posters of Walt Whitman and Ernest Hemingway. Tim liked to have things to look at on his walls—a variety of different things could be inspirational, he thought.

When he moved into the apartment, he had placed his desk so that he could sit at his computer and at the same time peer out from behind the blinds to see what was going on in the courtyard—Paige strolling around half-naked, Linda stomping up the stairs, the strange men who came visiting them late at night. There was even a little dull smudge on the window where he rested his face while peering out.

But now it was time for a change. The webcam was coming, and Tim didn't want all the world's perverts to be distracted by a messy room while it watched him masturbate. The focus should be on his penis—modest though it was—and not on the mess. The things on the wall could stay—in fact, Hemingway would look good moved to the head of the bed, sort of gazing down at the—activity—but the beer cans, full ashtrays, and miscellaneous trash had to go. And maybe Linda would be impressed—favorably impressed. Maybe. That was the important thing.

Chapter Seven

Grackles

AFTER DROPPING OFF THE DEED AT THE TRAVIS COUNTY Clerk's office, Gilbert went for a look at his new property. The directions Billy Johnston had given him seemed simple enough, but Gilbert quickly became confused in the tangled network of narrow roads that crossed the hills southwest of Austin. There wasn't any rush, though. Gilbert circled around in his fat red Cadillac, enjoying the day off, and when he somehow ended back up on the highway, he decided, what the hell, to stop at a convenience store for a six-pack of beer.

But as he came out of the store with his beer he spotted a billboard on the other side of the highway that ruined his mood. It was a close-up photo of a smirking, snotty-looking white girl, blond, and the caption, DAD ALWAYS KNEW YOU'D DO GOOD. Dad always knew you'd do good. The billboard was by a homebuilder pushing a new development out on the southeast edge of town—apparently aiming it at rich white kids just out of college. The same ad was plastered up all over the city, and Gilbert couldn't avoid seeing the smirking blond girl somewhere, every day, and every time he saw her he got mad. Gilbert had been a senior in high school when his own father had died of a heart attack, full of faith in his son's athletic ability but before he had seen him play a down of college ball, much less go on to actually do something with his life. Gilbert's mother died of cancer four years later, and after that, really, there wasn't anyone else, only a cousin in Athens and three more around Marshall, none of whom he knew very well. He was on his own. Dad always knew you'd do good. Shit. It was another thing that seemed to mock him—another reminder that people out there had things given to them—position, status, parental fucking support, goddamn TV-show lives—things that he would always have to struggle to get. He often wondered where that smirky little bitch actually lived—he felt like tracking her down and throwing a damn brick through her window, kick her all-knowing father in the damn nuts. Dad always knew you'd do good. The bitch.

Gilbert frowned in disgust and drove off, passing mobile homes and live oaks, mechanic shops, cedars and mesquites, dusty stray dogs, a fenced-in yard teeming with goats and chickens. Soon he opened a beer and felt a little better. Country, he thought, back out in the country—even though Austin was just over the hill, choked with traffic and smog and crazy people and messes and headaches, this was the country. It was nice out here.

Finally he saw Johnston's mailbox, dented and twisted around, a sad victim of mailbox baseball. A half-mile or so around the bend he found a simple gate held shut with a chain and padlock.

Gilbert got out of the car. The land at the front of the ranch was plain enough, cedar and mesquite and dusty brown grass, with clumps of prickly pear growing between outcroppings of limestone. The combination Johnston gave him opened the lock. Gilbert got back in his car and drove through the gate—and then had to stop the car and get out and close the damn thing. No good. Got to get one of those automatic gates, he thought.

The driveway was well-graded but dusty, winding through cedar thickets. Off to the right Gilbert saw a broad band of dense green—the line of the creek as it snaked across the property, he supposed. The driveway headed toward the creek, and as Gilbert rounded a bend he came across a red Nissan parked off in the grass. A young blond woman trudged up the hill toward it, backpack slung over her shoulder. Gilbert slowed his car to a stop, and a heavy cloud of white driveway dust blew forward and enveloped him. When it cleared he saw that the woman had dumped her pack on the Nissan's hood and was approaching his car. He hit a button and the power window slid down.

"Hello there," Gilbert smiled. "You look all hot."

The blond woman came over and looked inside the car. She seemed suspicious.

"Can I help you?" she asked.

"Maybe," Gilbert said. "I'm William Johnston's attorney."

"Oh," the woman said. Then something clicked. "*Oh*—I heard there was some sort of trouble."

"Yes, there was some sort of trouble," Gilbert said. "In fact, Mr. Johnston is in a *lot* of trouble."

"I'm sorry to hear that."

"Well, we're doing what we can," Gilbert said gravely. "We're doing what we can."

The blond woman didn't say anything. She kept peering into the back seat of the car.

"Want a beer?" Gilbert asked.

"Uh, no," she said, squinting.

Gilbert watched her. After a moment he said, "And you're out here...."

"Oh—I'm here checking the water quality."

"The water quality," Gilbert repeated. He stared at her from behind his sunglasses and took a long drink of beer.

"In the creek." When Gilbert just stared at her, she added, "I'm a grad student? Working on a project?"

"On water quality?"

"Yeah."

"Is it good?"

"Oh, yeah, it's excellent up here. Further downstream you get runoff from housing developments, golf courses, that sort of thing. But up here it's really—remarkable."

"Got a lot of crawdads in there, huh?"

"Crayfish?" the woman asked. "Yeah, sure, and a lot of aquatic insects—some plecoptera, some ephemeroptera—"

"And that's good?" Gilbert was grinning at her.

The woman nodded. "They're indicators of clean water."

Gilbert nodded, pondering the clean water. He took another long drink of beer, then asked, "So, how far is it up to the house?"

🍺🍸🍻🍷

When she got home from the Four Seasons, the cab driver and Paige had followed her wobbling up the stairs. Linda remembered that much. Tim was there, too, looking concerned and scared. There was some cursing. Then they prayed—she remembered praying. Linda was in bed, and they all prayed.

"We prayed last night, right?" Linda asked.

Quincy looked at her in the mirror. "You said you needed some help with some enemies."

"Right!" Linda smiled. She remembered stretching out in bed, Paige holding one foot, this cab driver guy holding another, Tim in the middle linking them—Tim staring at her crotch, too, it seemed like. The driver prayed. Linda tried to remember. "I will not be afraid of the thousands arrayed against me? Something like that?"

"No, no, no," Quincy said. "It goes, Lord, I will not be afraid of the ten thousand people who are set against me. Arise, O Lord, and *save* me, and smite all my enemies upon the cheek bone, and break out the teeth of the ungodly, for those that are not with me are *against* me!"

"Yes!" Linda laughed, delighted. "That's it! Damn straight."

"Smite the bastards," Quincy said. "Teach 'em the Lord's lesson."

"So you're some sort of man of God, right?"

"Shit, we're all people of God, you know?"

Linda smiled. "You cuss a lot for a preacher."

"What the hell," Quincy said. "All have sinned and fallen short, you know?"

"Oh, sure." Linda threw her cigarette butt out the window. A convenience store was coming up. "Pull over here," she said. When the car stopped she went inside and bought a four-pack of wine coolers and another pack of cigarettes. The clerk glanced at her black eye and then looked away. Linda looked back out through the window at the taxi. The driver seemed like he was a little pissed off, though maybe that was just his nature. It was silly, but the praying thing *had* made her feel better—as far as Linda knew, no one had ever prayed for her before, at least out loud. The blurry memory of Paige and the driver each holding a foot—peeking down at them and Tim through her spread legs—was somehow comforting. Outside, she got back into the cab and stretched out across the back seat. She opened a wine cooler and took a sip. Quincy backed out of the parking space but then stopped.

"So where do we go now?"

"South," Linda said. "We've got to find the Suburban."

"South. Shit." But Quincy pulled back out onto the street and headed south.

🍺 🍸 🍻 🍷

"You know, my life really sucks," Linda said.

"Yeah? Yours and mine both, man. My damn lawyer didn't even show up in court today. I'm being abused, you know, I'm being left to my oppressors. And now I have to go *back* to court in September!"

"So what? I'm supposed to go back to court tomorrow," Linda said. Probably won't, though, she thought.

"And that charge is *bull*shit to begin with!"

Linda shook her head and looked out the window. That's what they all said, the criminals. Some lied, some told the truth. Either way it was sad.

"Listen," she said, "I really can't care about your problems right now—I can only care about *my* problems, you know?"

The driver snorted and didn't look back at her. Linda wondered if he was offended. Some people were so petty. She sighed.

"Well, look, I'll *care* about your problems, as long as I don't have to *talk* about them, okay?"

Quincy said, "Shit."

"You have a very nice way about you," Linda said. For a criminal, she thought. A pleasant criminal. "I trust you. I liked the way you held my foot."

"Yeah?"

"You know that fat little judge?" Linda asked. "Richard Cantu?"

🍺 🍸 🍷 🍷

"Not to mention all those dildos," Raul said.

Paige shook her head. All those dildos, all those dildos, all those dildos—to hear Raul talk about it, when he was growing up there were dildos sticking out of every drawer, hanging in every closet. All those dildos were one of the reasons Raul had turned out the way he did—or so he always claimed. Paige had heard the story over and over again, for years, and had often wondered how many dildos Raul's mother needed, anyway. Mrs. Ledesma was a lovely, sophisticated woman from a very wealthy family, and Paige thought that while she no doubt had a demur, easily hidden vibrator stashed away somewhere, a whole house full of *dildos* was absurd.

"Paige! I *saw* them!" Raul said. He was sitting on Paige's couch looking at the television. Paige was in the kitchen washing dishes. "There were dildos everywhere! And every time I passed a closed door I was scared—scared there was something weird going on behind it."

Paige laughed. Raul's father was a distinguished professor of Spanish at the university—a poet, a translator of Neruda, of Borges. Paige had had a class from him years before—years before she met Raul—and had thought him foppish and vain and annoying. She loved the idea of Raul's parents doing weird things behind closed doors.

"It's not funny, Paige—I was scared."

"Poor baby," Paige said.

"I know. And then they wonder why I grew up the way I am. It's all their fault."

Raul was depressed. He had gone to his mother asking for money and she had been curt with him—she'd given him the money, but a lecture, too. She expected more out of Raul—everybody did. He had barely graduated from high school, had flunked out of the university after a semester, and had spent the last ten years smoking pot and having sex with older women—and men.

"It's all their fault," Raul said again. "They had to buy that house right next to the park—what did they think was going to happen?" The Ledesma's house was on a hill overlooking Pease Park, a popular cruising ground for Austin gays. Young Raul started hanging around the men's restroom at a very early age, though he always qualified his behavior, saying that he wasn't gay or even bisexual—that he never did anything to other men, he just had things done *to* him. He had been arrested once in a police sweep of the park, but had escaped and run home as the officer was checking his ID. Of course, the officer was left holding Raul's drivers' license in his hand, and soon a police car pulled into the Ledesma driveway to cart young Raul off to jail. His father had never forgiven him.

"They hate me," Raul said.

"Oh, they do not hate you," Paige said. She remembered Raul as he had been when she found him—dirty, unshaven, depressed, sitting behind the Kwik-Wash smoking marijuana with some other young losers. Paige had done several huge loads of laundry and didn't feel like lugging it all back up to her apartment. "Which one of you is man enough to carry my laundry?" Paige asked. The boys all looked at the ground. Finally Raul said, "I'll do it for five dollars," and he carried her laundry home—and he never left. For over ten years he'd been hanging around, even during Paige's short, disastrous second marriage. She hated to admit it, but Raul had become her main companion in life, even though he was annoying, argumentative, rude, opinionated, and stubborn—and, at times, incredibly and unreasonably and *violently* jealous of her other boyfriends and lovers. At least he was clean, now, most of the time.

"Yes, they do. They hate me."

"No, you're just a major disappointment, is all," Paige said. "They're both successful, and worldly, and your brothers and sisters are all successful, and you're just—you. Can you blame them for being disappointed?"

Raul didn't answer. After a moment, Paige looked around the corner. Raul was staring at the television—CNN again, showing some old women in a gym doing aerobics. The sound was off; Raul was staring at the old ladies jumping and kicking. He was holding a newspaper over his lap.

"Are you okay?"

"No!" Raul glanced at her darkly and then looked back at the television.

"Poor baby." Paige dried her hands off and went over to Raul and kissed him on the forehead. "Listen, it's okay if you're a disappointment. That's just the way you are."

"Great." Raul pouted out his lower lip. "That's just great."

"It *is* just great." Paige took the newspaper from Raul, and, as she expected, found that he had an erection. She settled in on his lap. Raul sat there, uncomfortable, and Paige kissed him again, and ran her fingers through his hair, smiling. "You perform a great service to the community. You mow old ladies' lawns, and then you fuck them—*somebody* has to do that!"

"No, not always. Not all of them."

"But sometimes." Paige fell backwards onto the couch, pulling Raul on top of her. "And that makes the old ladies excited," Paige whispered. "They think they're living an exciting and dangerous life. Sex with the lawn boy—oh my!"

Raul was silent. In a moment they were naked on the

couch, and Raul was on her, taking his time, as usual, and Paige said, slowly smiling, "And just think of all those dildos I'd have to have if you weren't around!"

🥃 🍸 🍺 🍷

The great-tailed grackle had adapted very well to city life and was the most common bird in the city, able to live on bugs or garbage or almost anything. They were large birds with black, iridescent feathers and bright crazy reptilian yellow eyes, and the males were larger than the females and carried an impressive fan-shaped tail: they fought for the best position in the highest branches of trees or the loftiest arch of a streetlight and they posed there, bills pointed toward the sky, gasping and croaking and hissing, shitting on anything that happened to be beneath them. Quincy Whittaker loved the grackles and he thought they were just like—life.

Quincy's cab was parked outside the office shack of a big towing company on the south side. The cab's meter was up to $64.25 now, and still running, clicking up another quarter every forty seconds or so. He could see the crazy woman through the shack's window, waving her arms and jabbering about something. Behind the shack was a fence enclosing a vast field of cars and trucks, mostly dead and partially disassembled, rotting under the hard harsh sun. In front of the shack, by a ditch, stood a giant lone sycamore, filled with grackles. Quincy was parked in the tree's shade, enduring a steady rain of grackle shit—just like life.

This is how it will all end, he thought, the World will come to a damn end while I sit in a car getting *shit* on. This is how it is.

For months Quincy had been anticipating the end of the world. There was a psychic who came on the radio late at night when Quincy was sitting alone in his dark, quiet cab, and every night the psychic seemed a little more worked up about the end times. He had a vision of a fungus that was going to kill all the planet's plant life, leaving no food for humans or domestic animals—no food at all. There was going to be an explosion of x-rays from the sun that would fry whatever side of the Earth was facing the sun at the time. The U.S. economy would collapse because of a mystery illness that would leave millions of people too ill to go to work. The dark star would swing in through the solar system, Nibiru or Marduk or whatever it was called—Planet X!—setting off a vast cataclysm of floods, winds, earthquakes, volcanoes—the end of the world, the end of the world, at last, and it was all tied in, somehow, to the Third Secret of Fatima, which was somehow connected to the Book of Revelations. Quincy was back on familiar ground, there, in Revelations. It was his favorite book of the Bible. He loved the part where the angels floated around streaming tears, crying "Woe! Woe! Woe, to all the inhabiters of Earth!" Sitting in the dark Quincy fondly imagined the skeletons of trees left leafless by the fungus, with great clouds of dirt and dust—no longer held fast by grass—blowing through the air, settling in dunes among the cars abandoned along the highways, Escalades, Navigators, Range Rovers, great huge SUVs like dead dinosaurs, bleached bones of the drivers behind the wheels, corpses cluttering the streets, food for the grackles. Then Marduk would loom on the horizon and there'd be an earthquake or two, a typhoon, a tidal wave, and the Earth would be washed clean. Woe to all mankind! Woe, you motherfuckers! Woe! Day and night, driving his battered cab through the streets of the city, Quincy pondered the end of the world—there were signs everywhere, he could see it coming, looking off at the expressways and strip malls teeming with rude goddamn rich people, thoughtless bastards worried more about their taxes than their souls, preening, cocky, ignorant of their fate, shitting on everyone below them—just like the damn grackles. Just like life. The end of the world! Quincy *wanted* it to happen. He wanted it. He couldn't wait.

Linda came out of the shack. "This is the wrong place," she said. "They don't have my truck."

"I was lookin' at those cars," Quincy said. "Those trucks over there." He pointed with his chin across the fence at the endless field of broken-down dead vehicles.

"Yeah?"

"Those were all peoples' lives, once. You know what I'm saying? People were *proud* to have those cars then, new cars, drive 'em all day, happy. Now they all a bunch of junk—worthless, nothing, dead. That's how we're *all* going to end up, you know?"

"Yeah?" Linda asked.

Quincy nodded. "Soon, too."

Linda looked out the window. She'd barely noticed the piles of dead cars, but now that Quincy pointed them out—hard afternoon sun glaring off the broken glass and twisted metal of the vehicles as they slowly returned to their base elements—they were, really, terribly oppressive. Junk. Lost dreams. Lost youth. Death. Linda flopped back in the seat, suddenly depressed.

"Good Lord," she said. "Take me someplace to get a drink."

The name of the girl biologist was Jennifer Berg. Gilbert was amused when she refused a beer a second time; she seemed to mistrust him. Still, she got into his car to guide him up to the house.

"So Johnston didn't do much with this land, huh?" he asked.

"Well, he just inherited it, I think," Jennifer Berg said. "But, no, the family didn't—hasn't—done anything with it in years and years. It's like a little wildlife refuge back here."

"Wildlife refuge," Gilbert said. "Huh."

The driveway circled up around the edge of a bluff, then ran almost straight down to the creek. Gilbert stopped the car by the water, deep in shade from sycamores, willows, cottonwoods. Wildlife refuge—people would like that.

"I guess this is where it happened," Gilbert finally said. "The murder."

Gilbert got out of the car. Clear water bubbled across the low-water crossing. In the pool above the crossing small fish darted around, and a turtle swam awkwardly for cover. Jennifer got out of the car and stood looking at Gilbert.

"The cab got up to here," Gilbert said. "And the driver, he didn't want to cross the creek—he couldn't tell how deep the water was."

"Yeah," Jennifer said. "It gets dark out here."

"It was dark out here," Gilbert said. "It was nighttime. The driver didn't know what was going on. So Mr. Johnston got out and started walking away across the creek without paying his fare. Then the driver got out and yelled something, maybe tried to stop him, and Johnston pulled out a pistol and capped his ass."

"Wow," Jennifer said.

"Then he took the driver's wallet and rolled him into the water." Gilbert stepped over next to Jennifer and looked at the downstream side of the crossing. The tall bankside grass had been beaten down and there were a number of tire tracks. "Then he got in the cab and drove it on up to the house."

"Wow," Jennifer said again. "That's just so—sad."

"I know that's right," Gilbert said.

They got back into the car and Gilbert drove over the crossing, clear shallow water splashing at the wheels, and then up the bank and around some trees, coming out into a large clearing. The house was there, long and low, built of limestone, solid and permanent-looking, though the windows were dark and the surrounding lawn needed mowing. Gilbert got out of the car. Everything was very quiet. A pair of vultures swooped low over the house and then out over the creek canyon, circling and rising on the hot breeze.

"What's going to happen to all this?" Jennifer asked.

"Oh, it'll probably get developed," Gilbert said. *Justice Estates*, he thought. Dad always knew you'd do good! Justice fucking Estates.

"Son of a bitch." The girl shook her head sadly. "Son of a fucking bitch."

Chapter Eight

Pave it All

HOME FROM WORK, TIRED, RICHARD CANTU TRIED dozing in the bathtub, soaking in warm, soapy water, but it seemed like every few minutes someone—his wife, his daughter—would come knocking at the door.

"Are you *still* in there?" This time it was Kelly. Amy was still too young to challenge him so openly; she'd usually knock and then whine about needing to pee and how she couldn't use the other bathroom because Davy was in there and and and—*kids*. Whiners. Crybabies. Where the hell did they get that from?

"Yeah, I'm still in here. I'm taking a *bath*."

"Well, I *want* to take a bath, okay?"

"I'll be out in a minute." The room was dark—lights out, shades drawn. Richard sank as far into the water as he could, a washcloth over his face.

"What's with this bath thing, anyway?" Kelly asked. "Most men take showers—you always take a shower."

"Well, now I like taking a fucking bath," Richard said through the washcloth. He didn't even open his eyes. "Okay?"

"Since when?"

Richard didn't bother to answer. After a moment or

so of silence he ran some more hot water into the tub. The "bath thing" began about the same time he had started seeing Giselle, of course. She loved a hot bath. Richard thought of Giselle, Giselle—soapy, slippery, tattoos, breasts, thighs, painted toenails—*damn*. His sore penis started to stiffen. He was in pain, but it was a good pain—his dick was red, chewed on, bent, the muscles in his butt ached, his thighs burned. Giselle was wearing him out. He'd never been so happy. Richard gently squeezed his penis, thinking about the first time he had seen Giselle's pussy—the first time he'd really taken the time to *study* it. She had three labial piercings, which—in his unfortunately limited experience—were strange, but strange too were the tattoos on the inside of her thighs: little John-John Kennedy on the left saluting across the way to Mao Tse-tung, on the right. He considered them for some time—aware, nervous, that Giselle was also considering him.

"Is it political?" he finally asked.

"Political?" Giselle asked. She reached down and touched herself. "My *cat*?"

"The tattoos," Richard said. "The Mao."

"Oh!" Giselle laughed. She rubbed at one of the labial studs and grinned at Richard, heavy wet lips, white hard teeth. "I saw one like that on Mike Tyson—the boxer. I had to have one like it."

"The boxer," Richard repeated.

"Kiss it," Giselle said suddenly. Before Richard could ask "Kiss what?" she lunged up and grabbed him by the ears, falling backwards, pulling his face into her crotch. He found himself eye-to-eye with young John Kennedy. He could remember the President's funeral, sort of, just a child at the time, in kindergarten, no cartoons on the television, the grown-ups all solemn and grave. But now he laughed, kissing little John-John, turning to kiss Mao too—

A loud knock—*bam*!

"Richard! What are you *doing* in there?"

"Taking a fucking *bath*!" Richard pulled the wet

washcloth from his face and hurled it at the door, glaring. It struck with a soft plop, then fell to the carpet.

"Well, hurry up. And don't curse at me." He heard Kelly close the bedroom door.

"Christ." The bath was ruined. Richard let go of his dick and hit the drain lever. The water began to gurgle out and the cool air felt good on his wet skin. When the water was gone he heaved his sore butt out of the tub and dried carefully. He slapped on deodorant and baby powder, and dressed in an old, loose-fitting pair of shorts and a t-shirt he had brought out earlier. He listened by the door for a moment—silence, for once—and opened it.

The bedroom was empty. He glanced at the bed—the square, stiffly-made, immaculate bed where he slept with Kelly—glancing at it with mild guilt, but with mild revulsion, too. Kelly. Jeeze. He crossed the room and went out into the hall. The doors to Amy's and Davy's bedrooms were shut. He could hear a television playing in Amy's room. Davy's room was silent. Suddenly full of concern for his son, he knocked on Davy's door, a soft *tap-tap*. A friendly knock, he hoped. After a pause, Davy—his voice thin and scared-sounding—said, "Yes?"

"You okay, boy?" Richard asked.

Another pause, and then, "Yes."

"I'm just checking on you, you know?"

"—Thank you."

Richard thought for a moment. He wanted to say something else. "Hey, you want to go to a football game this fall?"

"*Football?*"

Richard himself hadn't been to a football game in years, but it sounded like a good father-son thing to do.

"Yeah," he said, "I'll get some tickets, we'll go see the Longhorns. They're gonna have a good team this year, you know?"

He could really hear the fear in his son now. "That'd be great—*Dad.*"

"Okay, then." Richard went on down the hallway, disturbed. What did that boy do in there all day? Whack off? Davy was thin and gangly, with huge brown eyes like a starved dog, and it was hard to imagine him masturbating. *Distasteful* to imagine that. Jesus. Richard went into the living room and found his wife watching television—an ancient rerun of *That Girl*. He asked, "What's that boy do in there all day?"

"You leave Davy alone," Kelly said. "You know how sensitive he is."

"Well, yeah," Richard said. "But I was just wondering...."

Kelly looked up at him with dull irritation. "Are you through with your *bath* now?"

Richard said, "Yeah, I'm through."

"You probably used up all the hot water." Kelly got up and passed Richard, keeping her distance, and he watched her go up the hall and to the bedroom. When he heard the water running, he went to the phone and dialed Giselle's cell number. It rang twice, then dropped to voicemail.

"Hey, babe! See you at 8:30, at Ceasar's!"

Richard hung up, and turned to find his daughter, Amy, staring at him. Startled, but he forced a smile and said, "Hey, girl! How's it goin'?"

Amy turned without speaking and headed back down the hallway to her room. Richard shook his head. Family life—it was a fucking prison.

🍸🍺🍷🍶

Linda paid off Quincy—the meter read $112.75—and tipped him and watched him drive away. They had not found her truck—that could wait until tomorrow, or something. Later. She tried stuffing the fare receipt in her bulging purse but it popped back out and blew off down the street. Whatever. She turned and went into the Little Wagon.

"Linda!"

Linda heard Paige's voice but could not see her. The Little Wagon was dim—hell, dark—and it took her a moment for her eyes to adjust. Then she saw Paige sitting in a corner with Charlie Bessent. She went over and dropped her purse and phone on the table.

"I think I've figured things out," Linda said, digging around in her purse and pulling out some money. "I think I've got a plan."

"How wonderful," Charlie said.

Linda ignored him and went up to the bar and ordered two glasses of wine. The barmaid, a dark-haired, motherly-looking woman, looked at Linda's black eye, and asked, "Are you okay?"

"Hell no," Linda said. She carefully carried the glasses back to the table, only spilling one a little. "Listen—we're going to destroy Richard Cantu."

"We are?" Charlie asked.

"We are," Linda said. "Paige had the right idea all along. We're going to find out everything about the little creep's girlfriend, and then we'll blackmail him!"

Paige didn't say anything.

"Blackmail," Charlie snorted. "Who cares if he's got a girlfriend?"

"His wife!" Linda said.

"Actually, probably not," Paige said. "She's probably glad she doesn't have to sleep with him herself. I mean, think about it."

"I thought you were on my side," Linda said.

"I'm always on your side!"

"Blackmail," Charlie said. "What do you think you're going to get from him?"

"Oh, I don't know," Linda said. She thought for a moment. "Actually, I guess don't want anything from him—he just needs to be destroyed because he's a rude little shit. He's my enemy, right?"

Charlie shrugged. "Maybe you could just fuck him."

Linda looked at him, squinting her bad eye.

"I'm quite serious," Charlie said. "You know, you'd have to see each other every day—think of all the stress he'd be burdened with. He'd never know if you were going to say something to someone, never know if you were going to tell his wife—every day would be a torture."

"Too much trouble," Linda said. She sat quietly, shot down, and sipped her wine. There had to be some way of destroying Cantu.

Paige leaned forward. "We'll come up with something."

A loud voice came out of the darkness. "Hey! I've been looking for you all day!"

🍸🍺🍷🍾

Linda looked up and—well, yes—there was Gilbert Hardison, holding a mug of beer in his big hand.

"I thought you were sick," Linda said. "One of your clients told me you stood him up."

"Aw, all those criminals do is complain. Bitch, bitch, bitch." Hardison pulled out a chair from another table and sat down, squeezing between Paige and Linda. "Listen, I've been trying to get hold of you so I could apologize about the other night."

"I should hope so." Linda looked at Charlie. "This is the guy that knocked me in the face with his goddamn forehead."

"I've seen you on television," Charlie said. He reached across the table to shake hands. "I like the commercial where you help the little old white lady cross the street." He laughed. "'*I* will help you!'"

"Yeah, that's one of the new ones, the Good Deed series." Gilbert said. He looked at Linda. "Listen, baby, I'd like to make it up to you. Okay?"

"It's all your fault," Linda said. "Everything's all your fault."

"Well, maybe. But like I said, I've been trying to get hold of you. I called, left messages."

"I don't check messages anymore," Linda said.

"Since when?" Paige asked.

"Since Saturday," Linda said. "Someone might want me

to call back. I turned the ringer off on my phone, too."

"Well, hell," Gilbert said. "There you are—I've been trying to get hold of you, and you've been unavailable."

Linda frowned. "Where's the evidence?"

"Check your damn messages," Hardison said. He looked at Paige. "And I think—"

"Maybe I *will* check my messages."

" —I think I found that tattooed bitch."

"See if you really called."

"She works at the Hyatt," Gilbert told Paige. "I knew she was at one hotel or another. Tends bar there, has this big bird tattooed all over her back. First time I saw her, I thought she was wearing some sort of camouflage bodysuit, you know, but it turned out to be all her—those tattoos. I don't think she likes me." He looked back at Linda. "So why don't you let me buy you dinner?"

"I need to do laundry," Linda said. "But it'd be nice if you'd do it for me. Have you learned how to iron?"

🍸🍺🍷🍹

The jukebox faded out. Gilbert looked at Linda for a moment: her eyes were bright and alert behind the swelling. He looked over at Charlie.

"You do real estate–development law, right?" he asked. "Municipal Utility Districts, Public Utility Districts, stuff like that?"

"Oh, I do many things."

"Yeah, I'm thinking about branching out, you know? I've got some opportunities." Gilbert stopped. He wasn't quite ready to tell people about the ranch—about Justice Estates.

"There's always opportunities," Charlie said airily. "'Texas is built on opportunities.' That was one of my lines when I ran for the legislature. Went over big at the Comanche County Chamber of Commerce. 'Texas is *built* on opportunities, and we Texans make our own opportunities.'"

"I'd probably vote for you," Linda said.

Charlie smiled. "You're not even registered."

"Too much trouble," Linda said. She shrugged. "Don't you have to get up in the morning to vote?"

"The census says eighty-one people a day are moving to Austin," Gilbert said. "All those people'll need houses, stores—"

"Seventy-nine of them will be criminals at some point in their lives," Paige said. "You'll do fine."

Gilbert shook his head. He'd seen the huge houses—palaces, really—going up around Lake Travis. The people in those palaces wouldn't likely turn to The Justice Store when they were arrested for DWI or spousal battery, or when they needed a will or a deed drawn up. No, the trick was to get their money before then—to *build* the damn palaces—to build Justice Estates.

Charlie said, "Whenever I see a developer, I think, Let's go find something to pave and make some money!"

"Pave it all," Gilbert nodded thoughtfully. "Yeah, make you some money."

Linda looked away and frowned. Any way you looked at it, building or selling, real estate was boring. There was money to be made with it—but so what? Linda lived just west of downtown in the central part of Austin, never straying far from a path that led from her townhouse to her office to the courthouse to the Little Wagon and back again, and the relentless spread of Austin west into the Hill County—the endless fights between environmentalists and developers—was all just a rumor to her. Pave it all, she thought. Who the hell cares?

"See," Gilbert said, "when I set up my practice, I figured I could either be Neiman-Marcus or Wal-Mart."

"Neiman's!" Paige said. "There's no choice!"

Charlie said, "Honey, I hate to say it, but I think Sam Walton made much more money than Stanley Marcus."

"But the class of people you have to deal with...."

Linda realized that everyone was looking at her. Oh, she thought.

"Goddamn criminals," she said aloud, and everyone laughed.

"Developers aren't necessarily nice," Charlie said, "but I suppose they're somewhat cleaner than the average crack addict you people represent."

"They can always shower at the country club," Paige said.

"On the other hand," Gilbert said, "my clients may not be clean, but there's a lot *of* 'em."

Linda thought of the parade of criminals that marched through her life—most of them poor, dispirited, downcast, shabby—all of them guilty. How depressing. Maybe *she* should have gone to work for real estate developers. As far as she knew, she had no moral reservations about paving over birds and trees. If Charlie ever went to hell, she thought, it would certainly be for crimes against nature—but for sodomy, not suburban sprawl.

"And you have three convenient locations," Paige said.

"Right, but I got this problem—with all these opportunities I'm getting, I'm running into the laws of physics—I can't be in more than one place at a time."

Linda thought about developers. She could do MUDs and PUDs just as well as Charlie could, probably, if she paid attention, and she could spend the rest of her time hanging around country clubs. But—well, hell—there really wasn't anything for her to *do* at country clubs. Linda didn't play golf or tennis. She might as well stay home and watch Court TV and let Paige go to the country clubs. How irritating. Real estate law was probably just as irritating as criminal law—even without the criminals. They probably called meetings in the mornings, too.

To hell with it, she thought. To hell with everything. Why bother?

"So, I'm sort of thinking about expanding—about bringing on some more attorneys," Gilbert said, looking at Linda. "You know?"

"To hell with it," Linda said aloud. "I think—what're we talking about, anyway?"

"Sounds like he's offering you a position at The Justice Store," Charlie said. He smiled his thin smile and poured some beer.

Linda frowned. "Why?"

"You speak Spanish?" Gilbert asked.

"No," Linda quickly lied.

"Oh, please," Paige said. "You speak excellent Spanish."

"Yeah, I thought you did," Gilbert said. "Anyway, all you really need to know is guilty and probation and be able to count how many months until they get out."

"*Culpable*," Paige said. "*Libertad condicional.*"

"Too much trouble," Linda said. "I'm thinking of going into real estate law with Charlie."

Charlie laughed into his beer. Linda glared at him.

Paige said, "*Uno, dos, tres....*"

"Well, hell," Gilbert said. "We might go that way, too—real estate law. You never know. The opportunities are endless at The Justice Store. Sometimes we even make our own opportunities, you know?"

"I told you, I have to do my laundry," Linda said. "Well, I mean, *somebody* has to do my laundry. You didn't answer my question about ironing."

Chapter Nine

Almost Relaxed

A YOWLING YELLOW TOMCAT—SOMEONE'S CURIOUS PET— followed Linda and Gilbert into her condo and resisted Linda's half-hearted attempts to chase it back out. After a few minutes Linda gave up and sprawled back on her couch, trying to rest, hoping to sleep. The living room was dim, gloomy and comfortable, except that the yellow cat kept trying to hop up on her belly. After getting tossed off three times the cat sat on the floor near Linda's head, staring at her.

"If you're looking for those parakeets, they're gone," Linda said.

From a distant part of the townhouse she heard a washing machine start, and in another moment or two Gilbert bustled in with a bottle of wine and a glass.

"Here," he said, filling the glass. "I started your clothes, I got you this drink, and in a minute I'm gonna get to work on those steaks. Okay?"

"I'm not in the mood to eat," Linda said. But she took the wine glass from Gilbert and rested it on her belly.

"That washer you got's complicated but I managed to figure it out," Gilbert said. He stood looking down at her. "You know, you really got a lot of dirty clothes. You need to get a maid or something."

"A maid?" Linda asked. "You go and hire me one. Why the hell should I have to pay someone to do my laundry?"

"Maybe you should take a vacation," Gilbert said. "Ever think of that? Maybe I can sneak away, too, we can go to Mexico or someplace, sit on the beach and relax."

"The beach," Linda snorted. "Bunch of goddamn *sand*. I'll never understand why people want to go some weird creepy foreign place and sit on a pile of goddamn sand."

"Take my word, baby," Gilbert said, "you need to relax, some. You're on edge—you're getting to the point where you make *me* nervous. So drink your wine and relax."

"Relaxation is the next thing to death," Linda said. She turned her face away from Gilbert.

"You're crazy," Gilbert said. He walked off, and soon Linda could hear some banging around in the kitchen.

Linda took a deep breath and slowly exhaled, almost relaxed, not quite dead, probably depressed. The beach, she thought. Goddamn. Sand. Ridiculous. Oh well. She closed her eyes. The couch was very comfortable, and she might have had a pleasant time lounging there, dozing—except for that damn cat staring at her, and Gilbert. Gilbert would probably want to use his man-meat on her after dinner; that would have to be avoided. But at least she was getting her laundry done—that was the important thing, clean clothes, maybe even *ironed* clean clothes. It was almost worth putting up with man-meat for.

Paige was restless. Monday evening at the Little Wagon was not a busy time: construction workers, a few businessmen, a very few graduate students from the nearby married student housing, losers, losers, losers. Nobody worth fucking with—or fucking, for that matter. Paige was restless, and reckless: she felt like causing some trouble.

"That blackmail thing," Paige said. "I just meant that as a

joke, sort of. I didn't think she'd take me seriously."

"Linda can be strangely obsessive at times," Charlie said.

Paige frowned. Like the trip to see Madame Bustos, the search for Judge Cantu's probably imaginary girlfriend—and the idea to blackmail him—was intended to get Linda out and about and distract her from her depressing thoughts. It hadn't seemed to work, though.

"So this judge of Linda's," Paige asked Charlie, "how fat is he, really?"

"Oh, he's not grossly obese or anything," Charlie said. "He's just sort of—round. You know? Linda should just roll him away and forget the whole thing."

"Linda needs someone to blame," Paige said. "For everything."

"Perhaps that's it."

"Maybe *I* should sleep with him." Paige pursed her lips, thinking. Not to blackmail him, but to get the judge involved in something—something weird, maybe, something weird that would help Linda. "If I slept with him, it'd make Linda feel better."

Charlie laughed. "You could take up missionary work."

"Missionary position, unless he's *really* fat," Paige said. "It might even be fun."

"Suit yourself," Charlie said. "I wouldn't bother. He's not my type."

Paige smiled. "I guess that rules out a three-way, huh?"

Charlie sighed dreamily. "Yes, dear, I suppose it does."

Charlie was on his third big pitcher of beer and seemed pleasantly drunk and content. He probably had nothing more pressing to do than wobble home and take a Xanax and drink vodka and watch "Oriental Anal, Part VI." Paige, though, wanted something more—exciting. She finished the last of her wine and stood up.

"I have to go."

"Well," Charlie said. "If you must."

"If you see Raul, tell him to call me later—a lot later."

Outside, Paige got into her car and headed toward town.

The car, a battered green Jaguar, was a relic of her second marriage, and she felt comfortable driving it—reckless, restless—cruising slowly along the lake, watching people jogging or walking their dogs, crossing the First Street Bridge to the Hyatt. Paige was too easily bored—she knew it was her biggest fault. She moved from one fascination, one obsession, to another—failed first marriage, disastrous second marriage, career as a stock broker, career in marketing, career at a dot-com, grad student in math, grad student in philosophy—almost-finished dissertations abandoned on the hard drives of her computers as her interest faded—body builder one year, tennis player the next, then with little preparation on to the nationals in her age group in the heptathelon. Always the interest in men, sex, drugs, rock'n'roll—reckless, restless trouble. She was a natural at whatever she attempted, but too easily bored—a situation she sometimes regretted, but not for long. Regret was boring.

The Hyatt lounge was quiet and cool, and mostly empty. Paige went over and took a seat at the bar. A woman came around a corner and stood over the sink, rinsing glassware. Paige caught a glimpse of a tattoo—a dark red mark, at least—at the collar of her blouse. She looked up at Paige and smiled.

"Hi," Giselle said. "Can I help you?"

Maybe, Paige thought, maybe. She ordered a cognac and watched Giselle go down the bar to get it. Giselle was about the same height as Paige but far fleshier—heavier breasts, wider hips, wild thick hair. Still, when Paige studied Giselle's face she recognized the hungry, sexual look. If this woman was sleeping with the judge, then she was almost certainly sleeping with another man—shoot, other men—as well. Unless this fat judge was really something special.

"Thanks," Paige said, when Giselle brought the cognac. She didn't offer to pay for it, assuming that Giselle would give it to her free, or run a tab, or something. "I thought my boyfriend would be here waiting for me. He better not stand me up."

"Men," Giselle agreed.

Closer, directly across the bar, Paige could see hints of the tattoos around Giselle's neck and at the top of her chest. Other tattoos peeked out from beneath her rolled-up sleeves. Red, black, blue, Paige couldn't make out what they formed but they were quite startling—and, maybe, for some men, sexy—against Giselle's pale skin.

Paige watched Giselle sway down the bar, hips and hair, and noticed that a man three or four stools away was staring back at her. White guy, lean and athletic, well groomed, mustache, pale blue eyes. He was watching her.

Paige smiled at him—reckless, restless. "Hello!"

🍺 🍺 🍸 🍸

Linda slept, but at some point she was aware that Gilbert was leaning over her, saying something about dinner. Dinner! Too much trouble. She waved him away. Then, later, she felt a hand—hands, maybe—squeezing, feeling, sliding down her belly to her crotch. It didn't feel like the yellow tomcat so it must have been Gilbert, though she didn't know for sure—she didn't even open her eyes. Sex was *far* too much trouble. She pushed whoever belonged to the hand (or hands) away, and slept on.

When Linda finally woke up, it took a moment or two for her to realize where she was. It was dark outside and inside, and very quiet: no television, no radio, no dishwasher. Linda remembered, Oh, this is *my* place. She stood up, unsteady at first, and stumbled to the bathroom and turned on a light. It was surprisingly clean. Tim, she thought, thank God for Tim. But when she was through she looked in the utility room and saw her clothes—some wet, some dry—strewn all over the floor, spread across the washer and the dryer, mostly unwashed or half-washed or something weird, everything all ahoo and unironed and wet and mildewing. Goddamn Gilbert! After all these years he still did everything half-assed.

Back in the kitchen she found a big, broiled rib eye in the refrigerator, along with some uncooked broccoli. There was a bottle of wine on the table. Linda heated the broccoli in the microwave and ate the steak as it was—cold. It tasted wonderful—much better, too, for not having to be shared with inept lazy failed househusband Gilbert Hardison. She saw a note under the wine bottle: "Enjoy your dinner—G."

"Enjoy you not being here," Linda said aloud. "And what the hell am I supposed to do about those clothes?"

She opened the bottle and poured a glass, and ate the broccoli and the beef and felt fine until she noticed her bulky cell phone sitting on the kitchen counter. A cold feeling of dread settled over her—she could feel it in the pit of her stomach, in her shoulders. The phone was a threat: she hadn't checked her messages since Saturday. There was no telling what was in there—no telling who had called. She dreaded the damn thing.

After a moment she took the phone and dialed her voicemail. An almost human-sounding computer told her she had 13 messages. Only thirteen! It could have been much worse. Linda positioned her forefinger over the delete button to erase the messages as fast as she heard them.

Gilbert Hardison. "Sunshine? Hey, I'm sorry—"

He sounded drunk. Delete.

Gilbert. "Baby, I'm tryin to get hold—"

Still drunk. Delete.

Gilbert. "Hey, Sunshine, I've got a serious sort of business proposition for you, you know, I think you're gonna love it. Call me."

He sounded sober there. But what business proposition? At the bar Gilbert had said something about expanding opportunities at The Justice Store. Still, they hadn't really talked. Delete.

A woman's voice. "Linda, this is Raycene." Raycene was the receptionist at Foster & Moomaw, a rude trashy bitch. "You're supposed to call in if you're not going to be here."

"Oh, go to hell," Linda said. Delete.

Raycene again. "Linda, nobody knows where you are! Please call in. Mr. Foster wants to talk with you. Call in!"

"Go to hell!" Linda said again. Delete.

A man's rather passive voice. "Linda, this is Jeff Foster. We're very worried that you haven't called in. Or come in, either. Is everything okay? Please call."

Linda could almost picture the watery do-gooder eyes of Foster, the senior partner at the firm. Having him call was a bad sign. The dread settled even more heavily into her gut. Delete.

Don Frazier, a crack dealer. "Say, did you call that probation officer for me?"

Not until you pay me the money you owe me, asshole. Delete.

Paige. "Linda! Charlie and I are going to the Wagon—why don't you join us?"

Old news. Delete.

"Linda, this is Jeff Foster again. It's—well, it's just very important that we talk. Please call or come on in."

Delete.

"Linda, this is Karl Moomaw." The other partner, a harsh voice. Having him call was even worse. "You need to contact Jeff or myself immediately. Call my pager, call my cell phone, call me at home, call the answering service. We need to speak to you as soon as possible."

Linda took a deep breath and thought about that. "Oh, bite me," she finally said. She was starting to get pissed off. Why the hell were these people calling? Delete.

Linda thought for a moment and then hit the delete key again—and again, and again, deleting all the remaining messages before she even heard them. It crossed her mind that the delete key was a wonderful invention: there were whole passages of her life—of human existence—that would be better off deleted.

"To hell with everybody." Linda took the bottle and glass and headed back toward the darkened room and her comfortable couch and the cat.

Chapter Ten

Too Much Trouble

RICHARD FELL ASLEEP AT SOME PPOINT BUT WOKE up confused. He was being *kissed*. Kissed—Giselle, he realized, quickly recognizing her thick hair, her scent, her touch, kissing her back.

"You weren't asleep—you were faking," Giselle said.

"I'll give you faking."

Giselle laughed, "Fake me!"

Richard rolled Giselle over and took her from behind, reading the designs on her back in the dim light coming from the bathroom. Sometimes it was like—well, maybe there was a message written there for him, something hidden and secret burned into Giselle's flesh. Richard ran his fingers down her back, from her shoulders to her hips—soft, soft, surprisingly cool.

"Richie," Giselle said.

Richard slipped out then, his cock rubbing against her ass, and Giselle reached for him; but he was tired and he rolled Giselle over and covered her.

"Baby, you're heavy," Giselle laughed. Richard didn't say anything. Exhausted, milked dry, drained, he slowly slowly humped away until he finally came. Giselle kissed him. "Baby, get off—you're *heavy*."

Richard rolled away. Good God! Never—never—*never*—had he felt so—

"I'm so relaxed," Giselle said. She put her head on his chest, thick hair spraying up into his face. Richard held her close, but with his free hand he fumbled around on the nightstand looking for his watch.

Coming up on three o'clock. Good God! He'd never stayed out past midnight before. What would Kelly—well, no, *fuck* what Kelly would say. Still—

"It's time to go," he said.

"Mmmm. When're we going to really spend the night together?"

"I don't know."

Giselle lifted her head and looked at Richard. He couldn't make out her expression in the dark. But then she took his left breast in her mouth, softly sucking—then biting. *Hard.*

"Ow! Hey, cut it out!"

"Someday I will," Giselle said. "Someday I'll cut your fucking heart out and I'll *eat* it—and then where'll you be?" She went into the bathroom and closed the door. Richard lay in the dark fingering his chest. Moody. Damn, she was moody.

When it was his turn in the bathroom, Richard showered quickly, examining himself as he soaped. There was going to be another big bruise. What would Kelly think? Well, it didn't matter what she thought, as long as she kept her mouth closed. Richard made up his mind, once and for all: Fuck Kelly. As for Giselle—she was moody.

Richard came out of the bathroom, buttoning his shirt. Giselle was dressed, sprawled out across the bed, eyes shut, the bottom of her blouse pulled up, exposing her navel. Tattooed flames shot out of it, like a volcano. Richard was tempted to stick his tongue into the flaming crater, but settled for placing his hand on her hot belly. She covered it with hers.

"When're we going to spend the whole night together?"

Giselle asked again, eyes closed.

"Soon...."

"You lie." Giselle jerked away and got to her feet. Moody.

But out in the car she was different again—kittenish, cuddling, scrunching up close, her head on his shoulder, hand running down his belly to his crotch. What was the deal? Richard was baffled. Either she was pissed off or she wasn't. His experience with women—sadly limited to Kelly, his mother, his daughter, his sisters, and his one serious girlfriend before Kelly—had led him to believe that all women were more or less permanently pissed-off. Pissed-off, and demanding. So Richard could live with Giselle's bad moods: they were normal. But that she got over the bad moods so quickly, that she could almost instantly switch back to being playful, sexy, fun-loving—*that* had him baffled.

"Baby," Richard began, then stopped. "You—you don't know how much you *mean* to me."

Giselle laughed. "I think it's funny, you never know what to say." She gave his dick a squeeze.

They came to a stoplight. Richard looked over at Giselle and saw a police car pull up alongside them. The policeman glanced back at him. Richard panicked.

"Jesus! Get your seatbelt on!"

"What?"

The cop seemed to be staring at them.

"Get your fucking seatbelt on! He'll give us a fucking ticket!"

"Fuck you!" Giselle said. But she straightened up and slipped behind the seat belt, the strap pushing apart her breasts.

Richard could just picture the disaster—ticket, arrest, newspaper coverage, Kelly, Kelly, Kelly, divorce, bankruptcy, humiliation. Kelly. He imagined his wife's face before him, acne pocks burning as she yelled, screaming—or worse, pouted. Yeah, silence would be worse. Fucking Kelly.

Then he saw Giselle's window sliding down. "What're you doing?"

"Hey!" Giselle was waving at the cop. "Hey!"

The cop's window came down. He was a young white guy, broad dull face, powerful shoulders, buzz-cut hair. Probably juiced on steroids, like most of the cops he knew.

"We just had sex!"

The light changed to green. The cop looked at the light, then back at Giselle.

"Hey, officer—we were *fucking*!"

The cop nodded and gave a thumbs-up and pulled ahead. Richard was aghast. The light turned to yellow and he just barely made it through the intersection.

"What the fuck did you just do?"

"You're a fool," Giselle said. "The best thing that would ever happen to you would be if your stupid wife found out about us. You'd be lucky! You could live! But no—you're too stupid to see that."

"Baby," Richard said. He shook his head—those damn moods! "Giselle—"

"And how do you think it makes *me* feel? Most men would be proud to be with me. Instead you're ashamed—you won't even spend the night with me. You're a total fucking fool, Richie."

♀ ♂ ♀ 🍺

When Gilbert got home he could hear Delia's bedroom television playing. The rest of the house was dark and quiet. Gilbert dumped his bags of groceries and presents on the kitchen counter. He turned on a light and dug around in the bags until he found the stain remover—a little blue can that came with a brush. The burned steak was easy enough to find on the floor beneath the window, and there were grease stains on the drapes and carpet. Gilbert sprayed the remover on the spots and stood back, waiting for the stuff to work.

"Those drapes'll have to be dry-cleaned," Delia said from behind him. For a big woman she was light on her feet.

Gilbert turned and looked at her for a moment. Then he

reached up and started un-hooking the drapes.

"Not now," Delia said, "not tonight—you can do it tomorrow."

Gilbert shrugged and sat heavily on the floor to scrub at the stains.

"What's all this shit?" Delia asked from the kitchen.

"I was gonna fix you dinner," Gilbert said.

"I already ate."

Gilbert heard a package open. He said, "Don't look in that one—"

"Shit. Are these for me? Chocolates. I guess you must feel some special need to apologize."

"That was supposed to be a surprise," Gilbert said. He twisted around and looked at her. "But, yeah, I do apologize, you know? I'm really sorry about yesterday."

"You're a big lyin' phoney." Delia stood in the doorway, fumbling at the box of chocolates. "What you say doesn't mean anything. You're just a big liar."

"I'm sorry, baby."

"Everything you say is a lie." Delia ate a chocolate and watched Gilbert scrub ineffectively at the stains. She said, "You're doing that all wrong."

"I'll get it."

After another moment or two Delia couldn't stand it. "Oh, get on in there and fix me dinner," she said. "I'll scrub the damn stain—you'll never get it out."

Gilbert got clumsily to his feet and smiled at Delia. "I'm sorry," he said. "I *will* help you."

"Don't provoke me," Delia said. She pushed by him, reaching for the can of stain remover.

The rest of the evening went according to plan. Gilbert could actually cook, and the big, grilled steaks came out fine, with broccoli and baked potatoes, nothing very fancy but quite good. After several drinks Gilbert led Delia upstairs and they fell onto the giant bed, Delia such a big wide soft armful, soft and yielding and warm. Linda was a little scrawny boney girl compared to Delia, and crazy. Linda was crazy. Depressed all the time. Thinking about herself all the time. *Talking* about herself all the time. Who the hell could ever live with Linda? Delia was smart and independent, demanding but forgiving, up front except when she wasn't. Love Delia. Linda. Linda. Gilbert rolled back with a sigh, quickly falling asleep, drifting dreaming back, way back, back into a game he'd played against UT his senior season, late in the game, losing, and the UT tailback came around the end—and then dreaming drifting even further back, to high school, a Friday night game in the rain, another little tailback, scooping the little guy up and just *pounding* him into the damn mud. The hardest hit he'd ever made. It was cold, November, and the misty rain made glowing halos around the stadium lights, and people were screaming. Oh yes. Oh yes. Gilbert drifted off to sleep, happy, happy, holding Delia close, in love.

♀ 🍷 ♀ 🍺

Paige, feeling frisky and cheerful, with an unexpected $250 in her pocket, was unlocking her door when someone called her name. She turned around and saw Tim, standing in the courtyard shadows just outside his door.

"Paige!" he called again.

"Hello!" Paige pulled her key from the lock and walked over to him. "What're you doing up so late?"

"Messing around on the computer," Tim said. He looked thinner in the dark, thinner and somehow—cleaner. Neater, at least: hair washed and combed, his wispy mustache shaved away, torn jeans replaced by ironed khakis, torn flannel shirt replaced by a red-and-white striped cotton Oxford. Even though the shirt was a tad wrinkled, and worn outside his belt, Paige realized she was looking at a completely new Tim.

"So," she said, slowly, wondering at the change, "are you finding me some good porn?"

"Not exactly," Tim said. "Come on in."

Paige followed him into the apartment, and again was surprised—everything was changed. Hemingway and

Whitman were still on the walls, but everything else was different. Tim's bed had been moved to the center of the room, beneath Hemingway, and was covered with a heavy purple bedspread. The bookshelves and computer desk were cleared of clutter and empty beer cans, and the books and papers were neatly shelved and stacked. And it was all clean.

"Good God," Paige said. "What's going on with you?"

"I just straightened up a bit," Tim said. "I decided I'm going to use this for a studio, and I wanted it to look, you know, better." He showed Paige his webcam and the plans for his new site. "I'm going to try to get this up by Wednesday."

"And people are going to pay to watch you masturbate?"

"Yeah, I hope so."

"How wonderful!" Paige was delighted. "We'll have to tell Linda."

Tim sat in his computer chair and wheeled around. "Yeah, she's at home, I think," he said. "She had company earlier, though, some big black guy. She getting a new househusband or something?"

"That was probably Gilbert," Paige said. "You've seen him on TV—The Justice Store? 'I will help you?'"

"Oh...."

"He's married, anyway—married to Dr. Dee. I love Dr. Dee." Paige spotted a copy of the alternative newspaper, *Metropolis*, next to Tim's bed. She grabbed it and fluttered through the pages until she found the DateLine ad. "See? Dr. Dee's DateLine, featuring Dr. Dee's Dating Do's and Dating Don'ts."

Tim took the newspaper. "Wow."

"I love Dr. Dee's Dating Do's and Dating Don'ts," Paige said. "They're the secret of my social success."

"'*Do* curb your passions,'" Tim read. "'Don't let your passions curb *you*.'"

"Sometimes I have to go other extreme, sort of." Paige looked over Tim's shoulder. "'*Do* be exclusive, but *Don't* talk about yourself exclusively.'"

"'Weekly High-Tech Happy Hour.'" Tim looked at the

photo of Dr. Delia, a striking black woman with close-cropped blondish-red hair. Married to this Gilbert. Huh.

"I've thought about going to one of those," Paige said. "I bet I could stir up all kinds of trouble."

"*Do* try," Tim said. "These people are obviously insane."

"'*Don't* be judgmental.'" Paige stepped back outside. "I think Linda's awake—there's a light on up there."

Tim said, "I'm not supposed to judge—things?"

"Who knows?" Paige grabbed a few pebbles and threw them at Linda's townhouse. The stones rattled and clattered off the building. "Linda!"

Sitting at his desk, Tim was still looking at Dr. Dee's ad—the Do's, the Don'ts, the photos of satisfied customers—men with expensive-looking haircuts, women with gleaming toothy smiles. The busy business leaders of today. Busy but—lonely. "It's scary to think there're people like this out there."

"Linda!"

Linda's front door opened but Linda herself stood back in the shadows. She quietly said, "What?"

※※※※

"Wow, it's clean," Linda said, looking around. "I still need a drink, though."

"Sure." Tim ducked into the kitchen and came back with a can of cheap beer. Linda frowned, but at least it was cold. She sat in a folding chair at the end of the desk. Tim sat on the edge of the bed, a bit uncomfortable, sipping on a beer.

"So what am I supposed to be so impressed with?" Linda asked.

Paige said, "Tim's got this computer deal—"

"Not more internet porn," Linda said.

"No—"

"I'm tired of internet porn. All those—*penises*."

"You can always look at lesbians," Tim said. "Paige likes lesbians, sometimes."

"*Big* penises!" Linda said. She thought about that, and

frowned.

"I just uploaded forty new Swedish girl-on-girl shots," Tim said. "Want to see?"

"What's wrong with big penises?" Paige asked. "Don't tell me you get bladder infections, either."

"I get bladder infections!" Linda said. "It's ridiculous. You get some big cock with a big girth, and you feel like you're getting ripped half apart, and if it's a long one all it does is bang away at your cervix and the guy's hips aren't close enough to stimulate your clit or anything, and so you can't get off, and it doesn't matter anyway because you end up with a damn *bladder* infection."

"Well, *I* always manage to get off," Paige said.

"I'm sure *you* do," Linda said. "But I can't be bothered with big dicks—well, I can—I *have* been—but I don't *want* to be. They're too much trouble."

"I thought you didn't like to get off, anyway."

"I *don't*," Linda said, lighting a cigarette. "Orgasms are a complete waste of time." She shrugged. "I guess it's complicated."

Paige snorted, "I guess!"

Tim stood up and kicked off his sandals and then slid the new khakis down his narrow hips. He folded the pants neatly and then sat on the edge of the bed in his underwear. He took a sip of beer and pointed at the computer next to Paige.

"That's why internet sex is such a big deal—it's not complicated at all."

"Yeah?" Linda asked. "So?"

"Tim's going to be rich!" Paige said. She explained about Tim's webcam—other webcams—his plan for online masturbation.

"People will pay for this?" Linda asked.

"Some people will," Tim said. "Sure."

"There're a lot of perverts out there," Paige said.

"I wouldn't know," Linda said. "I don't hang out with perverts."

"You hang out with us," Paige said.

"Yeah, well." Linda sighed. First criminals, now perverts. Paige went on describing how the webcam worked, and how it was going to make Tim rich, but the whole thing reminded Linda of her ex-husband, R.L., who had sort of become a pervert in the last year or so of their marriage. He was always wanting Linda to screw guys—or girls—while he hid in the closet and watched. The pervert. Gilbert, though, was reasonably normal. He was a big, clumsy fucker—literally— but probably not a pervert. She didn't want to talk to Paige about Gilbert's job offer, not until she knew if it was real or not. Working for Gilbert Hardison—working *under* him, Jesus! Now *there* was an image. Bleh. It wasn't tempting. But then those messages from Foster, from Moomaw—those messages—they weren't encouraging at all. Hell, they were *dis*couraging. They were pissed at her, no doubt about it, pissed and fed up—she could tell, even over the cell phone. If only those idiots had made reasonable accommodations for her sleep schedule, everything would have worked out. If only she could get up in the morning and get to work on time. No, if only she'd kept her mouth shut with that columnist. It was all the newspaper's fault. No, no, really, it was really all the fault of the goddamn criminals—and that judge—fat little Richard Cantu—he made her life miserable—they all did, all the sad, messed-up people—victims, criminals—lock 'em *all* up—strap 'em to the damn gurney, stick a needle in their arms—Gilbert, too—*and* everyone else—

"Linda?" It was Paige.

"Huh?"

"Tim's ready to show you."

Linda suddenly noticed that Tim had slipped off his briefs and was standing there in his striped shirt and socks. His penis—pink-white, circumcised and modest—was half-erect, maybe, and tilted off to the side, peeking from under the shirt-tail.

Linda looked at Paige. "*What?*"

"Tim's going to masturbate for us."

"I'm going to need another beer."

"Sure." Tim went into the kitchen, penis bouncing, and came back with another can of beer.

"Put your pants back on," Linda said.

"Oh, Linda!" Paige shook her head.

Tim sat on the bed and leaned back, reaching for a green plastic bottle. He said, "Hair conditioner makes a great lubricant."

Hair conditioner! Linda looked away. She opened her beer, took a sip, stared at the door. After a moment she heard the squelch of damp, slipping flesh, could smell the light lavender scent of the hair conditioner. Crazy.

"Linda, pay attention," Paige said. She was obviously delighted.

Linda risked a glance. Tim lay back, eyes closed, almost serene, one hand behind his head, the other vigorously kneading—himself.

"Hurry up and come," Linda said. "I don't have all night."

Tim looked at her and blushed. He rubbed harder.

"Maybe this will help." Paige lifted her shirt up, exposing her perfect breasts, swelling softly out and down.

"Stop that," Linda said. "You're being ridiculous."

Tim glanced at Paige, smiled, shut his eyes again. In a moment his hips moved a little, then some more—then he arched over and bucked into a pillow, toes curled.

Linda stood up. "Can I go now?"

Paige lowered her shirt and looked at the computer monitor. The camera had caught a nice shot of Tim's butt.

"Don't turn away when you come," Paige said. "You need to catch that money shot."

"Yeah, well," Tim said, "I guess I need to practice a little."

"You're both crazy," Linda said. "Masturbation is ridiculous."

"To do or watch?" Paige asked.

"Both! Either way it's too damn much trouble."

"But Tim will be rich!"

"Good luck." Linda opened the door and looked out into the courtyard. She suddenly thought of the laundry—*her* laundry—that goddamn Gilbert had left to mildew and rot and stink. She turned around.

"Tim," she said, almost sweetly. "Do you think you could do some laundry for me tomorrow?"

"Sure," Tim said. He sitting with a washcloth draped over his groin.

"But wash your hands first," Paige said.

"God yes!" Linda thought—Hair conditioner! Sperm!

Outside the night was quiet, though Linda could still hear a few cars racing up the expressway, and the sky was tinted a soft peach color from all the thousands of street lights reflecting upward. Linda went up the steps to her townhouse and saw the empty birdcage sitting next to the door. Poor goddamn birds, she thought. Gilbert was a fool. No pearls or anything. She suddenly grabbed the birdcage and hurled it down the steps—crash, bang, rattle—and she saw the yellow cat dash around the corner. A light went on in one apartment, then another. Linda let herself into her home, smiling, as cheerful as she had been for some time.

Chapter Eleven

Fitting

THE LAW OFFICES OF FOSTER AND MOOMAW WERE located just down the hill from the courthouse, in what had been the home of a mid 19th-century merchant. The old house was constructed of red brick and was well shaded by a magnolia and a live oak, and had an air of shabby stability. Foster Moomaw occupied the first floor of the house; on the second floor was the office of a psychiatrist named Rebecca Crutchfield, who was usually seen leading an angry schnauzer around on a leash. The last time Linda had visited the office—Thursday, Thursday, it seemed so long ago—she had encountered Dr. Crutchfield in the cramped parking lot behind the building.

"Are you depressed?" Dr. Crutchfield asked flatly, staring at Linda with cold grey eyes. The schnauzer was staring at Linda, too, and growling.

"Depressed?"

"Your—appearance—suggests you might be depressed," Dr. Crutchfield said. "I was just asking."

Linda had been without a house-husband for well over a week, and her blouse and skirt did not match and were more than usually wrinkled, and her hair was sticking out, and she was hungover, and of course she'd had to get out of bed *far* too early—but, still, the question irked her. She wanted to say something nasty and cutting, but her mind blanked and she ended up saying, "Oh, yeah?"

"Yes." Dr. Crutchfield turned and began walking toward her car, yanking the angry growling dog along. "Call me sometime if you want to talk," she said over her shoulder.

But today—thankfully—the grim psychologist and her deranged schnauzer were nowhere in sight. Linda went up the back steps, heart full of dread, knowing this was something she had to do.

"Linda!" Raycene, the receptionist, flashed a wide—very fake—smile. She was only in her late thirties but already had a full set of dentures, dentures that were several sizes too big, and far too white. The teeth dominated her face. "Mr. Foster's been really wanting to see you."

"Okay," Linda said. It was annoying—beyond annoying—that Raycene always referred to Jeff Foster as *Mister* Foster while Linda just rated—Linda.

Of course, Linda suddenly realized, she didn't know Raycene's last name at all—or even if she had one. Oh well.

"Also, you have a client," Raycene said. "Mister...."

Linda turned to look. A heavily bearded white man was sitting by the door, scarred prison tattoos on his forearms, bright pig-like eyes lost in folds of fat.

"Wilson," the fat man said.

"Mr. Wilson."

Linda glanced at Raycene. Even the fat criminal got a "Mister" from the toothless bitch.

"I'll go see Jeff," Linda said. She took a step toward the back of the house.

"Mr. Foster's with a client," Raycene said quickly.

"Oh." Linda paused. "I'll guess I'll talk to this guy...."

"Mr. Wilson," Raycene said. "But I'm not sure that Mr. Foster wants you to see any clients until *after* you've spoken with him."

"Well, shoot," Linda said. "That's certainly a waste of my

time. I'm here now."

"So?" Raycene asked. "Since when do you care about time? You weren't even *here* yesterday. Nobody knew where you were or anything."

Linda ignored Raycene and gestured at Wilson. "C'mon," she said.

Raycene said, "I listed you as 'sick' on the time and attendance report. I bet you really *were* sick, huh? Sleeping sickness, I bet."

🍺 🍸 🍷 🍷

Linda sat behind her desk and wheeled her chair around to stare out the window. Goddamn Raycene. Goddamn Foster and Moomaw! Linda was filled with a sudden disgust for the whole firm, for everyone in the whole building. They—all of them, Raycene, the lawyers, Dr. Crutchfield, her growling dog—pretended to be such good-hearted do-gooders, and really all they were was a bunch of prissy paper-pushers, not much better than bureaucrats. Time and goddamn attendance sheets! It was maddening.

Linda's window looked out into an alley. She watched a thin young brown-haired woman slowly bicycle by until she disappeared beyond a row of oleanders. Bicycle. That reminded her of—something. Something she was supposed to do. What, though? A bicycle. After a moment she became aware of a slight wheezing sound behind her, and she wheeled her chair back around again. There was a fat man standing in her doorway. Oh. The client—the criminal.

"Yeah?" Linda asked.

The fat man drew himself up. "My name's Marvin Wilson."

"Yeah? So what do you want?" There was no use being friendly with a criminal.

"I need legal representation," Marvin Wilson said.

"Oh," Linda said. "Well, sit down."

Wilson sat down, and Linda turned away and went

back to looking out the window. The alley was empty. A hot breeze stirred the oleanders. Gilbert Hardison. The Justice Store. Are far as Linda could tell, all the convenient locations seemed to be in strip malls, which probably meant that there wouldn't be any windows to stare out of. Which was okay—windows were a distraction, and besides, criminals could look *in* them, and often did. Especially serial killers. It seemed like they were always going around peering in windows. Ah, well, hell. The Justice Store. Gilbert probably wouldn't mind if she didn't come in until noon. To hell with this getting up in the mornings. Maybe she could arrange it so that all her hours would be in the afternoons, from one o'clock to four o'clock. Maybe four to eight to service criminals who had jobs. Four hours of—serious—work was better than eight hours of slack work or 13 hours of hanging around the office getting pissed at Raycene. And it was truly unbelievable that Karl Moomaw had once hinted that he *expected* her to work 10 or 13 hours a day! Doing what? Jesus Christ! Was he insane? Damn. Madness. At any rate, fewer hours were better hours. That's the sort of true fact Gilbert would understand.

Marvin Wilson shifted nervously in his chair and Linda wheeled around and looked at him.

"What do you want again?"

"Legal rep—"

"No, no—what were you arrested for?"

"Making a terroristic threat." Wilson lifted his chin and frowned. He blinked his tiny eyes, fighting back tears. "And destruction of personal property."

"Oh." Linda was not moved by Wilson's tears. This was the part of the job she hated—well, no, she hated *all* aspects of the job, but this one—talking to the goddamn criminals about their goddamn crimes, getting sucked into the dreary vortices of their sad, stupid, messy lives—this was about the worse. "Okay, so tell me what happened," she said dully.

"I got this neighbor," Wilson said, "and there's like this fence—well, there *was* a fence—running between his house and mine, and he's got this fucking *tree*—"

"Good fences make good neighbors," Linda said.

"Well, he's not a good neighbor, he's an arrogant son of a *bitch*!"

Linda looked down at her cluttered desk and nodded. She said, "Okay."

"And he's got this fucking *tree*, and it leans over the fence, and it drops its goddamned leaves in *my* yard, and I have to rake 'em up. And then when I told this son of a bitch—"

"How long has this been going on?"

"For years!"

"How long?" Linda asked again.

"Well, two years, maybe." Wilson frowned, thinking. "Yeah, I've been livin' there about two years, I guess."

"Okay." Linda looked at her desk calendar to see what month it was. "Okay, it's July. I guess that's why it's so hot out, right? It's summertime. It's *July*. Those leaves aren't going to fall off that tree until November—until *Thanksgiving*. So what's the big deal?"

"Well, it makes me mad." Wilson's eyes teared up again. "I look out the window and I see this big ol' tree shittin' on me like that, and I get to thinkin' about it, and it makes me *mad*."

Linda nodded. "Well, okay."

"So I cut the son of a bitch down," Wilson said. "Except I fucked up. I was out there—"

"Were you drinking?"

"Oh, well, I had a couple beers, but I wasn't drunk or anything."

"Right," Linda said. "You just drank a few—*several*—beers and you decided to cut the tree down."

"I decided it was the right time, you know? Except, like I said, I fucked up." Wilson shook his head. "I was out there with my chainsaw, and I was tryin' to hurry, and that asshole next door was out there yellin' at me, and so I cut the tree all wrong. I wanted to drop it on his fuckin' house, but I got all agitated—I get nervous, sometimes, you know—and instead I dropped it on the fence, and it flattened *that* fucker out, and then it got tangled up in the electric line to my house, so I lost my power, and then it poked a hole in the roof of my carport. It was a big ol' sycamore." Wilson paused to catch his breath, wheezing.

"Sycamores," Linda said, thinking. "Aren't they the ones with the big—"

"Yeah! They got big ol' leaves! Big ol' leaves all over my fuckin' yard—every year. You'd get mad, too."

"Maybe," Linda said. Probably, she thought. Maybe I should get a chainsaw myself, bring it into the office, take it to Raycene's desk, maybe carve her some teeth that fit....

"Yeah!" Wilson said eagerly. "And so the asshole next door, he's out there yellin' at me, and my ol' lady comes out and starts bitchin' about the electric, and her fuckin' kids are bitchin' about no TV, and I start gettin' this damn migraine—I been gettin' these crazy bad headaches ever since I was in prison, and I—"

"You were in prison?" Linda looked at the scarred and illegible tattoos on Wilson's forearms. "What for?"

Wilson sighed. "Oh, they said I was runnin' a speed lab. I wasn't runnin' no speed lab—I was just in the wrong place at the wrong time."

"Oh, I know," Linda said. "So many people *are*."

"Yeah," Wilson said. "Fuckin' cops." He was blinking back the tears again. "Fuckin' cops."

Linda said, "So...."

Wilson sighed. "So, the fuckin' cops came, and I told 'em, I said, 'If you don't shut that asshole up, then I'll burn his damn house down!' And so then they arrested me."

Wilson folded his hands across his big belly and looked at Linda.

Linda was strangely moved. Wilson was obviously an idiot, a fat and stupid criminal, but he also seemed to be a man suffering genuine grievances. Poor dumb slob.

"So that was your terroristic threat?" Linda asked.

"Threatening to burn the asshole's house down?"

"Yeah," Wilson said. He shook his head slowly, looking at the floor, amazed at the state of his life. "Austin fucking Texas. I *hate* this fucking town. If I could build me a bomb big enough, you know, I'd just blow it all to hell."

The door opened—no knock—and Raycene stuck her head in.

"Mr. Foster can see you now," she said, smiling, red lips pulling back from her giant white dentures.

Linda looked at her levelly. "Anybody ever tell you those teeth are about five sizes too big?"

"Yeah!" Raycene said, smiling wider. "Except they're actually only *three* sizes too big—just like the ones James Brown used to wear!"

"James Brown was an old black man," Linda said. "He was in show business. He could carry that off. You're a fat white woman who sits behind a desk—and you *can't*."

Raycene's lips closed around the teeth and she ducked back out of the office.

"Bitch," Linda said.

Marvin Wilson pursed his lips and looked back at the floor. Linda suddenly realized that he had dentures, too. Oh well. At least his fit.

"I'll be back in a minute," Linda said.

Outside Raycene was sitting at her desk, staring into her computer screen. Linda walked past her, headed to the rear of the old house.

"At least I didn't run into any *doorknobs*," Raycene said. "At least I don't smell like a *locker* room."

Linda paused. What the hell? Doorknobs? Locker room?

"Whatever," she said. She came to Jeff Foster's door. As she raised her hand to tap on it, it opened. Foster, an elegant dapper little man in shirtsleeves and suspenders, stood back as if surprised.

"Linda!" he said. "Are you all right?"

"Yeah," Linda said. "I guess." She walked past him and sat down. Jeff was staring at her face—Raycene had been staring at her face, too. Doorknobs! Oh. Linda hadn't bothered with makeup in the morning—*why* bother?—and her eye was still bruised and swollen.

"I've been trying to reach you since Friday morning," Jeff said. He walked behind his desk and sat down. He looked at Linda, then looked away. He sniffed a little.

"Yeah, I didn't check my messages until *this* morning," Linda said. "Is there some problem?"

"Well...." Jeff was very bright and quick-witted—he could be a bully in the courtroom, Linda had seen it herself—but she also knew that, for some reason, he was scared of her. She made him very nervous. "Well, you need to check you messages more often."

"Oh," Linda said, nodding. "Okay, I'll remember to do that." She stood up to leave.

"No—sit down, please." Jeff looked at her again—then away. Linda sat. "That article in the paper—we're concerned about that article." Jeff took a deep breath. "I'll be blunt: the firm was very—embarrassed—by that article."

There it was, what Linda had been dreading since Friday: "The firm was very—embarrassed," and that little hitch in Jeff's voice just before the word "embarrassed" meant more than the word itself did. She could feel that little hitch hit her in the pit of her stomach, like a punch. Still, Linda was able to force a phony laugh.

"Oh, heck, you know how the media distorts everything." Linda waved her hand aimlessly, wishing for a cigarette. "Crazy, isn't it? It's like a damn feeding frenzy or something."

Jeff produced a newspaper clipping—the column—and flattened it on his desk.

"'We might as well kill 'em all,'" Jeff read. He had a strong reading voice. "This article quotes you as saying that. This article quotes you as saying, 'I'd strap 'em to the gurney myself.' Did you really say that, Linda? Did you really—*say*—

that you'd like to strap someone to a gurney and *kill* them?"

"Oh, of course not!" Linda rolled her eyes like it was the silliest thing she had ever heard.

"Sexy," Jeff said. He read, "'I'd stick the needle in their arms—wouldn't that be sexy?' Did you really say that? Did you really *say* that you would find it sexually—stimulating—to *kill* someone?"

"Oh, hell no." Linda rolled her eyes again. "Dead people are a definite turn-off—dying people, too, for that matter."

"Well, I should hope so." Jeff glanced at Linda again, then stared at the wall behind her. He couldn't seem to look at her for more than a second at a time. "You should be aware by now that the firm is professionally—and *morally*—opposed to capital punishment."

"Of course it is!" Linda said automatically. "Professionally *and* morally!" She thought, Goddamn criminals did this to me. Poverty and stupidity did this to me. Gilbert Hardison did this to me. Goddamn Richard Cantu, too.

"Are you happy here?" Jeff asked suddenly. Now he was staring at her chest.

Linda's heart skipped a beat. "*Right* here?" she asked, motioning to indicate Jeff's office. *Happy*, though—what a question! Mere existence took all her time—happiness seemed like far too much trouble, something far beyond contemplation.

"At the firm," Jeff said.

"I *love* it here," Linda said quickly. Then she wondered why she had lied. She wished—she needed—everything to slow down.

Jeff stared at Linda's chest. Linda was about to ask him why he was staring at her tits—try to put him back on the goddamn defensive—when he looked away and sighed.

"We always want the best fit with our personnel."

Fit. There it was. *Fit*. That was the word bosses used when they were about to fire you. Linda had never had a real job before, and so of course had never been fired, but still she knew it was so. Fit. "You're just not a good fit here," they'd say, or "You're a perfect fit, but—" But! But hell!

"Oh, I can pitch a pretty good fit when I have to," Linda said, trying to joke again and feeling criminally stupid.

"I wasn't really talking about that," Jeff said.

Jesus, Linda thought, what *are* you talking about? If you're going to fire me, goddamn go ahead and do it.

"And there's the matter of the McNair case."

"McNeil," Linda said, smiling. "Curtis McNeil, Love, I got him off."

Jeff shook his head. "James McNair, a DWI. You were supposed to see him in court this morning."

"Oh," Linda said. Morning—well, then. Goddamn mornings. "I guess nobody told me, or something."

"Karl went down to court to cover for you."

"Well, I guess that's good," Linda said.

There was a long silence. Jeff was staring at her chest again. Linda had had enough. She stood up.

"I've got a criminal waiting."

Jeff blinked his heavy watery eyes as if he'd just woken up. "Your client—oh yes. We can talk some more later. But think about what I said, Linda."

Just what the hell *did* you say? Linda wondered. She turned and walked out of the office, leaving Jeff Foster looking confused. Raycene looked up from her desk, looking past Linda toward the front door, smiling widely with her glittery hungry teeth.

"Why, here comes Mr. Moomaw," Raycene said. "I think *he* wants to talk to you, too."

Karl Moomaw came up the steps, into the office, sweating heavily. He had a shaved, lopsided head and wore glasses, and had a horrible complexion, ancient pink acne scars on his face and neck that glowed in the summer heat. They seemed to glow a bit more when he spotted Linda. He dropped his bulging briefcase on a chair and took a deep breath, staring at her black eye.

"Ah, well," Moomaw said. "I just got through seeing your client."

"I guess there was some sort of mix-up," Linda said. She heard Raycene cough behind her.

"Have you talked with Jeff yet?" Moomaw asked.

"Just now," Linda said.

"I'm so sorry it had to come to this," Moomaw said sadly, feigning sincerity. He was very good at feigning sincerity. Foster was an attractive little man who bullied people; Moomaw looked like a monster and pretended to be nice. "It's nothing personal, though, Linda—we care about you very much. It's just that we want the best fit for the firm."

"Yeah, I know, fit's very important," Linda said. She sighed. Apparently Moomaw thought that Jeff Foster had gone ahead and fired her. Oh well. "Actually, I was just telling Raycene how fit is very important."

Raycene adjusted a pile of paper on her desk and glared up at Linda. *Bitch,* she mouthed silently.

Moomaw fished a box of breath mints out of his pocket and popped one in his mouth. "Perhaps if you could have met with us earlier, you know, communication is so very important—" he sucked wetly at the mint "— perhaps we could have *helped* you...."

Help—to hell with that. Linda wondered why she didn't respect Foster or Moomaw. It wasn't their old-fashioned wimpy liberal politics; on the few occasions Linda had examined her own political beliefs, she had come to the conclusion that she was more or less a damn socialist. Maybe it was just that they didn't seem to *enjoy* being wimpy liberals. Gilbert, who didn't have any politics at all, enjoyed being sleazy, and wanted to become sleazy and rich. And Charlie, as conservative as he was queer, took great delight in making money and despoiling the environment. Jeff Foster and Karl Moomaw were just *there*: wealthy enough, politically conscious enough, but joyless and boring, bumps on a damn log. The thought depressed Linda: perhaps she'd end up becoming like Foster and Moomaw, merely existing. What a stupid goddamn life *that* would be! Happiness seemed like a hell of a lot of trouble, but maybe it was better than this.

"I feel very personally responsible for what's happened," Moomaw said. "I hope things work out for you." He put one of his sweaty hands on Linda's shoulder but she twisted away. Moomaw stepped back and sort of passed his hand under his nose, sniffing, glancing from Linda to Raycene, looking sick and ugly with his bumpy head, and Linda realized that other people were smelling her mildewed clothes. She hadn't thought anyone else would notice. *Locker room!* Goddamn Gilbert—how come he couldn't wash her clothes like a normal househusband?

"Whatever," Linda said. Again Linda felt disgusted—with all of them. With everybody! She turned away and walked into her office and shut the door. Marvin Wilson was still sitting there, beefy arms folded across his belly.

"So," Linda said. She sat down, looked at her desk, then up at Wilson. "Okay. You've got this bomb you want to build to blow up Austin—how long you think before you can get that thing put together?"

Chapter Twelve

Brains

THE REMOTE FOR LINDA'S TELEVISION BROKE. IT wouldn't turn the TV on—maybe the battery was dead or something. Linda was already stretched out on the couch, and now there wasn't anything for her to do but stare at the blank screen, or at the ceiling. The evening wore on and the room got darker; the television and the ceiling above her were lost in shadow. Every now and then Linda tried the remote, but it refused to work. There was a working television up in her bedroom, but getting off the couch and going upstairs was too much trouble. Getting off the couch and turning this broken downstairs set on manually was *way* too much trouble. Linda reached for her cell phone and tried calling Tim, hoping to get him to come over and turn the TV on, but the number rang and rang without an answer. He was gone, or asleep—or masturbating, or whatever—the little traitor, and he didn't even have an answering machine for her to bitch into.

Linda rolled over and tried to sleep. For some reason as she drifted away she thought of Dr. Crutchfield and her angry schnauzer. Maybe I *am* depressed, she thought.

Linda was sitting outside in the dark with a bottle of wine and a mug when the black cab pulled into the parking lot. She was off the steps and halfway down the path before Quincy even honked his horn.

"Hey there," she said, getting in.

"Staying up all night?" Quincy asked. "For they sleep not, when they have done mischief."

"Mischief?" Linda asked. "I just woke up. I slept six whole hours."

"I guess that means you're well-rested," Quincy said. "Great. So where we going?"

"Oh, I don't know," Linda said. "I just feel like driving around."

Quincy looked over his shoulder at Linda and very deliberately hit the meter. "Drive around?"

"Around." Linda shrugged. "My TV's broke—I feel like looking at things."

"Around." Quincy shook his head and backed out of the parking lot and drove around the corner onto the expressway frontage. Soon they were headed north, lost in the late-night traffic.

"I was driving up this way New Year's Eve," Quincy said. "There was these three cabs in front of me, and every minute or so one of them would pull over to the side so the passengers could throw up."

"Don't worry, I'm not going to throw up," Linda said flatly.

"I didn't say you were—I was just telling a damn story. Jesus." Quincy glanced at her in the mirror and then back at the road, his jaw set.

"Oh." People were so sensitive. Linda filled her mug and took a sip of wine. She didn't say anything more. The expressway was pretty at night, she thought, following the railroad tracks, half-lit strip malls and office buildings along the way, puffy peach-colored clouds above floating up from the Gulf. In the morning—the dreadful morning, bright sunshine and heat—people would be going to work, going shopping, living miserable, messy lives, but now at night everything was—pretty.

They came up on a major interchange.

"Which way?"

Linda leaned forward to look out the windshield. "I guess go up 183, and head back south on 360," she said.

Quincy shook his head. "Why you doing this for?"

"Maybe I like your company." Linda sat back in the seat and took a long drink. "And like I told you—my TV's not working."

"Want me to take you to the 24-hour Wal-Mart to get another one?"

"Just drive," Linda said. Wal-Mart, she thought. Good Lord. Just think of all the unpleasant people who would be hanging around a damn Wal-Mart at three in the morning.

Quincy drove up over the fly-over and exited so that he could turn south on 360. The road was darker through here; only the lights of a few big houses flickered on the hillsides.

"Had this guy in the cab from Australia," Quincy said. "He works for IBM in Australia, they brought him over here for training or something. I picked him up out at the Salt Lick Barbecue, way out in the country, there, and I took him up through here to the Renaissance Hotel. The guy's all smiling and looking out the windows at all these damn dot-com houses, and he says to me, 'The amazing thing about your city is that there's no poor people!' It was crazy. I just thought—*damn*, you know?"

Linda said, "You tell him to look in the front seat?"

"I didn't say anything." Quincy shook his head. It didn't pay to get too pissy with customers—you set boundaries for your self-respect, of course, but since you needed their money too often you had to eat shit, or at least listen to stupid people and their stupid ideas. Like there being no poor people anywhere. Or this afternoon, there had been a woman in the cab who didn't like that the city was so spread out. "Austin should be more like Baltimore," she'd said. "You could have row houses, people could live upstairs from their shops. Everything would be so much more convenient." Quincy wanted to tell her—*Fuck, you want row houses, go live in goddamn Baltimore—this is Texas, we like cars.* And who wanted to live upstairs from a fucking shop? But, well, shit, he didn't say anything, he just shrugged at her stupidity and kept on driving.

"He was one of these damn foreigners."

"Idiots," Linda agreed.

Quincy thought about his late-night psychic and the coming end of the world—no more pretty, twinkly lights at night, and in the day dry dead leafless trees amid the smoking half-burnt skeletons of the dot-com mansions. It would be something to see. Men would seek death and not find it. Men would seek death and not find it. He said, "You know, someday all this is gonna be dust."

Quincy turned the radio on, hoping the crazy woman wouldn't mind listening to some prophecy. But the radio was tuned to his favorite afternoon Motown oldies station—The Supremes, "Baby Love."

Linda sat back and looked out the window. Too often as a child she jolted awake in the night to screams, shouts, crashes, bangs—her parents fighting. She had a cat that slept with her, a skinny black cat named Russy, and she'd pull Russy tight to her chest and try to sleep. "You're my only friend," she said to the cat as her parents screamed and threw things. "You're my only friend." One time there were four or five big crashes in a row—her father kicking a door in, she later figured out—and a disbelieving scream from her father: *"You fucked him in this house?"* Hey, that was something to wake up to. Linda remembered rolling over to face the bedroom wall, holding Russy close. Those night she always had her radio playing softly, tuned to a Top 40 station when the Top 40 was fun—Motown, Beatles, Rolling Stones, Frankie Valli, Gary Puckett, Mitch Ryder, dozens of other nearly forgotten one-hit geniuses—and Linda would hold the purring cat close in the darkness, trying to ignore her parents, and she would drift back to sleep listening to the stupid songs—how those guitars would lift her, though, how the lyrics would take her away, touch her girlish heart, make her almost believe that somewhere out there was a place that was bright but not harsh, a place where there was peace, tranquility, fun, a special guy, love—*happiness*. She believed it—all of it! Now, years and years later, Linda would often find herself bullying through traffic in the big black Suburban, half-listening to the oldies station, and a song would come on that she hadn't heard for thirty years or so, and she'd find her eyes suddenly flooding with tears. What was *that* all about? Some ancient half-lost memory of banging and screaming, of nights where her only friend was a loving cat, dark nights where a stupid song gave her a glimpse of some place she'd never see again, a place she'd look for but never find, and now instead of making her happy it was taking her back to the darkness—no, *hell* no, best not to *think* about that. Best to wipe away the tears and drive on. Better to think about the damn criminals, and their tawdry sad lives, and the sad ruined lives of the people they screwed with—think about all the sad lives, all of them, all of them.

"Can you turn that off?" Linda asked.

🍸 🍺 🍷 🥂

They passed south through a rocky defile and crossed the lake on a high bridge.

"So," Linda asked. "What were you in court for?"

Quincy glanced at Linda again. "Shit, I thought you didn't care about my problems."

Linda thought for a moment, trying to remember. "No, I think I said that I cared about your problems, but that I didn't want to *hear* about them. But I just now changed my mind."

"Shit," Quincy said. They passed another new shopping

development, lit with amber lights. "I was downtown and I picked up this drunk white guy, and we didn't go two blocks before he said, 'I'm gonna fuck you over, boy.' That's all he said, 'I'm gonna fuck you over, *boy*.' And I said the fuck you *are*, motherfucker, and I stopped the cab at this bus stop and told the cocksucker to get out, and he didn't, so I grabbed my maglite and I got out of the cab and went around to the door to pull his ass out, and all of a sudden the guy's flashing a badge in my face—and it's goddamn Evan Black, the District Attorney."

"Jesus!" Linda said. Evan Black was a well-known rude drunk who had been in office mis-handling cases forever. Linda had never met him, and, based on his reputation, didn't want to. "What happened?"

"He's just laughing at me, says, 'Why don't you hit me? C'mon, go ahead and hit me, let me put your ass in jail,' but I backed off and didn't do anything, and he got on his cell phone and called some cops and I end up with a goddamn ticket for callin' him a motherfucker at a bus stop. Whoever heard of a ticket for verbal assault? That's just—*fucked*."

"That son of a bitch," Linda said.

"So then I needed to get me a damn *lawyer*," Quincy said. "I seen them ads on TV for The Justice Store and call them, and that goddamn Gilbert Hardison—"

"Oh, yeah," Linda said. "Him."

"Yeah, him, he wants $2500 up front before he'll take my case. Which I don't have, right? So he goes to court and delays the case until I can pay him, and I end up paying him $50 a week for almost a damn *year*, and then when he gets the money he stands me up."

There was a gap in the hills and they could see Austin in the distance, all the new buildings glowing cheerfully on the horizon. Quincy gripped the steering wheel with both hands and accelerated.

"*Damn*," Quincy said. "Don't *ever* get a lawyer that advertises on the Jerry Springer show."

"I *will* help you," Linda said.

"Bull*shit*."

"Don't worry," Linda said. "That charge will get dropped. Black doesn't need any more bad publicity, and it's a stupid goddamn charge, anyway. Verbal assault."

"Yeah, that's what that Hardison says, but I'm still out $2500. God*damn*, you know, that's some fucking racket you people got going on."

Not any more, Linda thought, not for me. Which might not be a bad thing. Might not!

Going south in the dark, passing the mall, Linda spotted a familiar billboard lit with floodlights. DAD ALWAYS KNEW YOU'D DO GOOD. That blond girl with the stupid, almost sluttish sneer on her face—how was she going to persuade someone to buy a house? She made Linda mad—her youth, her arrogant sneer. What the hell was *she* doing buying a house? Where was a little bitch like that going to find some guy to mow her yard or unclog the toilet or undo whatever goddamn disasters afflicted houses? She had no business buying a house, anyway, trapped as she probably was in some dreadful high-tech job, having to get up in the morning, driving around in a great clumsy SUV, working in some immense open-air room with low-walled cubicles, noisy, brightly lit, people stomping back and forth clutching faxes or cell phones or their skulls, people going mad, stopping to chat about nothing nothing nothing, televisions in the corners with stock tickers careening across the bottoms of the screens—with the sound turned down, though, mute newscasters reading the war news, more bombs and dead people and stock market catastrophes—all of it utterly ignored by the frenzied, caffeine-addicted workers. Linda had seen offices like that—they were a vision of *hell*—that was it, that smirking girl was trapped in hell and probably didn't even know it, or else maybe she enjoyed hell, maybe she was a goddamn demon herself, with a 30-year adjustable-rate mortgage on some grotesque huge box-shaped house out on the edge of town with an uncut, weed-infested lawn and a clogged toilet. Damn!

Quincy drove past the mall and headed east on Ben White. Another one of the billboards loomed up by Manchaca Road. Linda shook her head. Dad always knew you'd do good. What bullshit. That made Linda mad, too, the *Dad* part. Goddamn Dads, what the hell did they know about anything? The whole thing preyed on the average young would-be home-buyer's sick quest for Dad's approval, no doubt after Dad ditched Mom and ran off with some young hootchy. Linda's own Dad—Jesus Christ. What a mess *that* whole thing was—her family. An allegedly cherished only child, Linda had grown up wanting nothing more than to get away from her bickering parents and go off to her room with Russy and read and watch some TV or listen to the radio—she wanted quiet, she wanted peace, she wanted *solitude*—but her parents seemed wholly intent on dragging her back into the middle of every damn thing. Mom especially seemed convinced that Linda ought to be involved in school shit—drama, debate, volleyball, the goddamn Latin Club. Linda always hoped that *her* Dad would sober up enough to run off with a young hootchy—she would have run off with them. But Dad just spent his time being a big shot at the bank or a big shot at the country club, drinking, drinking, whoring around a little, chortling with his cronies, until Linda was out of college and married to R.L. and Mom died in an auto accident. *Then* he found a young hootchy and married her—far too late to do Linda any good. What a stupid goddamn life.

🍸🍺🍷🥃

Almost home, Linda needed to stop at the store to get some cash and buy some cigarettes and maybe a couple of batteries for the TV remote. When Quincy pulled up to the Super Stop, Linda saw Raul Ledesma standing inside at the store counter, shirtless and shoeless, wearing only a pair of tight-fitting jeans. He was staring out at the cab.

"So, where's my bicycle?" Raul asked when she came inside.

"Oh, I don't know," Linda said. "Still in the truck, I guess." She walked over to the ATM to get some cash.

"Are you ever going to get it?" Raul was buying two cans of no-bean chili, a bag of Fritos, and a bottle of Big Red. His dinner.

"I'll get it when I get it," Linda said. "I've been extremely busy."

When Linda paid for her cigarettes and batteries she found Raul standing outside next to the cab.

"So, are you at least going to give me a ride home?" Raul asked.

"Home?" Linda asked. "What home? *Which* home?"

"Paige's."

Linda snorted. If Paige had ever heard him refer to her home as *his* home, she'd be furious. It sort of made Linda mad, too. The little leech.

"It's only five blocks," Linda said. "You can walk."

"I'd ride my bike if I had it," Raul said. "But since you're responsible for me not having my bike, I think you should give me a ride."

"Oh, hell," Linda sighed. She motioned for him to get in. "I guess we're going back to my place," she told Quincy.

Linda moved her bottle and mug aside so that Raul could sit down. The mug tipped over and wine spilled across the floor of the cab. Linda glanced up at Quincy but he didn't appear to notice. She found some tissue in her purse and tried wiping it up. Raul just watched her, without trying to help. Quincy backed the car out of the parking lot and the cab jolted as it hit the street—Linda banged her head against the hard door and the rest of the wine spilled. Damn! Oh well. To hell with it. She sat up and looked over at Raul.

"So," she asked. "Are you still depressed?"

"What?" Raul asked warily. "What do you mean?"

"I asked if you were still depressed. The other night

Charlie said you were depressed. Saturday, I guess—he thought you were very depressed and withdrawn." Linda looked out the window and sighed. "I was just *asking*."

Raul shrugged. "Why should I care what Charlie thinks? It's just what he thinks."

"Charlie likes you, for some reason."

"So? That doesn't mean that what he thinks isn't anything more than just what he thinks."

"Huh," Linda said, looking over at Raul, thinking. "That's kind of wise—I think." Maybe.

"It's his brain, let him think what he wants. Why should I care what goes on in his brain?"

"That's pretty good," Linda said. It sort of made sense. Why should anybody care about what anybody else said or thought? Ever? It was just something in somebody's brain—electrical impulses, or something, flashing around in a mess of blood and goo. "You know, I always thought you were retarded."

"So? Why should I care what you think?"

"It's my brain."

"It's your brain," Raul said. He shrugged and looked away. "Think what you will, even if it's something incredibly stupid."

Linda wondered if Raul was insulting her. Maybe—probably. But what did it matter? It was only his brain—his blood, his goo—let him think what he would.

"So you're not depressed?"

"I didn't say that," Raul said, taking another deep breath and sighing. "Actually, I'm a *very* disturbed individual."

Quincy looked at them in the mirror and shook his head. He said, "No shit."

Chapter Thirteen

Down to the Limestone

LATE THE NEXT AFTERNOON RAUL WOKE UP AT WORK, alone. Everyone was gone. He worked—was employed, at least—at an upscale garden-supply store just a few blocks from where Paige and Linda lived. Raul was officially a shade tree salesman, but he spent most of his time sleeping out behind the store in the soil additives section, curled up on the soft, warm bags of peat moss and sheep manure.

Raul was always annoyed when he woke up alone after closing. He didn't get on well with the other workers, who were all jealous of the time he spent sleeping, and even more jealous that the bosses—who liked Raul, for some reason—let him get away with sleeping. If Raul was sleeping at the end of a workday they all left very quietly, creeping away and locking the gate behind.

On most evenings after work, Raul would hitch a handmade wooden wagon behind his bicycle and cruise back by the nursery to pick up a tree or two, or some shrubs, that he had discreetly set outside the nursery fence. His goal was to re-green Austin—to plant shade trees, fruit trees, and ornamental shrubs. Already, since he had started in the spring, he had set out a fine row of trees for five blocks along the east side of the expressway frontage, alternating magnolias and Arizona ash. On the west side, along the hike and bike trail, he had planted several little clusters of peach trees. In ten or fifteen years, there would be a fine, high row of shady trees growing all year, with the peach trees blossoming pink in the spring, the magnolias white, and no one would know where they had come from.

Except Paige and Linda. Paige knew about the trees, and she thought that the freelance gardening was an absurd waste of time. But what Paige didn't know, Raul thought, was that *her* life was itself so absurd that everything she thought was absurd—wasn't. The same with Linda: though her life wasn't quite as ridiculous as Paige's, it affected her judgment just the same.

She was hard to argue with, though. Raul was often intimidated by Linda—he'd been intimidated by her ever since she passed out beneath him once while he was trying to titfuck her. They'd been out having drinks somewhere or other, Raul and Paige and Linda and Linda's then-househusband, and Linda had called Raul "the Mad Gardener."

"Look at the Mad Gardener," she said. "He goes around planting trees nobody wants."

"They're good trees," Raul said. "They keep the city cooler in the summertime. And they look nice."

"Oh, please," Linda said, lighting a cigarette and smirking. She blew smoke at him. "Most people embezzle money from work—you embezzle fruit trees. Tell me that's not crazy."

Linda was incredibly annoying. Paige was flirting with someone at the next table, laughing, and that made him mad, too. Paige, Linda—they both just pissed him off.

"You know what?" Raul asked, leaning over the table toward Linda. "I'd like to come all over your tits."

Linda sat back—surprised—a hand drifting to the top of her bosom. The fruit trees were forgotten.

"Oh—you'll have to ask Paige," she said.

"Paige!" Raul said loudly, still staring at Linda.

"What?" Paige turned from the guy at the next table.

"I want to come all over Linda's tits."

Paige laughed. "How wonderful!"

Raul didn't say anything. He just stared at Linda.

"Oh, all right," Linda finally sighed. "But you'll have to wait until I'm extremely intoxicated—extremely extremely *extremely* intoxicated!"

But once again Linda got a bit *too* intoxicated. By the time they got back to Paige's townhouse, Linda was staggering and stumbling around, mumbling under her breath, flopping back onto Paige's bed with her sweatshirt hiked up, exposing her soft round breasts. Raul slipped his pants off and sat on her belly, but before he could even get a half-decent hard-on Linda was asleep, snoring softly. Bitch. Raul leaned forward and slapped his dick against Linda's tits but he didn't—couldn't—get hard, and Paige stood in the doorway, laughing, laughing, while Linda's then-househusband—a wimpy little guy whose name Raul could never remember—sat downstairs on the couch, pouting. After a while Raul got off Linda—sleeping, snoring, she never moved—put his pants on, and left. A week rarely went by when Paige didn't tease him about—that. And Linda—Linda had never even mentioned it, ever, which was somehow worse.

Raul trudged up the last little slope to the condos. Paige's car was not in the lot. He went up to her door and tried his key. It didn't work—it didn't even fit. Paige changed her lock every couple of weeks, just to mess with him.

Raul looked around the complex. Paige wasn't home. Linda wasn't home. Raul had no interest in going on up to his parents' house and dealing with them—there was always the chance that he might walk in on something frightening or disturbing. After a moment Raul walked across the courtyard and banged on Tim's door. He waited in the hot sun and then the door opened and Tim stood there, pale and disheveled, in boxer shorts and a t-shirt. He was wiping his hand on a towel. Raul caught the slight scent of—lavender.

"Yeah?" Tim asked.

"You want to go to Happy Hour?"

Happy Hour at the Little Wagon was no more or less happy or dismal than any other hour of the week, but it always was just one hour per week, on Wednesdays, from seven until eight. The bar was always packed for Happy Hour, the usual regulars joined by various derelicts from the neighborhood to drink half-priced beer and imagine that they were getting something over on the usually tight-fisted management.

Quincy's cab did a tight u-turn on the street in front of the bar, pulling up at the door. Linda paid the fare, then added a ten-dollar tip.

"I'll probably need you later," she said.

"Yeah?"

"We still have to go look for my truck."

"Yeah, right," Quincy said tiredly. "The one that's down south somewhere."

"That's it." Linda got out of the cab and quickly took the few steps up and inside. The bar was dark, the air cold and heavy with the smell of smoke and spilled beer.

"Linda!"

Once Linda's eyes adjusted to the dark, she made out Paige sitting at a table with Charlie Bessent and a guy named Roy Weston, an old acquaintance. She got a mug from the barmaid and sat down at the table.

"We're trying to get Charlie to tell us about the governor's penis," Paige said.

Oh. Linda poured herself a beer. *That* story. Everyone knew that Charlie had been in a fraternity with the former governor. Linda wasn't impressed—it was ancient history, who cared about some old fossilized *thing?*—but Paige always wanted to hear about the governor's willie.

"You must've seen it," Roy said.

"What makes you think I *wanted* to see it?" Charlie sat back, a happy smile on his deeply lined face. "It's hard to understand now, but we were very modest in those days."

"Yeah, right."

"I slept all day," Linda said. She wasn't nearly ready to tell people about her fit—or her lack of fit, or her probable firing, or whatever it was—at Foster Moomaw, though it wouldn't hurt to show at least *some* suffering, a mild depression, a touch of weltschmerz. She took a long drink of beer.

"That's very healthy," Paige said.

"Honey, your face looks much better," Charlie said. "That by itself should make you feel better."

"That black eye scares people," Paige said. "Linda likes scaring people."

"She sure scares me," Roy said. "Always has."

"Oh, I don't care about my face," Linda said. "I just care about my life." She paused, not sure if that was true. "It's complicated," she added.

"Poor Linda," Paige said.

"I talked to this criminal yesterday," Linda said, "he wants to build a bomb and blow up the whole city."

"Now, *that* should've made you happy," Charlie said.

"Yeah, well." It *had* made her happy, sort of, for a little while, but it hadn't been enough to offset the annoyance—anxiety—goddamn complication—of talking to Jeff and Karl about her goddamn fit at the firm. Assholes. "Actually, I'm kind of pissed off," she said. "In a general kind of way."

"We should run this client of yours for mayor," Roy said. "I'd vote for 'im. We could blow everything up and get rid of all those damn new ugly buildings."

Linda tilted her head and blew a cloud of smoke toward the bar. The morning's newspaper had run a story about the ugliest buildings in town, picking on used-car lots, strip malls, and trailer courts. Apparently it offended Roy, somehow; Linda was just glad it pushed her article back into history a little bit.

"I *like* used car lots," Roy said. "I like mobile homes. If you're looking for an ugly building, look right in the middle of town—look at the capital building."

"I like the capital," Paige said.

"As a building, it's fine. But it takes up too much space, and it's poorly located. I'd like to get in a D-9 Cat and knock the son-of-a-bitch down."

"We could put up some condos and make some money," Charlie said.

"It's a fine site for condos," Roy agreed. "Very centrally located."

Linda liked the idea of a D-9 Cat—a very big bulldozer, she assumed. She swallowed her beer with satisfaction. A very big bulldozer—yes. She could get into it and cruise around, knocking things over. Start with the Little Wagon itself, knock the dearly beloved beer joint—and all the drunks and losers—into the river. Then start over. Reduce whole neighborhoods to rubble, scrape everything down to the damn limestone—and start over. Hell, Linda thought, that's what I ought to do with my damn *life*—scrape it all down to the limestone, yes, and start over. And—

"I'd save the Texas Tower, though," Roy said.

Do absolutely *nothing*. Ever! Do nothing but watch goddamn television. Maybe read a little. Linda almost laughed out loud thinking about it—start life over and do absolutely *nothing*. Why not? She had the resources—a trust fund from her mother left her in a position where she didn't have to worry about a paycheck, ever. Linda knew how lucky she was to have a rich dead mother. There were plenty of other people out there who were sad and messed up and still had to soldier off every goddamn morning to work in some dreadful job or other. There were some brave people out there. Heroes. Linda was glad she didn't have to be one of them.

"It's a good tourist attraction," Charlie said. He noticed Linda smiling. "I guess you like the tower, too, huh?"

"What?" Linda asked. Oh, the UT Tower. She set her mug of beer on the table. "Yeah," she said. "Well, you know those stupid confederate statues they have on mall at the university?" Everyone nodded. "When I was a freshman, a boy took me out once and showed me where one of the sniper's bullets hit right next to the statue of Jefferson Davis. He stuck his finger in the hole—I guess he thought it'd turn me on." Linda pursed her lips, remembering. "It didn't."

Linda thought of herself as she had been in those days—lonely, depressed. What the hell—disturbed. So many wasted years! The boy who showed her the bullet hole had been one of a group of bozos that played croquet out on the university mall every Friday afternoon in a sad attempt to be colorful; now he was a big-shot political consultant in Washington, a media advisor to the president, a talking head on CNN, and very rich. Still a boob, though, and dull, as far as Linda could tell. So many wasted years. Roy Weston, sitting across the table from her, was a link to those days: he had been roommates with her ex-husband, R.L., back when they were dating. Roy was an unhappy student, drunk and depressed much of the time, often too depressed to get out of his bed to go to the bathroom. Instead he would just kneel on his bed and pee out the window. Every time Linda came over to visit R.L. she had to step over puddles of Roy's pee—or sometimes dodge golden showers from above. So many wasted years—too many! Goddamn, Linda thought. Now—now was the time to start over and do things right. Do *nothing* right. Linda gazed smiling over at the fat butts of the men sitting along the bar. Oh, she thought, for a D-9 Cat—or a chainsaw! Or a big ol' bomb, blow it all to hell—

But then her view of the bar was blocked. She recognized the bulging jeans in front of her face and looked up—yes, Raul.

"Paige," Linda said. "Your boyfriend's here."

🍺 🍷 🥃 🍸

"Which one?" Paige asked hopefully. She twisted around and saw Raul. "Oh, that one."

"Yes, I had to come looking for you." Raul grabbed a chair from another table and crammed in between Roy and Paige. Tim stood awkwardly for a moment, then went to the bar to get another pitcher of beer.

"You smell like you've been sleeping in the compost stacks again," Paige said. She looked disgusted.

Raul pursed his lips. "I told you—we call it the Soil Additives Section."

"You still smell. Why don't you go take a shower?"

"How can I shower? You changed the lock on your door."

"I don't want you showering at my house!" Paige said heatedly. "You use my towels!"

"Does he use your towels, too?" Charlie asked.

"Yes! I always set out towels for guests to use—"

"I'm not just a guest," Raul said.

"And he never uses them!" Paige was getting worked up. "He always uses my *personal* towels, and they always end up smelling like—like sheep shit!"

"It's very annoying," Charlie said. "At my home I keep a special bathroom for guests, and he never uses it."

"I'm more than just a guest," Raul said.

"You're a human fucking dildo, is what you are," Paige said. "Get used to it."

Tim brought over a pitcher of beer and two mugs. He filled one and pushed it over to Raul, who was glaring at Paige. He filled another for himself, and sat down next to Linda—but still a little apart, as if he might not be welcome.

"So, how're you doing?" Tim asked her.

"Miserably," Linda said. "My life is ridiculous."

🍺 🍷 🥃 🍸

"I spent the day masturbating," Tim said. "I bet your life isn't nearly as ridiculous as mine."

"I don't want to hear about it." Linda took a sip of beer. Tim was probably right, though: jerking off for a living was pretty ridiculous. "Did you finish my laundry before you—played with yourself?"

"Clean and folded."

"Goddamn," Linda said.

Tim blinked—at first he thought Linda was speaking to him, but then he followed her gaze up the bar to the door, where a massive black man stood wearing an expensive but ill-fitting suit. Tim thought he might be the same black man he had seen leaving Linda's townhouse Monday night.

"Friend of yours?" Tim asked.

Linda shook her head. Gilbert goddamn Hardison. This place, she thought—it's all the bar's fault. You came to a place like the Little Wagon to get a beer and not have to talk to anyone you knew, because the people you knew would never set foot in a place like the Little Wagon, ever. But then you'd somehow become involved with all the drunks and derelicts and losers who were hanging around, become part of their messy lives—and then the people you knew previously would for some reason show up, curious. It was disgusting. The place needed to be knocked down! Scraped to the goddamn limestone!

Linda turned to Charlie. He'd been coming to the Little Wagon for almost thirty years. She asked, "How do you *stand* it?"

"Stand what?" Charlie had been listening to Paige and Raul argue.

"You're an idiot," Paige said.

Raul shrugged and poured beer into his mug. "What's more idiotic?" he asked. "To be an idiot, or to hang around with an idiot? Huh? You, or me?"

"Stand what?" Charlie asked Linda again.

Before Linda could answer Gilbert had spotted them and was making his way down the bar.

"Hey! Here's the gang!" he said happily. "Got a bunch of lawyers sitting around getting drunk—is that old Austin or what?"

The gang. Linda looked away. Jesus Christ, she thought, if I wanted to join a gang I'd go over the Eastside and sell crack. The gang.

"Gilbert!" Paige looked up, smiling. "Get a mug and sit down. Linda and I were just talking about you.

"What were we saying?" Linda asked.

Gilbert found a chair and forced his way in between Tim and Linda, his jacket riding up on his thick shoulders.

"So, you enjoy your meal?" he asked Linda.

"It was okay," Linda said. "I was hungry."

"You must've been sleepy, too, the way you passed out like that."

Linda shrugged and looked away, dragging deeply on a cigarette.

"I should've been the one tired, the way I cooked your food, did your laundry...."

Tim had been sitting quietly, watching Linda, watching Gilbert. Now he said, "Laundry? You mean those clothes I had to re-wash?"

Gilbert looked over at Tim, frowning, squinting. "What?"

"Linda's clothes," Tim said. "The ones that were all mildewed and stinky and shit." Gilbert was still frowning; he was a scary-looking man when he frowned. Tim slacked back in his chair. "I, uh, had to re-wash some...."

"Just a minute." Linda pulled her giant cell phone from her purse and hit a button to speed-dial Quincy's number—she got his goddamn voice mail. What was he doing away from his cab? Eating, praying, smoking rocks—he could do all that in the damn car. "Hey, this is Linda. I need a ride. I'm still at that bar—the Little Wagon. So come get me." She thought for a moment, then said, "*Please* come get me," and hit the disconnect button.

Gilbert said, "You're not taking off, are you?"

"Oh, hell, I don't know," Linda said. She lit another cigarette. "Maybe. Why do you care?"

"'Cause I wanted to talk to you," Gilbert said. He was aware that the little white boy next to him was staring—along with Paige, and Charlie, and the others at the table. He lowered his voice. "Privately, you know?"

"I'm busy," Linda said. She didn't know what to think. If Gilbert was going to offer her a position with The Justice Store, she might end up taking it. She knew that she was sort of a sucker for his offers, especially when she was drunk. But working with Gilbert would also probably be a lot of trouble, and would obviously interfere with her new life of watching television and doing nothing. And he had that wife. "I don't know. I've got too much going on."

"You've got too much going on," Gilbert said. "You need to drink some more beer." He filled her mug. "Then we can talk."

Chapter Fourteen

Really Good Air Conditioning

GISELLE WAS TIRED OF MEETING AT CEASAR'S. SHE TOLD Richard that she was tired of meeting in a dark bar for one drink and then going off to a motel for fucking and fried chicken. Richard was a little surprised: Giselle had always seemed to enjoy the fucking—*and* the fried chicken. Personally, he liked a safe, orderly, repetitious life of comfortable routine. Kelly had taught him to be that way: ideally, every day should pass in the same manner, day after day after day after day. Safe, with no surprises. He didn't see any reason why he couldn't have an orderly, repetitious, comfortable and safe affair. But Giselle was—demanding. She wanted things. She liked surprises. Richard didn't know if he liked it or not, but there it was: Giselle wanted something more than just a drink at Ceasar's.

The big, popular nightclubs downtown, on Sixth Street, and in the Warehouse District, were out, though. Richard feared that he would see someone he knew—someone who would tell Kelly. That was something he couldn't risk; it was something he didn't even want to think about.

Still, by evening he was able to come up with an idea. Richard cruised up to the employee entrance at the Hyatt and found Giselle waiting impatiently, frowning at the flocks of grackles settling in the trees around the hotel.

"Richie, I'm getting shit on out here," she said, getting into the car. "And it's *hot* out."

"I know, babe," Richard said. Hot: he could feel the heat that Giselle herself radiated. He looked at her and smiled. "But don't worry, we're going to a place that has some really good air conditioning."

Richard turned the car around and drove out of the parking lot, hoping that he wouldn't be seen, heading for an old dilapidated beer joint on the west side, a place he'd gone to a time or two in college days, the Little Wagon.

♀ 🍷 🍸 🍺

"Remember the Alamo?" Roy asked. "The Alamo Hotel, I mean—and the bar? We used to go there with R.L." He looked at Linda, who shrugged. "I guess I didn't know you then," he said to Paige.

"Guess not."

"Too bad." Roy took a sip of beer. "Anyway, if you ever see the old Clash video, 'Rock the Casbah,' at the end of it, they're running down Sixth Street to the Alamo."

"I've seen that," Tim said. "That was filmed here?"

"I'm *in* it," Roy said. "Anyway, the Alamo used to be a great place, bunch of old drunks living upstairs—Lyndon Johnson's drunk brother died there a couple months after I moved to Austin. Downstairs there was a wonderful bar, where all the old drunks would hang out, hippies, bikers, lowlifes, scumbags—"

"God yes," Linda said, remembering.

"—and folksingers would play there, old-timey country yodelers, it was wonderful. They gave away free pretzels."

"They were stale," Linda said.

"The manager was a communist. Where would you find a communist bartender these days?"

"They used to be everywhere," Charlie said.

"He was a Trotskyite," Linda said. "His wife was a Wobbly—how's that for an anachronism?"

"Anyway," Roy said. "The Alamo got bought by a developer in the early eighties, and one of the old drunks, he got a goat and sacrificed it out on the front steps, he cut the goat's head off and squirted goat blood everywhere, he put a hex on the place. The goddamn developer managed to knock the place down but then he went broke and the place was a vacant lot up until last year."

"Jesus," Paige said.

"My first Saturday in Austin, I bought some speed at the Alamo. Actually, I met my man at the Alamo, and then we came over here to the Wagon to get the shit. That was my first time at the Little Wagon, too." Roy looked around at the smoke-stained walls. "I remember it was raining that day."

Linda looked around, too. "I think they've changed the carpet since then. Not much else."

"Sometimes I feel like an endangered species," Roy said. "You know? My habitat's getting destroyed bar-by-bar. Pretty soon I won't have any place to hide."

Charlie shrugged and poured more beer. "Pave it all," he said. "Pave it all."

When Richard's eyes adjusted to the sudden barroom darkness, he was shocked to see three people he knew—Gilbert Hardison, Linda Smallwood, and Charlie Bessent. They were sitting at table with some other people. Gilbert was staring right at him. Oh, shit. His instinct told him to turn Giselle around and push her back out the door. Run! He looked at her with his mouth hanging open.

"This is kind of a dump," Giselle said. "You said you come here for the air conditioning?"

"Judge Richard Cantu!" Gilbert said loudly.

Richard shrank back against the bar, against Giselle, licking his lips, at a loss.

Giselle looked across the bar. "What, you know those people?"

"Well, yeah."

"So what!" Giselle sounded pissed. "Remember I told you—most men would be *proud* to be with me!"

"Hey—your honor!" Gilbert shouted.

Richard looked away and ordered a pitcher of beer from the barmaid.

"Richie?"

"I know, babe," Richard said. The thing was, she was right. But she was wrong, too. Oh, hell, it was all fucked up. Richard suddenly felt like crying—a judge afraid of a bunch of drunk lawyers! Afraid of his own—mistress! Damn. He took a deep breath. No—can't give in. Fear nothing.

"You could've taken me to someplace *nice*," Giselle said. Sometimes her voice sounded so harsh—scratchy and hoarse from beer and cigarettes. And anger, too. "But no, you had to have some super fucking air conditioning."

The beer came and Richard paid for it. "Grab the mugs," he said to Giselle. He took another deep breath and headed for the table.

"Hey, Counselor Hardison," Richard said. "What're you doing here?"

"Drinking beer," Gilbert said. He sat back in his chair, grinning, looking delighted. "And you?"

"We're just hanging around."

Richard and Giselle stood by the table, and, in a pause from the jukebox, there was an uncomfortable silence.

Paige leaned around Raul and looked up at Giselle. "Don't I remember you from last night?"

Giselle smiled. "Yeah—you were at the bar."

"What bar?" Raul asked.

Paige ignored him. She asked Giselle, "Is this your boyfriend?"

"Why were you going to a bar?" Raul asked.

"Yeah," Giselle said. "This is Richie—he's a judge."

Richard looked embarrassed. Paige stuck out her hand

and introduced herself, smiling, eyes bright. Richard held her hand for a second after they shook—shocked, almost, by Paige's looks, flawless and athletic and so much finer than Giselle's. He didn't want to let go of her hand.

"Who were you talking to at the bar?" Raul asked, though now he was glaring at Richard.

"Well, Judge, join us," Charlie said. Like Gilbert, he looked delighted.

※

Linda was appalled, really. That idiot Cantu was sitting at their table with that tattooed floozy—that circus-girl—and all the men were staring at her, strange red and green feathers streaking up from her fat breasts. The whole situation was grotesque.

"Life has not prepared me for this," she said.

"What?" Gilbert looked at Linda, squinting. "Prepared you for what?"

"Life!" Linda waved a cigarette in the air. "What the hell else am I unprepared for?"

Richard Cantu got chairs from another table and wedged them between Linda and Charlie. Giselle sat next to Charlie; Richard sat next to Linda—she shrank away—and leaned around her to talk to Gilbert.

"I guess this is where Ms. Smallwood gets in those fist fights, huh?" Richard had to shout over the jukebox.

"What?" Gilbert had to shout, too.

"Those black eyes!" Richard jerked a thumb at Linda. "Those barroom brawls—she has those here?"

"Oh! Yeah, something like that."

Linda sipped her beer. She thought she'd like to blacken Cantu's goddamn eye. Charlie was saying something to Giselle, looking at her sideways, smiling gracefully. Giselle looked—happy. Happy at all the attention. Circus girl.

Richard leaned around Linda and shouted at Gilbert again. Louder. "Maybe we better go ahead and sign her up for Domestic Abuse Counseling!"

"What?" Gilbert hollered. "*Who*?"

"Ms. Smallwood—she looked like she's been abused!"

Linda set her mug on the table with a splash. "What the *fuck* are you talking about?"

Richard leaned back from her. "I was—making a joke!" He was still yelling over the jukebox.

"Well, it's not very goddamn *funny.*" Linda glared at him.

"Judge!" Gilbert shouted. He was leaning so far around Linda that his head was almost resting on her chest. "Hey, Judge Cantu!"

Richard didn't hear him. He was looking away, shouting something at Charlie, or Giselle. Everyone at the table—except Paige—was looking at Giselle. Paige was looking at Richard, amused. Linda sighed, and Paige looked at her and winked.

Linda thought of something. She silently mouthed, *This is our chance.*

Paige looked puzzled. She leaned forward, whispered, "What?"

Linda again mouthed, *This is our chance.* Paige shook her head and shrugged. *What?*

Linda said, "*Blackmail!*"

Paige said, "Oh!" She looked at Richard and smiled. "Oh—right."

Raul had been watching them. He asked, "*Black*mail?"

"Black *males*!" Linda shouted across the table.

"We're talking about miscegenation," Paige said sharply. "We're in favor of it, okay?"

Roy Weston was leaning around Charlie, talking to Giselle. The jukebox faded, and Linda could hear what he was saying.

"I know this guy, he's a fishing guide in Idaho, he's married to his horse."

"A male horse or a female horse?" Charlie asked.

"A mare, a filly—whatever," Roy said. "A female. The guy lives in a trailer, he's got a ramp up to the back door, and the horse just trots on inside, they hang out, they eat popcorn together, watch TV—"

"Screw?" Charlie asked.

"Of course!" Roy said. "They're married!"

"We've got to put a stop to this," Richard said. "We're officers of the court—we're defenders of civilization!"

"Does this horse have a brother?" Paige asked.

"Yeah!" Charlie and Giselle said at the same time.

"I'd like a horse like that," Giselle added. Linda noticed Giselle's hand slip away and disappear under the table—was she touching the judge? Good lord. Giselle said, "Maybe I got one, though."

"We're the defenders of—*civ*—civilization," Richard insisted. He was getting all red in the face.

Linda had had enough. Talking about sex with horses was okay, but this "defenders of civilization" bullshit was madness, especially when the prime defender of civilization was sitting there getting his dick squeezed by a tattooed tart.

"Tim!" Linda said. "Tim!"

Tim had been listening to the horse talk in an interested, professional way. He looked over at Linda.

"Are those green birds still around?" she asked.

"—birds?"

"Those green birds you said were in the park."

"Linda wants to see a bird," Charlie said. Everything came back to penises with him. Hadn't he noticed the judge?

Tim remembered. "Oh—the feral parakeets."

"Yeah," Linda said. "Those, whatever. You want to show them to me?"

"Uh, yeah, I guess I could." Tim stood up, rocking the table and spilling some beer.

"Sunshine?" Gilbert put his big hand on her wrist. "Baby? I thought we were going to have dinner."

Linda pulled away. "Tomorrow—maybe."

"No, I'm serious. I want to talk to you about some stuff."

"Oho!" Richard hooted. "Serious *stuff* talking time!"

"Will you just shut the fuck up?" Linda stood over Richard

looking down at him. "You're not making any sense at all. You're just being a fool." Richard closed his mouth, surprised. Linda touched Gilbert's shoulder. "Call me tomorrow."

"Tomorrow," Gilbert said. "You'll check your messages?"

"I promise," Linda said. She could see Tim waiting by the cigarette machine at the bar's door, and headed toward him—toward the light from the door.

"Hey, Linda!" Raul shouted behind her. "Why don't you go get my bicycle?"

Tim drove out the back way, cutting through the alley behind the bar and down by the park along the river. The evening was cooling off and joggers were out, men and women bouncing along the hike-and-bike trail. Linda had gone running with Paige a time or two—Paige didn't jog, she *ran*—hobbling along, trying to keep up, and she remembered the smell that lingered by the pedestrian bridge where many joggers passed: sweat, heavy sweat, the whole section of park reeking of damp sweaty people. It was sickening.

Now Linda looked out the window and saw two slender young women—college girls, probably—jogging along, long brown legs pounding down the trail, shiny hair bouncing. One of the girls had a red ribbon in her hair. Linda shook her head.

"I guess I'm not very feminine."

Tim looked at her and then back at the street. He glanced at her again. He said, "I guess there's different kinds of femininity."

Linda laughed. "What—did you read that somewhere?"

Tim shrugged. "I don't know. It just seemed like an appropriate thing to say."

"Yeah, right." Linda laughed again and shook her head.

Tim drove his rattling old Chevy across the Lamar bridge and into a park on the south side of the river. People were playing softball on wide, green fields. Tim stopped the car.

"What're we doing?" Linda asked.

"Uh, those monk parakeets," Tim said. "You said—"

"Are you serious about that?" Linda asked. "Men are so literal."

"You said—"

"Never mind what I said," Linda said. She thought for a moment. "You mean there really *are* some birds out here?"

"I think so. They're supposed to be around here somewhere."

"But you've never seen them."

"No," Tim admitted.

"Oh," Linda said. "So this could just be some big lie."

"Well, maybe," Tim said. "But I don't think so."

Linda got out of the car and followed Tim down the parking lot. She didn't expect to see any feral parakeets fluttering around—the birds sounded like an urban legend of some sort, just another vague disappointment. They climbed a rattling aluminum bleacher behind a backstop; a few people were seated there, boyfriends and girlfriends and mothers or whatever of the softball players, apparently, watching a co-rec softball team play.

"Paige says they're all lesbians," Linda said, pointing out at the field.

"Even the men?" Tim asked.

"The women—most of them," Linda said. "Paige knows about things like that."

Tim looked at the field. A male player hit the ball hard, and the player at third base, a woman, knocked the ball down. She wasn't able to make a play, though.

"Maybe some of them are," Tim said. That girl at third base—she was kind of square-shaped, with short black hair.

"Maybe *I'm* a lesbian," Linda said.

"Well—"

"No, I'm not," Linda said. "It'd be way too much trouble. Besides, I don't want to have sex with women. That's what lesbians do, right? Have sex with women?" Linda thought for a moment. "The thing is, I don't really want to have sex with *any*body. It's way too much trouble."

Tim frowned and sighed. He noticed two older women sitting on the row below them. They were apparently afraid to turn around and look, but they couldn't help glancing at each other and then leaning back a bit to listen better. Tim sighed again. He wanted to have sex with Linda.

"And even if I did want to have sex with a woman, I wouldn't know how."

Tim shrugged. "I guess it's sort of like masturbation, except on someone else."

"Even more trouble! Masturbation is a grotesque waste of time. It's stupid. Orgasms are stupid, too." Then Linda remembered what Tim was trying to do for a living. She asked, "How do you *stand* it?"

"It's good for me, I think," Tim said. "This doctor guy on the radio says frequent ejaculations are a beneficial form of prostate hygiene."

"I don't ejaculate," Linda said. At least, she didn't think so—she tried to pay as little attention as possible to what went on down there. She'd always thought of her *down there* as if it was some weird foreign country—like Uruguay or someplace. Who the hell paid attention to what went on in Uruguay? Still, she was pretty sure that she didn't have a prostate gland. Masturbation was just wasted effort. Linda shrugged and glanced at Tim. "What do you think about?"

Tim hesitated. "Well," he said, "*you.*"

Linda sat back. "Prostate *hygiene*," she said. "I'm the sweetheart of prostate hygiene. That's just great."

But she did smile—a little.

🍷🍸🍺🍻

Quincy stopped his cab in front of the Little Wagon and waited for the crazy woman to come out. The bar's door was made of heavy, reflective glass; he could see his cab reflected in the door, but he could not see though it. For all Quincy knew the bar could be empty—the cars parked out front along the street could just be—abandoned. The bar could be full of dead people and ghosts. He honked the cab's horn. No one came out. Bitch.

Quincy got out of his cab and took the hot, quick step over to the bar. He opened the door and was met by cool, smoky air, sweet with the smell of spilled beer. He took off his sunglasses, eyes adjusting to the darkness, but he didn't see the crazy woman, or any dead people, or ghosts. Just some drunks and the barmaid—a tall, chesty white woman with dark hair.

"I got a cab here for Linda Smallwood," Quincy said.

"Linda—she was here—she was over at that table." The barmaid pointed.

Quincy made another few steps toward the table by the jukebox. There was the other crazy woman—the hot-looking one—sitting there with his fucking lawyer, Gilbert Fucking Hardison, and that fucking pussy judge, and some bitch with tattoos.

Paige saw him first. "Hello!" she said. "Are you looking for Linda?"

"She called and said she needed a ride," Quincy said. The judge and Gilbert stopped talking and looked at him.

"Oh, she left," Paige said. "She didn't call you to cancel?"

"Fuck no!"

"I'm sorry," Paige said.

"Crazy bitch," Quincy muttered.

Gilbert was looking at him closely. He asked, "Don't I know you?"

Quincy stared at him for a moment. "Yeah, I'm a fuckin' client a yours," he finally said. "You was supposed to be in court on Monday. They said you was sick."

Gilbert sat up a little straighter and touched the loosened knot of his necktie. "Well, I *was* sick," he said. "Didn't we reschedule?"

"Yeah, for September twenty-third. You gonna be there?"

Gilbert stared at him. "The twenty-third," he finally said. "Yeah, I'll be there."

"Yeah, well, I hope so," Quincy said. "You know? Defend the poor and fatherless, and do *justice* for the needy." He turned and walked away. Behind him he heard Gilbert say, "—guy's a cab driver or something. I can't remember what he did—assaulted one of his passengers, I think, beat the shit out of some guy...."

♀ 🍺 ♀ 🍺

At the other end of the table, Giselle was talking about her body art. Roy and Charlie were watching her closely.

"My bird, he symbolizes freedom—he's got hold of me, you know, he's taking me somewhere that's good and free and safe."

"I assume all that really hurt, though," Roy said.

"Yeah, no kidding, it hurt like shit," Giselle said. "But it was worth it. See, I look at my body like a temple. You know those old Greek temples with those old white statues?"

"Of course," Charlie said.

"Well, they weren't always white and dead-looking—they used to be *decorated*. They were full of color, they had drama, they were *alive*." Giselle stood up and spread her arms, chest out, feet planted firmly, posing. The table rocked a little, and beer spilled, but no one seemed to notice. "I think my body's like that, you know? It's like a temple, it tells a story."

"Hey," Richard said. He was getting red in the face—agitated, embarrassed, jealous, something. "*Hey!*"

Giselle sat down. "My body art, it makes me feel like I'm really an important part of the world."

"Amazing," Charlie said. He gazed at her shoulders, at her back, trying to read the story. "Can I touch?"

"Sure!"

Charlie ran two bony fingers down Giselle's arm. There was a black Celtic cross peeping out from beneath the red and green feathers of the freedom bird. He said, "Smooth."

Giselle smiled at him. "My artist's been telling me he can get me on the cover of *Tattoo Magazine*—wouldn't that be so cool if he did? Like, that's my goal!"

🍷🍸🍹🍺

The more she watched the game, the more Linda became convinced that the women playing softball were lesbians. She was delighted; for the first time all day she felt happy.

"I doubt if they're *all* lesbians," Tim said.

"Of course they are—though there might be some who don't know it yet," Linda said. "And those guys are all hitting on them and not getting anywhere, and that makes the games more interesting. There's a sort of—sexual tension—on the field, you know?"

Then Tim saw the green parakeets, six or eight of them, gliding in quickly and settling on the wire backstop.

"Look!"

After resting a moment the parakeets took off and flew toward one of the light towers.

"Huh," Linda said. "And here I thought you were telling me a big lie."

"Oh, no," Tim said, "I read about this in the paper—they nest up in those towers. They have communal nests."

Linda said, "Communists."

"They're an intruder species," Tim said.

"I think I liked it better when I thought you were lying," Linda said. Her brief surge of cheerfulness was gone—flying off, maybe, with the feral parakeets. She wondered what happened to That One Bird. Maybe he'd found a home in the commune. She hoped so.

There was a dull *clung* from the field and Linda looked down to see the square-headed third-basewoman hitting a long drive to left-center.

"Only a lesbian could hit the ball like that," Linda said. She frowned, imagining herself with a heavy aluminum bat, smashing things. "I wish *I* was a lesbian."

🍷🍸🍹🍺

Charlie took drunk quite suddenly, spilling a mug of beer and then peering into the puddle, puzzled, wondering why his lap was so wet. He asked, "How did this *happen*?" He stood up and staggered back into the jukebox. "I'm—*wet*."

Paige didn't complain when Raul was recruited to drive him home: Raul had been a drag on Happy Hour—he wasn't even mildly cheerful—glowering at Richard and Giselle, at Gilbert Hardison, and most of all at Roy Weston. Roy's story about the guy who was married to a horse made Raul mad, probably because the story had delighted Paige.

"He's also mad because I changed the locks on the door," Paige said as Raul led Charlie out the door. "I came home yesterday and found these—*globs*—of pubic hair in my toilet."

"Oh, my God," Giselle said. She scooted her chair closer to Roy and leaned across him, listening to Paige. "What'd you even do?"

"I flushed the toilet!" Paige said. "I mean, I don't even know where that hair *came* from—"

"He doesn't look very hairy," Roy said.

"He's not. And I guess he's less hairy now." Paige took a sip of her beer, and frowned. "Of course, he's just going to wait until I'm asleep some night—"

"Or day?" Roy asked.

"Or day," Paige agreed. "And then he'll steal my keys and have them copied. So I don't know what I accomplish."

"But that hair thing is just so totally *gross*," Giselle said. She put her hand on Roy's arm. "You ought to go punch that guy in the nose or something."

Paige looked at Roy and smiled. "Or *some*thing."

🍷🍸🍹🍺

Richard and Giselle left the bar at closing time, leaving Gilbert behind, talking intently with the barmaid, who was an ex-client, or ex-secretary, or ex-girlfriernd, or—everything. The night outside was warm, and soft, and quiet, and Giselle held tightly to Richard's arm.

"See, baby," she said, "that was fun. You *can* take me out places—I told you, no one will stare at you or anything."

Richard didn't say anything. Of course no one was staring at him: they were all staring at *her*—at Giselle. And why not? Giselle had been posing all night, showing off all those crazy—weird, creepy—tattoos that he liked so much. *Liked*. Richard thought of Paige, how smart and fit and trim and clean she looked—she looked *normal*, and beautiful, and still she had a sort of mad crazy glint in her eyes. Giselle looked—strange. Plain strange.

"You're quiet, baby," Giselle said.

"Thinking," Richard said.

And there was Kelly, too. All evening while he had been in the dark, smoky bar, he had managed to push the image of Kelly out of his mind, but now, walking with Giselle in the soft night air, Kelly—with her pock-marked face, her sharp tongue—came back. Richard had told Kelly that he was going out to meet with some Republicans, to plan his re-election, and that was somewhat true, maybe—Charlie Bessent was a Republican, he must be, he'd been in a college fraternity with a former governor. So that wasn't really lying. But Kelly might not believe him, anyway. She was a suspicious-minded woman.

Giselle said, "Nobody's going to tell your stupid wife anything."

Richard looked at Giselle. He wondered, What are you, some sort of mind reader? But he didn't say anything.

"You're silly," Giselle said.

"Well, maybe." Richard frowned. Word might still get out—Linda Smallwood always seemed like a big-time gossip, and Gilbert Hardison was a—slippery character. He tried to push all that out of his mind. "Sometimes, I guess."

"Sometimes!" Giselle laughed. "All times!" She broke away from Richard and ran off down the hill to where he had left the car. There was a park at the bottom of the slope, with massive shadowy cottonwoods and a long, spring-fed swimming pool. The park was closed now, and dark, and

Richard's car was parked next to the entrance.

"Richie!" Giselle yelled. "C'mon!" She ran heavily down across the parking lot and threw herself across the hood of Richard's Buick. "Come on!"

Richard followed her, panting. He was too drunk—too heavy—to run well, but he lumbered along, thinking—dreading—that he would soon have to go home.

When he got to the car, Giselle was sprawled across the hood, legs spread wide, hands behind her head, eyes shut. She heard Richard plodding up and opened her eyes and smiled.

"What'cha thinking about, Richie?"

"Uh—you," Richard lied. But then Giselle reached out and took his hand and placed it over her crotch, and it wasn't a lie anymore. "Oh, baby," he whispered. "You're so—*hot*." He squeezed her pussy, feeling the hot hard bumps of the labial studs through the fabric of her shorts, then bent over her belly, kissing her—the tattoos again hypnotizing him—flames, swirls, feathers, signs of the zodiac radiating out of her navel, that fiery vortex, sucking him down and down and in forever, forever. He could just disappear forever. He could just disappear. Giselle said, "*Yeah,*" and sat up and kissed Richard, sinking back, pulling him on top—and then there were lights, red and blue—a Park Police car drifting slowly toward them. Richard hopped back off Giselle, hiking his pants, hoping his dick wasn't sticking out.

The policeman was looking out the car window. "So, what're y'all doing out here?"

"Just visiting," Richard said.

"We're fixing to fuck!" Giselle laughed.

"We're just visiting."

"We're gonna *fuck*!"

The park policeman—a skinny white boy, in his late twenties, maybe, with a long sad nose—looked from Richard to Giselle. Her blouse was half-open, dark tattoo lines showing in the flashing lights.

"Well, just don't fuck here," the cop said.

"I said, we were just *talking*."

"Yeah, right." The cop turned off his flashers. "Go on home and *talk*," he said, and drove off.

Richard looked at Giselle. "Jesus Christ! What the fuck are you talking about—we're gonna fuck?"

"I'm just more honest than you." Giselle slid off the car and looked around. She began walking down the sidewalk to the park.

"Where're you going?"

"He said not to fuck here!" Giselle ran off into the dark.

🍷🍸🍹🍺

Richard followed Giselle down into the park. There was a long, winding concrete ramp for wheelchair access, and Richard shuffled along, holding on to the steel railing so that he would not trip in the dark.

"Richie! Come on! Hurry!"

At the bottom of the ramp Richard stood beneath immense cottonwoods, panting. It was dark. But then he spotted Giselle climbing over the swimming pool fence.

"Giselle?"

"Come on!"

Richard trotted up to the fence. Giselle dropped heavily to the other side of the fence and staggered back a step.

"What's going on?" Richard gasped. His heart felt huge—he felt blood gushing through his chest, sweat running down his face. Yet, still, his dick—it was hard.

"Let's go swimming!"

"The pool's closed," Richard pointed out. He couldn't help it.

"That's what makes it fun!" Giselle disappeared into the shadows.

Richard put his hand on the fence. It was a standard eight-foot chain link fence with a gate for service vehicles to get and out. The gate—closed and locked—was where Giselle had climbed over. Richard remembered playing with other boys when he was a kid, they'd be messing around and come to a gate like this and all the other kids would swarm over it like it was nothing at all—except for young Richard, who would be worrying about getting into trouble. "If it's closed, we're not supposed to be there," he'd point out. "It's *locked*, too." The other boys would all jeer at him, "Go home, you pussy! Go home to your mother!" And Richard would go home, expecting to be praised for being good, only to find himself not praised for anything. His mother *expected* him to be good—what was there to praise? Thinking about it now pissed Richard off. As far as he could tell, being good had never benefited his life in any way—in any way.

"Richie!"

"I'm coming," Richard said. He more or less fitted his toe onto one of the gate's hinges and pulled up, scrambling, pulling, pulling, then heaving his right leg over the top. Damn. Something was ripping—his shirt, what the hell—and Richard rolled on over, landing on his feet like a cat but toppling backwards onto his butt with a heavy thump.

"Damn," Richard said.

Giselle laughed. "Richie, you're so fucking clumsy!"

Richard looked up, hurt. "I'm like a cat."

"Clumsy cat." Giselle had already taken her shirt off and he could see her breasts bob in the shadows. She slipped her shorts off—she wasn't wearing underwear—and crossed the soft grass to the pool. She hesitated, then jumped in.

"Ahhh! It's cold! Richie, you better get over here!"

Richard was still catching his breath.

"Richie! Get over here and warm me up!"

Richard had another flash of nerves—in the woods at night, with park policemen cruising around—but he took a deep breath and pushed it all aside. He took off his shoes and socks and stood up. He could feel his dick straining hard against the fabric of his shorts, his trousers. He loosened his belt.

"Richie! I'm cold!"

🍷🚽🍸🍺

Roy Weston's apartment under the bar was cluttered with fishing and camping equipment, books, papers, empty beer cans, pizza boxes—it was messy and cramped and moldy and somewhat claustrophobic. Paige liked Roy—he was funny, and she looked forward to seeing him again at least a couple of more times—but still she was glad to get back to her own home and take a hot bath and relax. She was just fixing to go to sleep when there was a knock at the door. Paige looked out the peephole and saw Raul, primping his hair.

Paige opened the door an inch. "What do you want?"

Raul smiled. "To come in."

"Why?"

"Well," Raul said. "Because I always come in."

"What about that hair in the toilet?"

Raul shrugged. "What hair?"

"That goddamn *pubic* hair you put in my toilet!"

"I'm sorry," Raul said.

"You certainly are." Paige slammed the door shut.

Raul thought about kicking the door in—he'd kicked the door in the time he stole Paige's mattress and threw it down the embankment onto the expressway. But Paige had called his father that night, waking him up, screaming at him until he agreed to buy her a new door and a new bed, and the whole incident had been too ridiculous and embarrassing to endure. He knocked on the door again.

Paige opened it a bit. "What now?"

"I said I was sorry."

"I don't care about that," Paige said. "I want to know why you did it in the first place."

"Did what?"

Paige restrained herself from opening the door to punch Raul. Instead she said, slowly, "For filling my toilet with pubic hair!"

"I didn't *fill* it."

"It looked full to me."

"Your perspective is skewed," Raul said. "Why aren't you accepting my apology?"

"Because you're not telling me what I want to hear!"

"I'm sorry," Raul said.

Paige slammed the door shut. Raul waited a full minute before knocking again. Paige waited two minutes before opening it.

"I thought it would be exciting," Raul said.

Paige nodded, staring at him. She asked, "Was it?"

"No," Raul admitted. "But I *am* sorry."

Paige shut the door. After a moment, she opened it all the way, and Raul stepped inside.

🍸🍷🍺

"I knew she'd let him in eventually," Linda said. "She always does."

Linda and Tim were sitting in the dark on the steps of her townhouse, quietly drinking beer.

"It probably has something to do with that penis of his," Tim said.

"Jesus Christ, it's got *everything* to do with that penis of his!" Linda thought of the night when Raul wanted to come on her chest. Thank God she'd had enough sense to play possum—once he'd seen that she was in no shape to notice his mighty cock he had lost interest and wandered off.

"Well, there's that gardening he does," Tim said.

"Gardening?" Linda asked. "How absurd."

Tim was sitting two steps below Linda—next to her knees. He wondered if it was time to move toward her—lean against her, put his hand on her knee, rest his head in her lap, maybe even put his hand up her thigh, stroke it, stroke it, up to her crotch. No, he thought. Give it time. Time and patience. He turned and smiled at Linda.

"What're you looking at?" she asked.

"Just checking to see if you're still there," Tim said.

"Where the hell would I be?" Linda frowned. Tim could be annoying. She finished the last of her beer and stood up. "Can you fix me breakfast in the morning?"

"Sure," Tim said. "What time?"

"Whenever I get up." Linda took two heavy steps to her door, and paused. She said "Good night, Tim."

Chapter Fifteen

Defenders of Civilization

"THOSE REPUBLICANS MUST GO AT IT PRETTY HARD," Kelly said when she found Richard passed out on the couch.

"What? Oh." Richard opened his eyes and closed them, quickly. Too much light. After a moment he managed to sit up and hold his head in his hands. His clothes were damp. What? Oh, we were—swimming. "Jesus."

"That election's over a year away," Kelly said.

"Can't be too prepared." Richard lifted his head and looked around, squinting. Kelly was standing in the doorway, frowning. The harsh morning sun made her look craggier than usual. He looked back at the floor. "Yeah, those Democrats," he mumbled. "Those darn *liberals*—they might try something tricky. Nobody cares about justice anymore."

"Justice? What?"

"We're the defenders of civilization."

"*What?*"

Richard shook his head. "Nothing."

"Are you going to work today?" Kelly asked.

"Yeah," Richard said. He made an effort. "Sure I am."

"Well, you'd better hurry—you'll be late."

Kelly stood in the doorway for another moment, then

padded softly down the hall. Richard continued to look at the carpet. Justice, he thought. Oh God. I'm sick. I'm weak. I'm tired.

"I'm under a lot of *pressure*," he said aloud.

🍺 🍸 🍻 🍷

It was nearly noon when Linda woke up. She glanced at the alarm clock through filmy eyes and rolled out of bed—Shit! I'm late! But then she stood there for a moment, realizing that she probably didn't have to work today—or maybe ever again. Well, good.

Still, she *was* employed—until they officially got rid of her. So maybe it was best to call in. Linda reached for her cell phone and dialed the office.

"Foster Moomaw!" Raycene answered. She sounded—cheerful. Linda could imagine Raycene's slippery pink tongue curling around those teeth. Big grinning teeth. The thought made Linda's flesh crawl. "How may I direct your call?"

"This is Linda Smallwood," Linda said.

"Oh," Raycene said.

"Yeah—*oh*," Linda said. "I'm not coming in today."

There was a pause. "Well, okay, you can come by and get your shit whenever you want."

"My shit."

"Your things—your *stuff*. I put everything in this big box just inside the back door," Raycene said. "When you come in you need to give your keys back, too, and sign the resignation papers I typed up. Mr. Moomaw's going to cover your cases."

"My cases?"

"Your clients. Your—"

Goddamn criminals. Linda punched the disconnect button on her phone, frowning. Goddamn Raycene. What a creepy bitch. Linda had once had a house-husband who'd had false teeth—Steve, a carpenter from three doors down. He was kind of creepy, too, a big, blond guy who had lost his teeth in a motorcycle wreck, or a fight—the story changed from time to time. Linda made him wear his dentures whenever he was in her home. "Go back to your own place if you want to be gross," she said. Still, Steve was an excellent vacuumer and a fair cook, and Linda kept him around for a few months, despite his annoying hints that he'd like to have sex more than once every three or four weeks. When he wasn't vacuuming or cooking or framing houses or timidly insinuating that he'd like to get laid, Steve would lounge on Linda's sofa watching Mexican television. He was in love with Veronica Castro, a soap opera star who also hosted her own variety show. Whenever Veronica Castro was on Steve gazed at her with a weird, almost drooling rapture. Linda pointed out that he might enjoy the shows more if he knew Spanish, but Steve said No—*Hell,* no!—Veronica would lose her *magic* if he understood what she was saying. Linda shook her head. Steve was an idiot, but she still kept him around—his skill with a vacuum cleaner outweighed his intelligence.

Then one evening Linda was in the kitchen, opening a bottle of wine, and she heard Steve softly say, "I wonder if she's a virgin."

"What?" Linda asked. A goddamn *what?*

Steve hesitated. He said, "I wondered if she might be—a virgin."

Linda came out of the kitchen and looked at the television. Veronica Castro was singing some upbeat little song, bouncing around in a low-cut, glittery gold dress.

"Jesus Christ," Linda said. "The woman's at least forty years old—she's probably been married six or seven times. And who knows *what* kinds of goddamn casting couches they have in Mexico."

Steve was silent. "Well, shit," he finally said. "Why'd you go and tell me that for? You *ruined* it."

"Goddamn," Linda said. Steve's blond, bland, toothless stupidity suddenly pissed her off. The weirdo. Virgins! Forty year-old Mexican TV virgins! She pointed at the door with the wine bottle. "Out! Get the hell out of here!"

Steve got up and left. Linda never spoke to him again,

and at the end of the month he moved out of his apartment and disappeared. Before Raycene, Steve had been the only person she'd known without teeth. Now there was that client, too, that criminal, the tree-chopper. The bomber. Goddamn, Linda thought, there was just something just weirdly disgusting about dentures and the people who wore them.

There was an unassuming knock at the door. Tim, Linda thought. She got out of bed and stumbled downstairs to open the door. Tim eased in past her with a handful of plastic grocery bags.

"It's about time," Linda said. "I'm starving."

"Oh," Tim said. He stood frozen, staring at her. "Oh. You look like you were asleep."

"Yeah?" Linda stared back at him. She ran a hand across her stiff hair. "So I was dreaming about food, okay?"

"Sure—I just had to do a little shopping," Tim said. He backed into the kitchen and began setting out eggs, bacon, canned biscuits, orange juice—

"There's some vodka in the cabinet," Linda said, spotting the juice. She went up to her bedroom and came back with a quilt and settled in on the sofa. "You don't watch Veronica Castro, do you?" she asked.

"Oh, sure, sometimes," Tim said. "She's hot."

"That's just great," Linda mumbled.

Tim brought Linda a mug of orange juice and vodka. "Sometimes I look at her website before I masturbate."

Linda pursed her lips. "I thought you were thinking about me when you masturbated."

"Well—" Tim said. "I usually look at Veronica *before* I masturbate, and I think about you *while* I masturbate. It's kind of complicated."

"Apparently so," Linda said. She took a long sip of her drink. "I think I lost my job—or maybe I quit. I haven't decided yet."

"That's good," Tim said. "You never sounded happy about it."

"Happy." Who the hell could be happy getting up in the mornings? Linda shook her head and frowned. "Well, anyway, now I think Gilbert wants me to take over one of his convenient locations."

Tim was clattering around the kitchen. After a moment he said, "Yeah, I guess you could make some money that way, if you wanted to."

"You don't like Gilbert, huh?"

"Yeah, well, he is fucking *married*."

Linda shrugged. "Thank God he's not married to me."

Dodged *that* bullet, she thought.

"But he is—married, I mean."

Linda laughed and turned around and looked at Tim. The little pornographer looked angry. "Yeah, so?"

"Well—he's *married*." Tim shook his head. "That's—well, it's not right."

"That's his problem." Linda shrugged. "*Marriage*."

As far as Linda had ever been able to tell, marriage was nothing more than an arena for conflict, with gladiatorial couples in a constant fight for moral superiority—or immoral superiority, sometimes—endless bloody warfare to get to the place where one could merely say, "I told you so," or "You're not going to tell me anything." Certainly that was the example set by Linda's parents, days of sickening drunken bickering followed by nasty, uneasy truces; her own stupid marriage with R.L. had followed that pattern. Paige's two marriages, too, as far as she could tell from the outside. Just having a—guy—was so much simpler. If you wanted masculine companionship, he was there; if you wanted to be alone you could send him away—and while he was away he could wash your damn car or something. And if he didn't return from a trip to the dumpster—well, there were always plenty of other guys out there lurking around.

Gilbert, though, was more than just a guy. Linda knew it was illogical, but she really did feel some sort of deep—

affection—for him. She *liked* him. Even if he was extremely irritating at times. And unreliable, and sneaky. He couldn't even be trusted to wash the damn car—the one time Linda had sent him off for a car wash, he had come home with the task uncompleted, the Suburban unrinsed, big blotches of detergent dripping from the fenders, the windows cloudy with soap. He'd run out of quarters, he'd said. *I will help you.* The big liar! The phony! As for Gilbert's marriage to that fat woman—well, that really was *his* problem. Linda brightened, suddenly realizing that Gilbert's marriage might put him at somewhat of a moral disadvantage.

Linda smiled at the television. Court TV. A rabbi was on trial for hiring a hitman to kill his wife. A schoolteacher was charged with fucking one of her students.

"Life sure is a mess," she said happily.

🍸🍷🍺🍶

When Richard finally made it home after a long, bad day, he was still quite ill. Something about the quantity of beer he'd drunk the night before—or maybe that cold water in the pool. It was all maybe too much. Giselle, too. In the past day or so she had developed a nasty habit of calling him at work—at court! He'd warned her—almost actually plainly told her more or less flat out—not to call him at work. Yet there had been seven calls from her he'd had to dodge during the day. Seven. Ms. Kreider, his secretary, was giving him a funny look. The situation made him—anxious. As well as sick. When Richard got home he just wanted to eat and go to sleep—to pull a blanket over his head, to hide—but then Kelly told him that her mother was sick and that she'd have to take the kids and go to Houston for the weekend.

A free weekend—Richard suddenly felt much better. He thought of Giselle. Then he thought of that woman from the night before—Paige. At some point Giselle had gotten up to use the restroom and Paige had leaned across Charlie Bessent and said, "You're kind of funny. You think maybe we could get together sometime for drinks?"

Richard had hardly believed it. He blinked in surprise.

"Be careful, Judge," Charlie said. "Paige can be a dangerous woman."

Richard said, "I'll be the judge of that," laughing at his own attempted joke, and then Paige pushed her business card across the soggy table to him. "Call me sometime," she said. Giselle came back then, and that Roy guy, and not much more was said, but Richard felt—Damn! He *felt*—that was the thing. Giselle was—*Giselle*. Legible Giselle, maybe the tattoos *were* a bit much. What normal person wanted to be on the cover of *Tattoo Magazine*? And those piercings, rivets of stainless steel running through her—stuff. Her thing—her *cat*. Was she crazy? Not crazy, maybe, but—disturbed. Why would somebody do that to their body, even if their body was a fucking temple or whatever, unless they were disturbed? Paige was so much more athletic and trim and fit—clean-looking, and smart. Sane. Undisturbed. Her somewhat soggy business card was in his wallet. I should call her, he thought—sometime. Maybe soon. Paige seems like a busy woman, she's popular, has lots of friends, maybe she already has plans for the weekend. Maybe I should call Giselle first, though, and get things straight with her. Seven calls! I wonder what Ms. Kreider thinks.

Richard heard Kelly rattle around in the kitchen and felt a sudden surge of guilt and fear. Not the time to call anyone right now. He decided to take a bath and a nap and to worry about the weekend later. He headed for the bedroom, turned a corner—and ran into his son, Davy. Davy was a slight, dark boy with his mother's sharp features, though fortunately without her complexion.

"Hey, boy!" Richard tried to put some heartiness into his voice. He put his hand on Davy's shoulder. "How ya doin'?"

"Okay." Davy shrank back away from his father. He always seemed so frightened, that boy. He cringed around like a depressed kicked dog.

"What'cha doin'?"

"—I was on the Internet," Davy said.

"Oh yeah?" Richard smiled. He wanted to be friends with his son. "You lookin' at some way cool sites?"

Davy shrugged. The door to Davy's room was open. Richard was not by nature a snoop, but he stuck his head into the room anyway, in what he hoped might be friendly, fatherly way. But before he could see anything more than a fuzzy glaucous blob on the monitor, Davy pushed by him and stood in the front of the computer desk, blocking Richard's view. Richard was almost shocked. Davy had never before been so—physical.

Richard stepped in and looked around. Everything was very orderly, for a teen-aged boy's room—the bed tightly made, books and CDs stacked, computer sitting in the middle of an otherwise empty desk. Richard could now see around Davy, see that the grayish blob in the center of the monitor was a bed—a bed, in a dimly lit room, with something in the bed—a person, maybe. There was a poster at the head of the bed, some guy with a bushy beard.

"What kind of site is that?" Richard asked.

"It's a—webcam," Davy said. "It just shows this guy—doing stuff."

"Stuff?"

"Living," Davy said. He glanced at the monitor and then at his father. "I guess he's sleeping right now. But sometimes you can see him, like, eating, or working at his computer, or watching TV. You know?"

"And that's it?"

"Yeah," Davy said. He seemed to relax a bit as he clicked the mouse to close the window. "It's sort of cool."

"Damn," Richard said. He shook his head, thinking, People are *fucked*.

"Richard!" Kelly shouted from down the hall. "Are you in there bothering David?"

"We're just looking at his computer." Richard felt another wave of guilt and fear rise up from within.

"Well, leave him alone so we can get packed," Kelly said.

Oh—the free weekend. Kelly's mother. Richard felt

sorry for her, being married to Kelly's dad, having Kelly for a daughter. No wonder she was sick.

🍺🍸☕🍷

Linda was irked. She wanted Tim to drive her down south to finally get the Suburban, but, no—Tim claimed he had to go masturbate and then head off to an appointment with some doctor, or something. Spurned for a webcam. Or else he was really mad about Gilbert being married, which was weird. Either way—damn. First he wasn't there when her TV remote broke, and now this. Tim's status, however vague and amorphous—however Tim-like—might have to be reconsidered.

And now there was Quincy. The cab driver seemed mad at her—and she hadn't done anything.

"I really do have to go get my truck today," Linda said.

"Yeah?"

They sat in the parking lot of the complex, the cab idling noisily. Every now and then the meter ticked up another quarter. Linda saw that Quincy was wearing his Justice Store t-shirt. I WILL HELP YOU. Good Lord. She rolled her eyes. The messy aspects of life that had cheered her earlier were now incredibly—annoying.

"Listen," Linda said, and paused. She wasn't used to making apologies—as far as she could tell, she interacted with most other people on such a slight, sketchy basis that she seldom did anything worth apologizing for. Paige was a friend, Linda knew she'd be lost without Paige, and Charlie was a friend, and her relationship with Gilbert was something very weird, but also very important. For the sake of her sanity, though, she tried to keep just about everyone else in the world so far away emotionally that they might as well be wild beasts, or robots. Like Quincy, here. He was evidently okay as a person, probably, for a criminal, and he had certainly been a huge help driving her around, and those prayers had made her feel better, and she actually really sort of *liked* him, but—well, it was complicated. Like everything else, it was goddamn complicated! All these—people! All their pain, their problems, their chaos, their messes. Linda couldn't cope with any of it—she didn't want to, either. How much more pleasant it was to stay at home and watch the world's messes on television.

"Listen," Linda said. "I'm sorry I left the bar before you got there."

"Drove all the way out there for nothing."

"I'm sorry. Okay?"

"I went in that damn bar," Quincy said. "And I saw that damn Hardison sittin' with the judge."

"Yeah, I know," Linda said. "And that tattooed woman was there, too—I had to get out."

"I hear that," Quincy said. He took a deep breath and Linda could see his neck muscles relax. "It's like they all conspiring against me."

"That's exactly how I felt," Linda said.

"Didn't know you *had* feelings."

Oh, well, maybe he was still a little mad.

Linda said, "My feelings are very subtle."

🍸 🍷 🍺 🍶

A stark black and white sign over the door read **THE JUSTICE STORE.** On the door itself was a smaller sign, black print on a lavender background, *Dr. Delia's DateLine*. Tim hesitated a moment, then went inside. A young Mexican woman behind a desk looked up at him with enormous, owl-like eyes. She didn't say anything. When Tim stepped over to her desk he saw that she was reading *Teen People*. Britney Spears was on the cover. Britney had an unusually meaty butt, Tim thought.

"Yes?"

"Oh!" Tim said. "I'm here for the—DateLine?"

The young woman slowly blinked and pointed. "Through that door over there."

Tim could feel a slight breeze coming through the open door the receptionist pointed at. When he went through it he saw four giant, industrial-sized fans in each corner of a long room, blowing at top speeds. Narrow multicolored ribbons were attached to the fan grills, blowing out in the breeze, and helium-filled balloons were bobbing at the ceiling. Tim looked around in wonder.

"Hi there! I'm Delia Huston Hardison." A big woman rose up from behind a desk and approached him. "Welcome to my DateLine!"

Tim smiled. Delia's photo in the newspaper ad didn't really capture her, he thought—she was a striking woman, tall and square-shouldered, broad-hipped, with a vast deep bosom. Her hair—dyed, probably—was reddish-blond and cropped short, showing her beautiful long skull, and her eyes—contacts?—were the same tawny honey as her skin. Tim kept on smiling, amazed. He tried to imagine her naked— naked.

Delia led Tim over to a comfortable chair by her desk. The desk—like all the surfaces in the room, seemingly—was covered with books and magazines, mostly self-help and relationship titles.

"Tim, Tim," Delia said. She sat down and punched a key on her computer. "Tim Newlin. I got your email earlier this afternoon. I'm just really pleased that you've trusted my DateLine with your social needs."

"Well, yeah," Tim said, squirming in the big chair. "I really liked your website."

After leaving Linda to her breakfast, Tim had gone back to his apartment to check out the DateLine website. He'd been impressed. It was very well put together and easy to navigate, with social schedules, personality tests, and plenty of Dating Do's and Dating Don'ts from Dr. Dee. There was also a selection of photos of alleged members, and all of them, both sexes, seemed reasonably young and attractive, shiny hair and sparkling teeth, their jobs heavily skewed towards high-tech—software engineers, website developers, tech writers, though he did spot a couple of accountants and a lone attorney. Tim was intrigued. Here were these bright, attractive, well-to-do young people searching for love, sex, affection, whatever. But Tim couldn't understand why they all had to go to the trouble and expense of signing up for the DateLine. The girls, especially. Why couldn't they just go down to Sixth Street and find some guy to fuck them? That's what Linda or Paige would do, if they felt like getting fucked. But they were older. These girls on the website, they were maybe trying to be safe, or maybe they didn't know how to find a guy to fuck them, or maybe they were looking for something more complicated than getting laid. Not that it really mattered.

"I thought about signing up online," Tim said, "but I thought it might be cooler to come down here and, you know, look at your office and everything."

"I'm so glad you did," Delia said. She leaned forward across the desk, warm, radiant, lively. Tim couldn't get over how her eyes were the same color as her skin. "Let me tell you something about myself," she said, smiling. "See, when I came to Austin I worked for ten years at the Internal Revenue Service. Started out as a Tax Examiner, and I worked my way up to become a manager in Human Resources. Then I went to work at in the private sector, at Nntych Software, and, again, I was in Human Resources. And what I saw at Nntych, Tim, was that we were hiring all these brilliant young people from all over the country, from major universities, from all over the world, really, and when they got here they were like blank slates—they had no relationship to this city, or to each other, or to anything. They were lonely, they were empty, they were needy. And *that's* where I saw my opportunity."

"So you made your own opportunity," Tim said.

"Make your own opportunity," Delia said. She sat back and looked a little puzzled. "That's the theme of my essay for next week! How'd you know that?"

"Uh," Tim said, "I don't know." He'd heard that line somewhere. From Linda, maybe? Where'd she get it? From

Gilbert? Charlie? Who knew! "I think my mom always said I was a little bit psychic, maybe."

"Well, maybe you are." Delia leaned back in her deep chair, studying Tim. "Anyway, I started my DateLine to fill those needs, and it's just been wildly successful—and it's *so* gratifying to help people."

"Oh, I bet." Tim glanced over his shoulder just as the bearish figure of Gilbert Hardison stalked past the door. He looked back at Delia and smiled. *I* will help *you*.

"Well," Delia smiled. "Would you like to get started?"

"Sure!"

"One of the great many methodologies we use here at the DateLine is the personality test," Delia said. "We use the results of the test to match you up with a date that we feel you might be compatible with. You can take it at home online, if you want, or you can take it here, now—"

"Here now would be great," Tim said.

Delia stood up and led Tim to a computer in the corner, near one of the giant fans.

"By the way," she asked, "how'd you hear about my DateLine? You've obviously seen the ads we run."

Tim took a deep breath. He'd been waiting for this.

"Well," he said. "I have this neighbor, Linda Smallwood? And, uh, she's good friends with your husband, I guess."

"Good friends." Delia's lively cheerful face went flat and expressionless.

"Yeah, very good friends, I think, you know, they're always hanging around together, and we were all having drinks last night at Happy Hour, and the subject came up—"

"The subject came up at Happy Hour—last night," Delia said. "Really."

"Yeah, and so, well, this just sounded really cool, like something I'd like to do."

"Huh." Delia glared at the office door. For a moment Tim imagined that she had some sort of penetrating x-ray vision able to see through all the walls all the way back to her husband's lair. Maybe the x-rays were even powerful enough to kill him—*dead*—right there! But then she turned and looked brightly at Tim, a small smile on her lips. "That's very interesting," she said. "Just let me know when you've finished your test."

"Sure."

Delia turned and walked slowly back to her desk. Tim watched her, watched the roll of her beautiful big round butt, his heart pounding. He thought, Gilbert Hardison, you are a greedy son of a bitch and I hope she beats the shit out of you.

Chapter Sixteen

Reasonable Accommodations

IN THE EVENING RAUL AWOKE IN HIS LITTLE NEST behind the soil additives section of the nursery. He urinated on some yaupon holly, then climbed over the fence and headed up the street to Paige's house.

But then he spotted Linda's truck. Linda's truck—finally. The big black Suburban was parked in the lot next to the nursery, covered with a heavy, plaster-like coating of white dust. Raul walked over and rubbed some of the dust off the back window: his bicycle was still there. He wondered where Linda might be. He tried the door but it was locked. The parking lot belonged to the grocery store next to the nursery, though people going to the restaurant across the street parked there, too.

He tried the grocery first. Just as he came in the door, though, he saw his mother in the produce section—no doubt sizing up the yellow squash or the cucumbers. Or maybe the celery. He made a quick turn and went to the back of the store, where the wine and meat were displayed—where Linda would probably be. No Linda, though. Raul quickly stuffed a package of organic, free-range chicken breasts down the front of his jeans and went back outside and crossed the street to the restaurant. He found Linda sitting with Gilbert Hardison.

"Oh," Linda said. "It's you."

"I saw your truck parked outside."

"Yeah, I picked it up this afternoon. Now go away."

"My bicycle is still in the back."

"I didn't notice," Linda said. "Right now we're fixing to have dinner. I'll get it for you later."

"Give me the keys and I'll relieve you of that burden," Raul said.

Linda sighed and reached for her purse.

"Hey, man," Gilbert said. "There's something dribbling in your pants."

Raul hitched up his dirty, crusty jeans. He could feel sticky chicken juice running down his leg.

"So why are you looking at my pants?" he asked.

"Because he doesn't want to look at your face," Linda said. She glanced at his groin and grimaced. "Goddamn—what *is* that? Are you infected? Does Paige know?"

"I got Paige some chicken breasts at the store."

"Shit," Gilbert grinned. "I bet she's gonna appreciate the delivery, there."

Linda pulled out her car keys. "So go get your bike and bring these back to me."

"I'll leave them with the valet parking guy."

"I said, bring them back to *me*."

Outside, Raul quickly got his bike out of Linda's Suburban—he locked it up, even—and then coasted back across the street to the restaurant. He handed the keys to the valet parking guy who stood in front.

"Give these to that loud female inside," Raul said.

"Which one?"

"The *rude* loud one."

Raul rode around to the back of the nursery, where his wagon had been waiting, loaded with four spindly peach trees, a bag of sand, a bag of sheep manure, a spade. He placed the chicken breasts on top of the sheep manure, hitched up the wagon, and pedaled off to the expressway.

Annoying as Raul was, Linda was so desperate for an interruption that she had rather welcomed his appearance. Almost as soon as they were seated, Gilbert made an official offer—partnership in The Justice Store, with an office at the "convenient location" on East Seventh Street, "just around the corner from the probation office."

"I need reasonable accommodations," Linda said. "I don't like to work in the mornings."

"Who does?"

"Lots of people," Linda said. "Crazy people. But I'm not one of them."

Gilbert shrugged. "We'll get you some very reasonable accommodations."

Linda felt a strange sinking, drifting sense of release. That's what work came down to, she thought—reasonable accommodations. If those idiot liberals at Foster Moomaw had been even partially accommodating to her sleep patterns, things might have worked out. But they didn't even try. The big phonies. To hell with them. Linda was starting to feel indignant, and she smiled grimly.

"Good to see you smiling again," Gilbert said.

"Huh?"

"You smiling like that—it's good."

"Oh," Linda said. "I guess so." Gilbert was smiling back at her, and he looked rather cute. Linda felt compelled to say something more. "I guess this will be fun, or something."

"Sure it will!"

Linda looked away and sighed. Feeling compelled to say something always irked her. Gilbert went on, talking about his big plans for The Justice Store, and that irked her, too. Men who had big plans were always very annoying. Even if they followed through on the big plans, they were annoying. Linda couldn't understand why men just couldn't go out and make a bunch of money without talking about it beforehand.

Of course, men who didn't—couldn't, or wouldn't—follow through on their big plans were even worse. What the hell. Generally, men were stupid—totally useless, unless laundry or auto repair was involved.

"And what about ol' Judge Cantu?" Gilbert asked suddenly.

Linda focused on Gilbert. "Hmm? What about him?"

"Him and that woman he was with?"

"Oh. She seemed to be—a colorful character."

Gilbert laughed. "Yeah, that's right. A lot of people might think ol' Richard might not have it in him, but not me. I *know* Richard Cantu."

"Lucky you!"

"No, I'm serious, I really know the man, you know. He's always been a good boy, always done what he's told, never made a mistake. But then he gets a whiff of the strange and his whole life changes."

Linda arched an eyebrow. "Sort of like you?"

"Shit, I've always known the strange."

"You went to a Baptist college," Linda said. "Baylor's very conservative."

"So? You better bet there was some Top *Secret* strange goin' on there—anyway, Austin was just down the road. Lots of strange in Austin."

"I know *that's* right," Linda said. She thought about what he'd said about the Judge. "Were *you* good when you were little? Did you always do what you're told? *Do* you?"

"Sometimes," Gilbert said. "If what I'm told isn't too fucking weird."

Linda laughed. He was such a nut. "You got it goin' on!"

"I do!" Gilbert smiled widely and leaned back in his chair. "You have *no* idea how much I got it goin' on—I got the power!"

🍸 🍺 🍷 🥂

The early dinner left Linda drowsy. She leaned against

the door of Gilbert's big car, barely awake, watching passively as they got on the expressway and headed south across the river. Gilbert glanced at her from time to time as he kept the car steady in the heavy traffic. Linda thought he looked pleased, though she couldn't imagine why. Gilbert exited at Industrial Oaks and pulled into a liquor store.

"You want anything special?" Gilbert asked. Linda shook her head no. Gilbert touched her unbruised cheek. He said, "Sunshine, cheer up."

"Why?"

"You were acting happy just an hour ago."

"Acting," Linda said. "You got that right."

Gilbert shook his head and went on into the store. He came back out a few moments later with three bottles of sparkling wine and a bag of ice. Linda watched him arrange the bottles in the backseat cooler.

"Planning a party?" Linda asked.

"I got all sorts of plans," Gilbert said.

"So I noticed." Men with plans, she thought. Save me.

Still, Linda perked up a little as they headed out of town into the hills. The broken, dusty country was quiet as twilight approached, and pretty. Linda spotted the billboard with the nasty-looking blond girl. DAD ALWAYS KNEW YOU'D DO GOOD.

"There's that bitch," Linda said.

"Oh—her."

"She's everywhere. Who do you think she gets to unclog her drains?"

Gilbert shook his head and they drove on. After a while he stopped the car in front of a gate. "I suppose you're not gonna get out and open this thing for me?"

Linda just smiled.

"At least you're cheering up some."

After getting out and opening the gate, driving through, getting out and closing it—all the time aware that Linda was smirking at him—Gilbert drove on up the dusty driveway. Linda stared out at the scrubby thickets of trees and cactus.

"Why are you bringing me out here?" Linda asked. "Kill me? Dispose of my body?"

"Why would I want to do that?" Gilbert sounded hurt.

"Oh, it happens all the time," Linda said. "Serial killers—they bring women out to places like this and kill them and dispose of their bodies."

"Now, why would I want to do that?" Gilbert asked again. "I just—"

"Because you're tricky."

"I just bought you a fucking ninety dollar steak," Gilbert said. "I got an investment in you, you know?"

"Maybe that's just one of your tricks."

"Tricks," Gilbert said. "Shit." They drove around a bend and Gilbert pointed to a dark line of trees. "That's the creek over there," he said. "The water quality's very good up here."

When they got to the low-water crossing the sun was hidden behind the hills and the creek's water was dark, dark, though white with foam where it poured over the concrete crossing.

"You know that murderer I'm defending?" Gilbert asked. "Johnston? Killed that cab driver?" Linda nodded. "Well, this was his place. It's mine now—his fee to me."

Linda looked out at the shadowy limestone cliffs above them. "You really *are* tricky," she said.

Gilbert smiled, pleased, and drove across the creek and on up to the house. There was a bit more light there, the house standing long and low and solid-looking. Gilbert parked beneath one of the oaks and shut off the car's engine. Everything was very quiet.

Gilbert said, "This is all mine, now."

🍸🍺🍷🍹

Linda wasn't sure how she felt about Justice Estates. Gilbert's plan was somehow grand and disturbing at the same time. Of course she understood the classic Texan craving for land—her own grandfather and father, respectable businessmen in oil and banking, had at times purchased plots of land out on the Edwards Plateau that they referred to as ranches, though they weren't working ranches at all but country houses, places to get away from the city on weekends. Linda hadn't much liked being trundled out to the ranch on weekends but the men all seemed to like it. There was no reason why Gilbert, black and from rural East Texas, shouldn't be as susceptible to this land lust as anyone else. The problem—the creepiness—came from how he had acquired the land and what he planned to do with it.

"Does your wife know about this place?" Linda asked.

They were sitting outside on the porch in the warm dark, drinking champagne from plastic cups, waiting for the air conditioning to cool the house. The sky was filled with stars; invisible in the city, hidden by city lights, they still managed to shine down through the haze.

"My wife," Gilbert said. The fabric of his lawn chair stretched, squeaked as he shifted his weight.

"Yeah," Linda said. The lassitude she'd felt during dinner and the drive out had disappeared and she smiled at Gilbert. "That woman you're married to—does she know about this?"

"The ranch is business," Gilbert said.

"Just for us Justice Store big shots, huh?"

"Something like that," Gilbert said. "Delia's not involved in this project."

"Not yet," Linda said. "But you *are* going to invite her out to your little lovenest, aren't you?"

"Little lovenest."

"That's what you've got here, right? Someplace you can bring your girlfriends to."

Gilbert stood up and dumped the last drops of his champagne onto a prickly pear. Then he refilled his cup, looking off into the darkness.

"Not that I care," Linda said. "Shoot, I think you *should* bring your girlfriends out here—*and* your wife."

Gilbert leaned against a roof post, shaking his head. "This is more than just that," he said. "It's a project."

"A stupid project," Linda said. "If you want to keep this place, just keep it the way it is. There's enough big houses being built already. And you're right on the creek, here—think of all the environmental lawsuits you'll have to deal with."

Gilbert chuckled at that. The linebacker in him still liked the idea of conflict.

"And what's with *you*?" Linda asked. "You're no goddamn builder. You like to tear things down. I don't get people like you who want to be something else. Goddamn architects want to be musicians, musicians want to be actors, barmaids want to be nurses, nurses want to be lawyers, and you want to be a real estate magnate. It's stupid. Nobody's content with their miserable goddamn lot in life."

"What about you?" Gilbert asked. "I remember one time you wanted to be a bail bondsman."

"Oh, that's not going to happen," Linda said. She was silent for a while. "You know that," she finally said. "It's too much trouble. All I really want to do is watch Court TV."

Gilbert set his cup down and stepped over behind Linda and put his big hands on her shoulders. Linda relaxed a little as he kneaded her back.

"No cable out here," Gilbert said softly. "But I'll get a satellite dish set up for you real soon."

"This is all your fault," Linda said. "You got me started on this whole legal thing."

"I'm sorry, Sunshine," Gilbert whispered. He bent over and kissed Linda on the top of her mussed head. "I'm sorry."

"Oh, well, goddamn," Linda sighed. "It's too late to change things now."

🍸🍺🍷🥂

Linda dozed for a while after the sex, then woke to Gilbert's heavy snoring. The bedroom was dark. She felt her way to the bathroom, stumbling and stubbing her toes on unfamiliar furniture, and then on out to the front of the house, where enough moonlight spilled through the windows to light her way. The murderer, Johnston, wasn't much of a housekeeper—there was a mildewy rotten smell coming from the kitchen, and the furniture that she kept banging into was ratty and tattered. In the moonlight, though, everything looked soft. Linda made her way through the living room and out onto the limestone-flagged porch and stood there nude in the warm night breeze. There were five or six deer in the yard cropping grass, and one of them snorted and stamped in alarm when she came outside. Linda filled a cup with ice and warmish champagne and sipped at it, listening to the creek, the deer, the night sounds—frogs, crickets, the ghost of the dead cab driver, maybe a few Comanches, who knew what the hell was lurking out there in the dark. Linda was a city girl, but standing naked on the porch was—pleasant. Standing around naked was the sort of thing Paige would do, and Linda was surprised that she sort of liked it, too. It was kind of fun. She felt, well, *relaxed*—an unusual feeling, one that didn't even approach being dead. Linda walked to the end of the porch, stepping carefully, and looked to the east. She could see the violet lights of Austin reflecting up into the sky. Really, she thought, this wasn't so far out in the country at all. Stupid idea to build big houses out here. Big houses, strip malls, bunch of ugly shit. This place needs to be left the way it is. Justice Estates. Gilbert's a goddamn fool.

Back inside Gilbert woke up as Linda slipped into bed.

"Here's my Sunshine," he said. "C'mere, baby."

"Go back to sleep," Linda said. She pushed his hand away. Sex had been as clumsy and ridiculous as usual, with Linda refusing to let Gilbert get on top of her, trying to keep him away from her still-bruised and tender face, forcing him instead to take her from behind—and having to remind him to stick it in her pussy and not anywhere else. Gilbert had been annoyed but he'd gotten over it.

"Feeling good?" Gilbert asked sleepily.

"I don't know," Linda said. "Maybe."

"Maybe." Gilbert chuckled softly. "Baby, you were thrashin' around like a wild mallard duck."

"A what!" Linda sat up.

"A bird, baby," Gilbert said. He sounded dopey, half asleep. "A beautiful wild bird...."

"A bird?" Linda asked. "Like a—*parakeet*?" A vision of the dead bird in its cage flashed in her mind—That Other Bird dead, That One Bird flying off into the trees, both of the birds alive at one time, such a stupid goddamn gift, no pearls, green birds over the softball field, the commune—*feral parakeets*. The phrase sounded more ominous than ever. Feral parakeets. She slapped Gilbert on his round belly. "A goddamn *parakeet*?"

After dark, Tim took a break from porn and rode his bike up to the Super Stop for beer and cigarettes. As he turned from Waterston onto West Lynn, he spotted Linda's black Suburban in the parking lot of the closed grocery store. He turned back and coasted into the lot.

It was her truck, all right. There was the familiar crease on the rear passenger-side door, where Linda had taken a right turn a bit too sharply and had banged against a telephone pole. The truck was covered with a heavy layer of white dust. It looked like it had been sitting somewhere a long time, though a little of the dust had been wiped off the windshield and off the rear window. Strange.

Tim looked around, surprised to find his eyes tearing in frustration. The restaurant was still open. Linda was probably over there, having fun with some people—with that big black guy, maybe. Well, maybe, probably, she wasn't having *fun*, exactly, but Tim was sure she was over there. With Dr. Delia's husband. Gilbert fucking Hardison. What a greedy bastard he was! Why couldn't he be satisfied with the incredible Dr. Delia? He had no business with Linda.

Tim pedaled on down to the Super Stop for his beer and cigarettes, and when he came back up the street, Linda's Suburban was still there. He circled it once, then leaned close and wrote in the dust with his finger: *Linda come home*. Then he coasted down the slight slope to the complex. There was a light on in Paige's townhouse—no telling *what* was going on in there—but the other windows were dark and quiet. Tim looked at Linda's door for a moment, until he suddenly felt silly and went inside to masturbate.

Chapter Seventeen

Poisoned

SICK WITH FOOD POISONING, PAIGE SLEPT POORLY. She kept having to get up to go to the bathroom or drink water, and by the time she got up for good, around noon, she was exhausted. Raul had not come back. Apparently he'd spent the night at Charlie's, and was now no doubt at work, dozing peacefully back in his nook in the compost stacks. The son of a bitch.

Stretched out on the couch, wrapped in a blanket, Paige felt alert and feverish—she felt like stirring up some trouble. She called Linda but there was no answer. After a moment, thinking, she dug around in her purse until she found Judge Richard Cantu's business card. She dialed the number, and after going through a suspicious-sounding secretary and holding for a few minutes, got the judge himself.

"Hello," Richard said. Paige liked the sound of his voice—rich, reassuring, and rather passive.

"Hey, hi, hello, this is Paige Davenport. Remember me?"

There was a meek pause. Richard asked, "—Yes?"

"From happy hour Wednesday?"

"—Sure. Well—yeah, I remember you." There was a longer pause. Paige could hear him swallow, trying to think of something to say. "Sure."

"I've been poisoned," Paige said cheerfully. "What should I do about it?"

"*Poisoned*?"

Paige frowned. "Do you really remember me?"

"Sure I do," Richard said. "You're the—you're very attractive, I think. I—"

"I guess that's a compliment," Paige said.

"Yeah, I saw you at the bar. We were at that table—"

"Are you certain?"

"Well, yeah—" He didn't sound certain, but he added, "I have your business card!"

"Are you sure it's really *my* card?" Paige asked. "Or is it somebody else's card?"

There was a long pause. Richard finally asked, "What?"

"Never mind," Paige said. "You remember that pretty boy who was sitting next to me?"

"Well, yeah—"

"That's Raul—he's the one that poisoned me. He cooked me dinner last night and I got poisoned—I could be dying right now."

"Dying?"

Paige was losing her patience. "Listen, do you have a sense of humor? At all?"

"Of course I do!"

"Really?"

There was another long pause. Paige could almost hear Richard thinking. Finally, he said, "I—I *think* so."

"Well, you're not showing it," Paige said. "Here I am in pain, dying of food poisoning and you're not even laughing."

"I—I guess if you think you've been poisoned, you should call the poison hotline or something."

"Oh, good lord!"

"Well," Richard said. There was another long pause. "Well, I mean, what do you want me to do about it?"

"You could maybe buy me some drinks and listen to me *talk* about it."

Paige could hear Richard breathing. Eventually he asked, "What?"

"You're not very decisive, either," Paige said. "I thought judges were supposed to be decisive. Maybe I've got the wrong—"

🍺🍷🍸🍹

"No!" Richard said. There was a large window in his small office that looked not outside, but inside, across the outer office, where he could watch the court employees bustle around their desks. Right now he could see Ms. Kreider, an erect middle-aged woman with a massive, solid-looking bosom—Ms. Kreider, who had been giving him funny looks. Funny looks—no fucking wonder! Five calls from Giselle already today, seven yesterday, surely everyone in the office knew about her by now, imagining much more, and now this Paige calling. But Paige! Damn. "No," Richard said, "it's just—I'm not used to getting calls like this."

"I don't wonder," Paige said. "You're not very funny."

"You want to have a drink this evening?" Richard blurted.

"Of course not—I'm dying."

"Oh, yeah," Richard said. Poisoned. Damn. That sucked. "Tomorrow?"

"Maybe," Paige said. "But only if you promise to be funny."

"Well," Richard said, "I can try to be funny."

"That's not very encouraging," Paige said. "Most people who try to be funny fail."

🍺🍷🍸🍹

There were only a few cars in the grocery store parking lot, and Linda did not see her big Suburban among them.

"Well, shit," she said. "It was here last night."

"They tow them cars, you know," Quincy said. "They get here in the morning, see some strange car, they tow it."

"Yeah." Linda felt her heart sink within her—to lose the truck just after she got it back. Goddamn.

"What'd you want me to do?" Quincy asked.

"Oh, I don't know. Make a block or something while I think."

Quincy pulled back onto the street and headed around the block. At the nursery, Linda saw Raul sitting on a stool amid rows of scrawny fruit trees. A tall woman with graying black hair was standing over Raul, talking intently—lecturing him, it looked like, an angry lecture. Raul just stared off into space. Linda suddenly envied him—envied that strange brilliant ability to just *turn off*, to not care what anyone else said or thought. Linda was working at it, but Raul was the master. What a talent!

The cab turned left and went past the other side of the nursery, and then left again, past some older apartments, well shaded beneath large trees. Then left again, back to the grocery.

"You truck's not anywhere," Quincy said.

"What?" Linda had been thinking, Why the hell do *I* care? About anything!

"Your truck—it's not here."

"Oh, I don't care," Linda said. "Just take me on downtown."

🍺🍷🍸🍹

Cox O'Brien was the largest law firm in the city, and one of the largest in the state, occupying five floors of one of the towers on Congress Avenue. Linda got off the elevator at some floor or other and stood in front of an empty receptionist's desk, looking puzzled. It was late on Friday afternoon, and most of the drones that the firm employed appeared to have already fled, or were hiding, or had dropped dead, or something—the whole floor was ghostly silent. Someone should have been there, though—Linda had talked to someone who promised to be there. She stood in front of the desk, frowning, until a beautiful young black woman came around the corner. She stopped and looked at Linda with surprise.

"Can I help you?" she asked.

"I have an appointment with Ed Waldman," Linda said. "He was supposed to be here, or his secretary, or somebody. I think."

"Oh—Mr. Waldman's down on thirteen," the woman said. She slid into a chair behind the receptionist's desk. "This is seventeen. You must've gotten off on the wrong floor."

"Oh." Linda turned and hit a button on the elevator.

"You can take the staircase, if you want," the receptionist said. "We have our own staircase for the office. Want me to show you down?"

"No, that's okay," Linda said.

"Oh, it's not a problem!" she said. Linda noticed that the young receptionist had real teeth, young and healthy. That was somewhat comforting.

"Whatever." Linda sighed and followed her to a staircase that spiraled down the west side of the building through the law firm's offices. The whole outer wall was made of glass and Linda could look to the west, see the river running through the city, the gray smoggy hills beyond, the hot hard afternoon sun glinting off everything.

"Quite a view, huh?" the girl asked.

"Yeah, it is." Depressing view, Linda thought. She looked to the southwest, toward Justice Estates. It was out there somewhere in the haze.

They came down around the spirals to the thirteenth floor. A tall, tanned young man with thick glasses was waiting. "This is Mr. Waldman," the young woman said. She turned and started back up the stairs.

"Linda, right?" Waldman asked. "C'mon back to my office." Linda followed him down a long hallway, past many closed doors. "I'm glad you caught me," Waldman said. "This was kind of at the last minute. Most of the receptionists and secretaries have gone home for the weekend."

"It looked deserted out there."

"We all try to be reasonably informal on Fridays—attendance, dress, that sort of thing." Waldman glanced at Linda and gave his head a sort of smirky sideways hitch. What the hell did that mean? Linda wondered if she was being insulted. Waldman was dressed casually in a polo shirt, jeans and sneakers, but Linda had tried to look serious and businesslike. She was wearing most of what had once been an assertive red suit, a suit that should have been dry-cleaned but had been washed and left to mildew by Gilbert, and then washed and bleached by Tim. It didn't stink any more but it had faded to pink and shrank a bit, and was unusually wrinkled.

"I looked on the internet," Linda said. "You're the guy who does golf course law?"

"That's me." Waldman smiled—wide, bright teeth, a frat boy's careless empty smile. He started walking down the hall again. "Somebody's got to do it," he said. "Maybe I'm being punished. You think?"

"Golf course law."

"Yep," Waldman said. "You might be surprised—there's a lot of liability issues with golf courses, environmental issues, all sorts of things. Plus I get to play golf just about every day."

Linda wondered who he was related to, to get a job like that—or, considering the relaxed, feminine roll of his hips as he walked, who he was sleeping with.

"This is my little bit of heaven," Waldman said at an office door. He stood aside and let Linda pass by. The office was tiny, cramped with a cluttered desk and shelves filled with golf trophies, and a big window looking east over the convention center and the interstate.

A woman was seated in the corner, wedged in between the desk and the window, a slender white woman, very well dressed, long dark hair with a trace of gray at her temple.

"This is Adele Stratton," Waldman said. "She's an executive with the Balcones Canyons Conservation Association, which our firm represents on a pro bono basis, so I've asked her to be here." Linda wasn't surprised at the pro bono mention: Cox O'Brien represented dozens of huge polluters—strip mines, smelters, chemical refineries—along with corporations that manufactured things like poisonous over-the-counter medicines or disintegrating SUV tires. Representing the tiny BCCA—even if it meant dragging Ed Waldman in off the golf course—was good public relations. Waldman said, "Apparently somebody over there asked you to call me—is that correct?'"

"Yeah, something like that," Linda said. She sat down in the other corner and struggled to pull a wad of paper out of her handbag, dropping an unused lipstick, her house keys, and a few coins. She unfolded the paper, a printout of a map she'd found on the internet, and asked, "You all are familiar with the Beitleman Ranch, right?"

Linda told Ed Waldman and Adele Stratton all that she knew about Justice Estates. It wasn't much, factually, but, still, she thought she made a good story out of it—the murderer, the ranch, Gilbert, Gilbert's crazy plans. Waldman and Adele were familiar with the property and at one time had even approached Billy Johnston about selling it to the Nature Conservancy. They hadn't heard of the murder, though, or that the ranch had changed hands. Waldman's office faced the east. As Linda talked she noticed a column of dark gray smoke rising far off. She fell silent.

"So what do you want us to do about all this?" Adele asked.

"*I* don't know," Linda said. "You guys are the ones that fight developers. I guess you should sue him, or something."

"Sue him, or something," Waldman said. He and Adele exchanged a look.

"I guess," Linda said. "As far as I can tell any development out there'll run into the watershed ordinances, and maybe the endangered species act."

"Right. But so far, all of this is just talk."

Linda shrugged. "Well, sure. And like I said, you also need to look into how he acquired the property—it's probably unethical or something."

Waldman nodded, "*Probably* unethical. Yeah, well." He leaned back in his chair, stretching his long, hairy arms. He looked at Adele and shook his head. "You know, I work these cases for you people—"

Linda blinked. *You people.*

"—and I'm *not* unsympathetic, really, but I also think all this anti-development activity is futile—I mean, *something's* going to be built out there. Why not some nice houses and a golf course? Thirty-thousand people moved to Austin last year, and people are *always* going to be moving down here, whether the economy's booming or busting, and they're going to need places to live and play golf, you know? I've lived here almost four years now and I've just seen incredible changes."

"I grew *up* here," Adele Stratton said. She was looking at Linda's wrinkled map. "I've lived here all my life. I remember when we had such a beautiful small city, back before everything—exploded."

Waldman cocked his head and smirked. "Hey, you know, young people today don't like hearing how great things used to be."

Linda and Adele slowly looked at each other. Linda looked at Waldman.

"Meaning we're old?" she asked.

Waldman sat back. "Well—"

"Why should anyone care what young people think?"

"Well—"

"Young people are *stupid*," Linda said. "Actually, I've always thought young people were full of shit. Even when I was young I thought that."

"Young people of a certain age, I mean," Waldman said.

Linda shrugged. Actually, she still remembered how she disliked hearing her father talk about how *bad* things used to be—another big lie, of course, since he'd grown up the son of a successful oil man during the Great Depression. How bad could that have been?

Adele Stratton said, "I wonder what's on fire over there."

The column of smoke was quickly growing heavier and darker, almost black.

"Where is that?" Linda asked. "East Seventh?"

"Somewhere on the Eastside," Adele said. Waldman just shrugged; in his four years in Austin he'd never gone east of the interstate, except to the airport.

Linda asked, "Isn't there a tire warehouse over there or something?"

More shrugs. Linda wondered if Gilbert's convenient location on East Seventh might be burning. She almost hoped so—it would save a lot of trouble, and maybe even some arguments and hard feelings. She glanced at Adele and Waldman, gazing out the window at the smoke. Apparently they'd already lost interest in Beitleman Ranch and Justice Estates. Oh well, Linda thought. I tried.

Chapter Eighteen

A Group Thing

ON HIS WAY OVER TO PICK UP PAIGE, RICHARD FELT A little nervous. Well, *very* nervous. He tried to calm himself, but there it was—tightness in his chest, tension in his shoulders. Nerves. Strange, because he knew he was safe: Kelly was away in Houston, tending to her sick mother, or whatever it was she was really doing, and Giselle was safely at work, serving drinks and letting drunks peer down the front of her blouse. Richard shifted a little in his seat at the thought of Giselle's heavy white-tipped breasts, the tattoo of John-John Kennedy on her inner thigh, feeling a little blood rush to his groin—Giselle—a twinge in his penis. Tonight, though, Paige. She was the first woman who'd ever really pursued him—though in his case, in this case, a single phone call was all that constituted pursuit. That was kind of scary right there, and a little depressing.

Paige answered the door wrapped in a sheet, sleepy-eyed, hair somewhat ahoo. She didn't say anything. She just stood there squinting at him.

"It's seven-thirty," Richard finally said. "I mean, I think it is. Am I early?"

"Nooooo," Paige said slowly. "I don't know. I was asleep."

She turned away from the door and walked back toward the kitchen. The sheet did not cover her rear—her behind, her *butt*—and Richard again felt the twitch of a sudden half-erection. Paige yawned, covered her mouth, said, "C'mon in."

Richard came inside and stood next to the little counter that separated the kitchen from living room, not quite sure what to do. He noticed that the house was clean—spotless. He looked in the kitchen, to compliment Paige on her lovely home, and saw that she was bent over, looking into the refrigerator. Bent over, the sheet falling away, her perfect, round, tightly muscled butt, the soft frilled edge of her cat. Richard just stared.

"I don't have anything to drink," Paige said over her shoulder.

"Uh, that's okay." Richard forced a smile.

"Well, I'm *thirsty*." Paige stood up straight and looked at him sharply. "Why don't you go to the store and get me a Diet Dr. Pepper? I'll be ready when you get back."

"Oh—okay," Richard quickly agreed. He stepped quickly to the door, trying to hide his growing erection. "Just the soda?"

"Yeah," Paige said.

"I'll be back in a few minutes."

"Take your time," Paige said. "I just woke up."

Outside Richard could scarcely believe his reactions—not just his heart rate, or the lump in his pants—but the whole sense of teenaged nervous giddiness that rushed over him. Paige Davenport—*damn*.

There was a familiar-looking red Cadillac parked in front of the convenience store. Familiar-looking, but Richard couldn't quite place it. When he got inside, though, he saw Gilbert Hardison and Linda Smallwood buying beer. Oh, he thought, them. He went around to the back cooler and got two bottles of Diet Dr. Pepper and headed for the register.

Gilbert saw him coming.

"Well, Judge!"

"Mr. Hardison," Richard said. He took a deep breath and drew himself up as straight as he could—the sudden erection had vanished. "Ms. Smallwood."

"You get around," Gilbert said. He paid for his items and moved aside so that Richard could get to the register. Linda opened the pack of cigarettes and pulled one out.

"I was just sort of in the neighborhood," Richard said.

"Going on your date with Paige?" Linda asked.

"What?"

"Paige isn't too discrete." Linda lit the cigarette. "She told me you guys had a date."

"Hey, no smoking in here," the clerk said.

"What—" Richard began. Discrete?

"City ordinance," the clerk said.

"Oh, please," Linda said. "I'm an officer of the goddamn court. I don't want to hear about any city ordinances."

"Sunshine...." Gilbert was holding the door open.

"It's my job," the clerk said as they went out the door. He rang up Richard's sodas.

Richard paid and hurried after Gilbert and Linda. That comment about discretion was frightening. Kelly. Giselle, too—Giselle had quite a temper. Frightening.

"Well, Judge," Gilbert said. "I hope you have a good night."

The look on Gilbert's face, eyes hidden behind sunglasses, like he was almost *leering* or something. Richard caught a flash of gold on one of Gilbert's teeth. Leering.

"Yeah," Richard said. "Okay."

"Be safe," Linda said, closing the car door.

"What?" Be *safe*? What? Richard took a step closer to the car, but Linda did not look at him. He stood watching the Cadillac lurch back out of the parking lot and disappear up the street.

"Damn," Gilbert said. "You rattled that poor man."

"The rude clerk?"

"Cantu," Gilbert said, smiling. "Shit."

"He's just a goof," Linda said. "An annoying goof. And besides, he did need to be warned. Paige can be a very difficult woman—in the wrong hands she can be dangerous."

"I thought Paige was your friend."

"Well, yeah," Linda shrugged. "She is. So?"

It was early evening, and the sun was warm behind them. Gilbert rolled down his window and let the heavy damp air blow in.

"You're a difficult woman, too. You know that?"

"Really?" Linda smiled. "You think so?"

"Yeah, I guess you do know that," Gilbert said.

When Richard returned Paige was dressed in tight white jeans and a sleeveless white blouse. She looked clean and pure—alert, alive, healthy—not at all dangerous, or even difficult.

"Thank you *so* much," Paige said. "I'm dying of thirst—it's hard to put on makeup when you're dying of thirst."

"Sure," Richard said. "I bet." He watched Paige duck into the bathroom and heard a hiss as she opened the bottle.

"Hey." Paige stuck her head out the door, an eyeliner in her hand. "Why don't you sit down or something—you're making me nervous."

"Oh—okay," Richard said. He sat on a barstool at the kitchen counter. "So, how's your day been?"

"Wretched," Paige said from the bathroom. She sounded cheery, though. "I've been sick, remember?"

"Oh, yeah," Richard said. "You told me you had food poisoning, or something."

"It's all Raul's fault, that poisoning." Paige stood in the doorway, an eyelash curler in her hand. "Listen, do you have any insight?"

"Insight?"

"Into men. I'm trying to figure out why that little shit does the things he does—like poison me, or fill my toilet with pubic hair, or masturbate on my barbeque grill when I'm entertaining."

"On the food?" Richard was aghast. "Jesus!"

"No, I wasn't cooking, I just had guests—*a* guest—in the house. But he's probably jizzed on my food, too, for all I know. Maybe that's the base for those sauces he uses when he cooks. Maybe that's what he uses to poison me—sperm. Bleh." Paige made a face and went back into the bathroom. Richard heard some water running. "Not to mention the time he kicked in my door and stole my bed and threw it out in the middle of the expressway, and all I was doing was—was—*visiting*—with his girlfriend. Why would he object to that?"

Richard felt uncomfortable. He nodded at the bathroom door and said, "Yeah."

Paige stuck her head out and stared at Richard. "The thing is, the man's a pervert, and he's incredibly and unjustly jealous, and I want to know why he's *persecuting* me!"

There was a long pause. Richard listened to the water run as Paige just looked at him steadily with those violet-blue eyes. Finally he said, "Well, most men don't really know what they want, I guess."

"So what exactly does that mean?" Paige asked. "Are you speaking for yourself?"

"I don't know," Richard said. "Maybe. I guess."

"And what does that have to do with pubic hair in my toilet?"

Richard shrugged.

"You're almost as useless as Raul," Paige said. She shook her head and went back into the bathroom. "So—tell me, why are you so mean to Linda?"

"What?" Richard hadn't expected a question about Linda Smallwood. "Mean?"

"Why are you so mean to Linda?"

"What do you mean—mean?"

Paige stuck her head out of the bathroom and looked at him again. "Those jokes you make—those little comments you make about her work, about her black eye. You really hurt her feelings. Don't you know that? Linda's going through a really rough time right now, and she's really depressed, and you're not helping her at all. You're not being mean to her on purpose, are you?"

"Well, no," Richard said, slowly. "No, of course not."

"I didn't think so," Paige said. "You don't seem to be the nasty type."

"No," Richard said. "I wouldn't want to be mean to—Ms. Smallwood." He was confused, though. In every encounter he'd ever had with Linda Smallwood, she had always seemed extremely, well, *unpleasant,* but still she had all these friends who were so apparently loyal—affectionate, even—toward her. Mystery. "No."

"Why don't you apologize to her?" Paige asked.

"What?"

Paige came out of the bathroom and passed Richard, trailing a light, flowery perfume. There was a cordless phone on a table next to the couch, and Paige brought it over to him.

"Apologize," Paige said. She punched a number into the phone and handed it to him. "Go ahead and tell her you're sorry."

🍷 🍸 🍺

Linda's cell phone went off as she and Gilbert sat silently at a stoplight. "Damn," Linda said. She dropped her can of beer—foam spritzing across the floor—before she dug down into her purse and got to the phone. "I thought I had the ringer turned off."

"Aw, shit," Gilbert said. He could smell the spilled beer. "Law office!"

"I just had this interior detailed," Gilbert said softly. The light changed to green and he drove on. The beer can rocked back and forth, emptying into the carpet."

"Law office!" Linda barked again, annoyed. "Who's there?"

"Ms. Smallwood?"

"Maybe?" Linda glanced at Gilbert. "Who're you?"

"This is Richard Cantu."

"Yeah?" Linda put her hand over the phone. "It's Richard Cantu."

Gilbert laughed. "What's he want?"

"What do you want?" Linda asked the judge.

"I was wondering—worrying. Uh, I was thinking about the other night and how maybe you were, or might be—offended, you know, by some of the talk at the, uh, table...."

"Yeah," Linda said.

"And I'd like you to know that it wasn't, you know, deliberate on my part, and I'm sorry if you got the wrong impression, or anything."

Linda frowned. "The wrong impression about what?"

"About, well—about being rude. I mean, I hope you don't think I was, and I'm sorry if you do and if I was."

"What the hell?" Linda covered the phone again and looked at Gilbert. "He's apologizing or something. I think."

"Hey."

"Wait a minute," Richard said. "Oh—Paige wants to know if you want to meet us somewhere for drinks."

"Drinks? No—maybe later."

"Maybe later," Richard repeated. Then, "What?"

"No—" Linda began.

"No, Paige says we'll be at the Days Inn later."

"The Days Inn," Linda said. She looked at Gilbert and raised an eyebrow. "What, y'all are having an orgy or something?"

"An orgy?" Gilbert asked.

"No, no," Richard said. He sounded confused. "I don't know—she, Paige, she just says we'll be there, I think."

"Maybe later," Linda said. She hit the disconnect button and shook her head. "*That* was weird."

🍷🍸🍹🍺

Richard held the dead phone in his hand. "She said maybe later."

Paige frowned. "That's all?"

"Just maybe later." Richard blinked and pushed his glasses back up his nose, thinking it over. "Well, she did ask if we were having an—orgy."

"An orgy?" Paige asked. She frowned and looked thoughtful. "I suppose we could, I could call some people—did she sound like she *wanted* an orgy?"

"No, I don't think so."

Paige took the phone from him. "Well, how *did* she sound?"

Richard shrugged. "Like she always does, I guess." *Cross,* he thought. Angry. Unpleasant.

"You're no help," Paige said. "The whole point of this evening is to help Linda, and you're not being very cooperative."

Richard sighed, suddenly depressed. He thought the whole point of the evening was to do—something—with Paige Davenport. But Paige seemed to have other plans. She really was a lot of trouble. She wanted cooperation, apologies, insight, *thought*. Jesus. Here he had thought Giselle had been demanding. Giselle might bitch about being tired of eating fried chicken three times a week, or about not being able to spend a full night with him, but she never made him make phone calls apologizing to unpleasant people, and she certainly never made him *think*.

"Maybe I should go home," Richard said.

"Home?" Paige looked puzzled. "How can we have fun if you go home?"

"Fun?" Richard asked. Making phone calls?

"It's fun to help people," Paige said. "It's fun to be nice. You'll see." She put her soft hand to his cheek. "And you've got such pretty brown eyes."

🍷🍸🍸🍺

Outside Richard stood sweating beneath the trees in the courtyard waiting for Paige to lock up her house. He could still feel the touch of Paige's hand on his cheek—his flesh tingled, almost, a soft numb tingling—and that damn erection was sticking up again. He shifted his pants, took a deep breath, exhaled.

"Coming!" Paige called. She locked her door, then hurried over. "I guess I'm obsessive-compulsive," she said. "I always have to look around and make sure everything's turned off and locked up."

"Safety's very important," Richard said.

"See?" Paige asked. They walked out toward the parking lot. "We have something in common—concern for safety." Before Richard could reply, she asked, "You're driving, right?"

"Well—"

"Tell the truth, I'm not a very good driver. I keep banging into things." Paige stood close, her soft arm brushing his. Tingling.

"Sure," Richard said, hitching his pants again. He looked over at Paige's ancient green Jaguar. Dents in the fender, in the doors, a headlight busted out, a shattered taillight covered with red plastic tape, the car a victim of many bangings. "Sure," he said. "We can take my car. No problem."

Richard unlocked the door of the Buick and looked up to see Tim Newlin gliding towards them on his bicycle, a plastic bag of beer and hair conditioner dangling from the handlebar.

Paige said, "Tim, you remember Richard—from Happy Hour?"

"Yeah," Tim said slowly. He looked from Richard to Paige and back again—slowly, slightly stoned but alert.

"We're headed out to have adventures on the Eastside," Paige said. "Want to come?"

Richard's erection vanished and he looked off toward the expressway. What the hell? Paige inviting Linda Smallwood and Gilbert Hardison to join them, now this Tim kid. This was supposed to be a damn *date*, not a—well, whatever it was. A group thing. An orgy. Giselle never pulled this kind of shit. Richard glanced at Paige—sculpted arms, tightly-muscled flat belly, hint of a nipple under her light white blouse. Once again he felt very sad.

"No, thanks," Tim said. "I've got a busy night ahead."

"Tim's a pornographer," Paige said cheerily.

"Oh—" Richard looked closer at Tim. A pornographer?

"Want to see?" Tim asked.

The new office was just as grim as Linda had imagined it: scruffy stained carpet, dented sheetrock walls, no windows. Gilbert kept mentioning how this convenient location was just around the corner from the county probation office, but Linda was not impressed. It was convenient for the criminals, perhaps, but it was damn inconvenient for her, and a dump.

"You could use a little paint around here," Linda said.

"Yeah," Gilbert said. "Well, you know how it is—I only come in here a couple mornings a week, so I never notice anything."

"Mornings," Linda said flatly.

"Don't worry, baby, you can set your own hours. I'm a firm believer in reasonable accommodations. Everything's going to be fine."

Linda frowned. The office didn't look too fine. The reception area had putty-colored metal folding chairs salvaged from some ancient government auction, an ashtray and a faded NO SMOKING sign, a few employment inserts from the local daily newspaper, an old *Field & Stream*, and two old copies of the Spanish-language edition of *People*. A large sign on the wall read I WILL HELP YOU.

"Miss Molina sits over there." Gilbert pointed to a window-like opening in the wall. Behind it was a tiny room filled with tiny stuffed animals—bears, giraffes, horses, lizards, a sheep, and more. Linda assumed that there was a desk underneath it all. Gilbert said, "Miss Molina's actually very efficient."

"Yeah, I can see she's got her own little zoo going on there," Linda said. "Does she have teeth?"

"Teeth?" Gilbert looked at Linda and saw that she was serious. He shrugged. "Yeah, I guess so."

"You're not very reassuring. I think you should check out her teeth." Linda looked around the scruffy room. "You could use some flowers in here, too."

"Flowers!" Gilbert laughed. "Since when did you ever care about flowers?"

"Since I first came in here," Linda said. "You need flowers, and paint, and a window, and a receptionist with teeth."

They went down the hallway, past a conference room—it had a long table like a conference room, at least. Gilbert opened a door and turned on a light. "This will be your office," he said.

There was an old gray steel desk in the middle of the room, a desk covered with plaster dust and air-conditioning ductwork. Stacks of dust-covered computer manuals rested precariously on a chair behind the desk.

"Well!"

"Oh, I know," Gilbert said. "It's a fucking mess—but look, we're getting the AC fixed for you, gonna get some paint on the walls, it'll be great."

Linda didn't say anything. Gilbert laughed again and stepped close, wrapping his big arms around her, holding her tight, squeezing.

"Ah, Sunshine, you're just depressed."

"Not—"

"I know this isn't some fancy office downtown, you know, but this is a place where you'll be doing real work helping real people—and making real money."

Linda had never been too interested in making real money, or in having an office in one of the big buildings downtown, even a big office with a view, like at Cox O'Brien, but she felt that if she absolutely *had* to work she might as well be comfortable. And the East Seventh Street location of The Justice Store wasn't too comfortable. At Foster Moomaw Linda could at least sit in a cushy chair and look out her window into the alley and watch the nosy psychiatrist walk her angry schnauzer past the oleanders. Here the only distraction would be the clients.

"If you say so," Linda said.

Gilbert kissed Linda on the forehead—not noticing or caring that Linda winced—and stepped away.

"Once you get moved in here, this place'll seem like home."

"Good lord!"

"I'm not joking. We're like family at The Justice Store."

"Goddamn dysfunctional family," Linda mumbled. "Incestuous, too."

*   *   *

"You really do have the cutest brown eyes," Paige said.

Richard looked at her, feeling that now-familiar tightness in his chest growing again. They were sitting at the foot of a large bed, facing some sort of fancy computer system. Paige bounced a little on the bed, like a kid, glancing over at him, trace of a smile on her lips. Richard could hear that Tim guy in the kitchen. Paige kept bouncing, glancing. What the hell?

"Your eyes are blue," Richard said, feeling lame. He wanted to say something like "violet" or "azure" or "oceanic" or at least "really, *really* blue," but it seemed like his heart was choking off his throat, or his brain, or something—he was nervous, with that Tim lurking in the kitchen, a stranger, a pornographer—so he just repeated, "Blue."

"So my drivers' license says." Paige kissed him—sharp, sudden.

"Oh!" Richard blushed, put a hand on her shoulder. Paige grinned at him, blue blue oceanic violet azure blue eyes sparkling.

"Here you go." Tim came back from the kitchen and handed Richard a can of beer. "I've got a really simple system going here, you know, but, like, it still brings in some—cash." He sat at the computer, his back to Paige and Richard. "I've got two sites, a gay site and a straight site—the gay site actually does better."

Paige kissed Richard again, slower, deeper. Richard sighed, fell back on the bed, careful not to spill the beer, Paige falling with him, warm, liquid. Lord!

"The overhead on these things is so low, you almost can't help but make a ton of money—"

Paige sat up as suddenly as she had first kissed him. "We'd better get this party on the road," she said.

In a quiet room in Houston, his grandfather's den, Davy Cantu sat in front of a computer screen, sat still as a statue, staring. *Dad.* At Tim's place! That hot chick, too—saw her before with her shirt off a couple of times.

But with Dad!

Gilbert spotted the four remaining cans of beer sitting on Linda's future desk, sweating. "We've even got a little galley in back, got a refrigerator, got a hotplate, a microwave. You can cook your lunch there or whatever."

"I doubt it." But Linda followed Gilbert down the hall, following a worn path in the sad beige carpet. A room opened to the left.

"That's the paralegal's office," Gilbert said. "You'll like Ray, he's kind of passive, easy to intimidate."

Linda saw an overturned Starbuck's cup on Ray's desk, spilling something brown and curdling. She turned away and followed Gilbert the rest of the way down the hall to the galley, a dark, moldy little room with a sink, a microwave, and a tiny refrigerator. Gilbert was kneeling in front of the fridge looking puzzled.

"I think it's broke," he said. "At least, it's not cold."

"I hope you didn't leave anything in there to rot," Linda said. "Where's the bathroom?"

Gilbert pointed. "That door."

Linda opened the door to the bathroom. It was closet-sized, the walls covered with a strange collage of naked women—*parts* of naked women, mostly—dozens and dozens of photos of breasts, vaginas and mouths clipped from magazines and glued to the wall. Linda slowly turned from the room of parts and looked at Gilbert.

"Oh, yeah," Gilbert said. "It was like that when we moved in, so we kept it as an artifact, you know? This used to be a pawn shop, and I guess they had it that way. But we'll get cleaned up for you."

"It's fine," Linda said. She went back up the hall to her new office and stood looking at the huge steel desk, at the AC ducts. At the dust. Actually, she thought, I don't care. Really. Why *should* I care? She smiled and shook her head. Damn.

"Baby, I'm sorry." Gilbert stood in the doorway. He was usually a chipper-looking and erect big man, but now he was sort of slumped over. "It doesn't look good now, but we'll get everything fixed up fine for you."

"I don't care," Linda said. "Really, it's fine. It's a workplace utopia." Unlike the Justice Estates dystopia, she thought.

"It will be," Gilbert promised. "I'm gonna make this place really nice for you. It's gonna be great."

Linda shrugged. She said, "Okay."

Gilbert looked at Linda for a moment, then stepped forward and kissed her, holding her tight in his big arms. He pushed her back onto the desk. A length of pipe was poking Linda in the butt, and she reached around and pushed it to the floor. A puff of plaster dust swirled around her ankles.

"Gilbert, no," Linda said.

"Sunshine, come on." Gilbert kissed her neck.

"No."

"Last night you said yes, baby."

Linda pushed Gilbert away. "Last night I didn't feel like

arguing," she said. "Tonight, maybe I do."

Gilbert smiled. "I'll make you feel good."

"I'm not interested in feeling good," Linda said. She got off the desk. Gilbert put his big right hand on her rear, but she ignored him, and after a moment it fell away.

"No," Linda said. "We won't fix anything up. We'll just leave it like it is—a dump. The criminals will be impressed."

Gilbert stood dark and frowning. "You know, I don't know what to make of you."

Linda laughed. "Well, goddamn, Gilbert, you never have. So what's new?"

※ ※ ※ ※

Richard drove slowly up a hill, passing blocks of abandoned buildings. He knew this was a bad area—he had seen it on the television news: Crack Alley. The TV reporter had stood at the top of the hill, with the Capital dome shining white over his shoulder, and then the camera panned around and showed some black people walking up the street, their backs to the camera. The implication was that these people were a bunch of crack dealers and hookers and outlaws and threats to society and whatnot, and that the Rapid Response News Team had them on the run. As a prosecutor and a judge Richard had dealt with many people from the Eastside—that is, black people—but he couldn't go along with the TV guy's assertion that *everybody* over here was a crook. Still, he couldn't remember the last time he had gone east of the highway to see things for himself. Had he *ever* gone east of the highway?

"Where're we going?" Richard asked.

"Just up here," Paige said. "I have to see somebody."

"Who?"

"I don't know yet."

Richard frowned but kept on driving. There were a lot of people—black people—sitting on the steps of the buildings, standing around, walking. Richard began to feel a bit apprehensive. He remembered what the TV guy said: threats to society. Outlaws.

"Turn here!" Paige said. "And slow down."

Richard made a left onto a side street, and as he slowed several young black men approached the car from both sides.

"Lock the doors," Paige said.

Richard punched the electric lock and the doors locked with a reassuring clunk. Paige lowered her window a bit.

"Hey," a familiar-looking young black man said. His hair was wild and frizzed, sticking straight up from the top of his head.

"Hey," Paige said. "Where's Shorty?"

There was a bang on the glass by Richard's head and he turned to see a large black man—bearded, red-eyed—glaring back at him. The man made a gesture with his hand: roll down the window. Richard looked away.

"*Shorty?* Ain't seen 'im."

"No?" Paige asked.

"What are we doing here?" Richard asked softly. He knew, though. This was—a drug deal. Damn, he thought. I am buying drugs. He was suddenly a bit scared—and thrilled. He looked at Paige, blinking, half-smiling. A drug deal! What a—woman.

"Why you want Shorty? You lookin'?"

"Maybe," Paige said.

"Say, I got better than Shorty's got! Shorty's got shit."

There was another bang at Richard's window. He turned to see the bearded black man saying something—

"Get in." Paige said. She reached around and unlocked the back door. The young man got in, hair brushing the door frame. To Richard she said, "Get going."

Richard put the car in drive and pulled forward, away from the crowd. The man with the beard—the drug dealer, Richard thought, *damn*—trotted after the car for a few yards before giving up.

"So you got better shit than that shit Shorty's got, huh?" Paige asked.

"Ah, yuh," the boy nodded. "Say, I seen you before, but not him. He a cop?"

Paige laughed. "A cop?"

Richard held onto the wheel with both hands. "Which way do I go?"

"Make a right," Paige said. "You really think he looks like a cop?"

"Naw," the kid said. "He looks like a—a—"

Richard waited. These kids from the Eastside often had very limited experiences in their lives. To the kid, he thought, he probably looked like a school teacher, a bank teller, maybe a lawyer....

"He looks like a barber."

Paige burst out laughing. "A *barber*?"

"Yeah, one of them Spanish barbers, cuts people's hair."

"You know, he *does* look like a barber," Paige said, glancing at Richard, smiling. "You don't look like you've seen one recently, though."

"You don't like—"

"Which way?" Richard asked.

"Left," the kid said. "You don't like my hair?"

"It's charming," Paige said. "I wish I could grow mine out like that—the Barber ought to grow his like that."

"He's ball-headed," the kid observed.

"He ought to try, though," Paige said. "Listen, what's your name?"

"Love," the kid said.

Richard stiffened and glanced into the mirror. Oh! He *was* familiar. Love—that kid. That kid with Ms. Smallwood. Oh shit.

"Hi, Love," Paige said. "I'm Paige, and that's the Barber."

"He's a barber for real?"

"He sure cuts 'em down to size," Paige said.

"That's cool," Love said. "What'd y'all want?"

"A rock," Paige said. "Maybe two."

"Three for fifty," Love said. "That's a good deal. You won't have to come back."

"Do you have twenty dollars?" Paige asked Richard.

There was a stop sign ahead. Richard stopped. He asked, "Which way?"

"Turn right," Paige said. "Do you have twenty dollars?"

Richard turned right. Giselle had opened up a whole world for him, sexually—wet hot damp sweaty gasping heavy-duty fucking, so different from anything he had known before, and now—Paige. Difficult, Linda Smallwood said. Difficult, and dangerous. On a drug deal. It was stupid, but there it was. A different life! Outside the car people stood on the street corners in the hot, heavy evening air, whole lives, whole worlds, so different, so much more—something. So *much* more something.

"Yeah, I guess," Richard said.

"The Barber's cool," Paige said. "He's been cutting some hair, he's good to go."

"Okay," Love said. "You know where you're at?"

In trouble, Richard thought. But—

"No," he said, waiting for directions.

Chapter Nineteen

Dad Always Knew You'd Do Good

GILBERT SAID HE WAS GOING TO THE OFFICE, AND DELIA assumed he meant the convenient location on South Lamar. But when she pulled into the parking lot she did not see his Cadillac, and the office was locked and dark. Delia stared at her reflection in the grimy glass for a moment, and then unlocked the door and went inside.

Delia had been running the DateLine for more than a year now, and she had put her whole life into it, trying to bring people together, trying to make people happy, and now—*now*—the one and only man she wanted for herself was slipping away. It was embarrassing. More than that, it pissed her off. The bright, cheerful colors of her office, an office she'd bragged on as a cross between a party and a preschool, seemed to mock her. Even worse were the poster-sized printings of Dr. Dee's Dating Do's and Dating Don'ts.

DON'T EVER COMPLAIN!
EVER!

Fuck *that*, Delia thought. Bad advice!
Delia sat at her computer, did a quick search, found

a website for Foster Moomaw, and, at the site, found an extension for Linda Smallwood. She dialed the number; no answer, phone not in service, transfer to voice mail.

"Listen, bitch," Delia said. "You go and tell my cheatin' *husband* that he—"

Delia stopped. What was the use? Fuck it. She hung up.

Don't ever complain. Ever.

Bitch.

Outside heat radiated from the pavement, the bricks of the strip mall, the cars, everywhere, hot and smooth, and the sun lit the hazy smoggy hills to the west, gold and warm. Delia got into the Lexus, air conditioner blasting, and drove north, thinking, not complaining, no, but *thinking*, thinking that the time had come to do something. Something. Something.

Do—be ready with a smile.

And a baseball fucking bat, Delia thought.

Ah, Lord.

Gilbert wasn't at the north location, either. It was located just behind a Popeye's Fried Chicken and next to a Korean restaurant, and had a smell that—lingered. Delia could always tell when Gilbert had been working at the north office, he carried home a strange odor of fry grease and kimchi. It occurred to her now, though, that maybe he was just covering that bitch's perfume. Fuck!

Delia blew off checking for Gilbert out at the east office—it was too much trouble, now. She knew he was shacked up with that bitch, that whore. Gilbert couldn't see it, what a whore she was, what a bad influence, a true enemy, couldn't see what she was doing, how she broke his heart the first time and now was back to do it again. Delia drove aimlessly west, crossing the expressway and then turning south through hilly, tree-shaded neighborhoods, fine houses set back from the street, nice cars in the driveways, people watering their green lawns, jogging, walking their dogs, living pleasant, healthy lives—and yet she could only think of Gilbert. Gilbert and that bitch. That bitch had him caught in a trap, and he was too stupid to know it, the fool. She was going to have to be confronted, sometime. Destroyed.

Delia noticed a golf course on her right and realized where she was. She picked up her cell phone and dialed a number.

"Terrie! This is Dee—I've got to talk to you. It's about Gilbert."

Raul braked suddenly to avoid hitting a silver Lexus that turned wildly across the street in front of him, heading into a big, gated apartment complex.

"People should just hang up and drive," he said. "Cell phones are dangerous."

"Oh, I quite agree," Charlie said. "Cell phones—they're just—a menace." Charlie had been drinking beer at the Little Wagon since mid-afternoon, drinking more than usual. When Raul stopped by to look for Paige, the barmaid enlisted him to drive Charlie home.

"So, you haven't seen Paige?" Raul asked again.

"Call her," Charlie said. "Call 'er right up."

"Paige doesn't have a cell phone. She's against people calling her whenever they feel like it."

"Call Linda, then," Charlie said. "Call her and tell her not to take that job. We'll get her a better job. We'll get her something that's reasonable. And accommodating."

They stopped at a light. Raul looked over and saw Charlie fidgeting, tugging at his seat belt.

"I *can't* call her," Raul said. "I don't have a cell phone, either."

"They're horrible things," Charlie said. "Be careful when you cross this bridge down here—it's deadly."

Paige and Richard sat in the darkened car, waiting for Love to return. Paige sat quietly, but Richard was nervous, adjusting his seatbelt, glancing into the rearview mirror, out the side, looking for Love, looking for the cops, for anything, everything.

"Keep your foot off the brake," Paige said.

"Sorry." That was obvious: red lights flashing from the rear of a parked car obviously meant something weird was going on, and in this part of town weird things usually happened for a reason. Richard shifted in his seat, careful to avoid the brake pedal. "What if this Love doesn't come back?"

"He might not," Paige said. "It's been known to happen."

"We could maybe call the cops on him," Richard said. Paige was silent. "That was a joke."

"Just sit still," Paige said.

Richard risked a glance at Paige. Soft light from the street lights filtered in through the leaves of overhanging trees and Paige almost glowed—curved nose, shining hair, smooth smooth cheeks. He wanted to touch her.

"So, you're done this before?" Richard asked. "Only with Shorty?"

"Shorty's made up." Paige smiled. "You come up to these guys and just ask for some crack, they'll think you're a cop. But if you go up looking for somebody—Shorty or Larry or Wayne or whoever—they'll think you're a good customer of somebody else and try to steal away your business."

"Ah," Richard said. He thought, Larry. Wayne. Damn. I probably had them in court, too.

"But, yes—I've done this before." Paige sounded suddenly cross. "Jesus."

"Well, at least one of us knows what's going on."

"Just keep your foot off the brake," Paige said.

Richard sat still, looking in the mirror. A shape—a person—came out of the darkness. Richard tensed but the person passed by. But then a second shape appeared, quickly, and the rear door of the car opened and Love got in.

"Just go," he said.

"Which way?" Richard asked.

"Just go!"

Down the hill from Crack Alley and across the interstate was the Marriott Hotel. There was a sports bar in the basement, a loud place that Gilbert liked, where he could watch two or three games at once and drink and relax. He and Linda sat in front of a television showing a meaningless NFL preseason game, Phoenix at Miami. Gilbert stared up at the TV, details of his face lost in the screen glare. Linda frowned.

"Can't we put one of these things on Court TV?"

"No, baby."

"We can watch *COPS* or something."

"This is a sports bar—you see that guy get hit? Those rookies are hittin' tonight!"

Linda did not turn to look at the hit. Instead she looked down at the table.

"You know, I really don't want to work for you," Linda said. "I changed my mind. I don't want to work at The Justice Store."

Gilbert looked away from the television and studied Linda for a moment. "Well, *shit*," he said, "I'll go find a goddamn bartender to put on goddamn Court TV."

"It's not that," Linda said.

"It's not that." Gilbert frowned. "You just said it was that—you just said you wanted to watch *COPS* or something."

"I can watch *COPS* at home."

"You want to leave?"

"—maybe."

"Maybe," Gilbert repeated. He considered her for a moment, then looked back to the football game. "You're all kinds of trouble tonight."

"I just don't want to work at The Justice Store!"

Gilbert's big shoulders slumped. "Hey, c'mon, I'm trying to watch the goddamn *game*," he said. "I thought we had all this settled."

"So I changed my mind, okay? I don't want to work *anywhere*—it's too damn much trouble."

"Too much trouble."

"And I don't want to be your *girl*friend, or whatever."

"You're more than just a girlfriend."

"That, too," Linda said.

Gilbert smiled. "We have a history together."

"That's the goddamn problem!" Linda lit a cigarette. "You want to know the truth? The only reason I got engaged to you in the first place was because of what people thought. You're this big, black, football-playing lawyer—getting engaged to someone like you is totally ridiculous for someone from my background."

"Yeah?" Gilbert was smiling—how annoying.

"Yeah," Linda said. "I mean, some of the other girls might be *sleeping* with big black men, but no one else was getting *engaged* to one."

Gilbert shook his head and looked back up at the game. "Ah, Baby, you treat me like an object."

"So?" Linda stamped out her cigarette in the ashtray, then pulled another from the pack. She looked at it and frowned. "And then I got rid of you because you were *too* damn outrageous—I made my point by getting engaged to you in the first place. And there was that business about starting a—family."

In moments of honesty Linda knew she hadn't ended her engagement with Gilbert because she'd gotten tired of him or whatever, but because she'd gotten *scared* of him. It had to do with—family. Gilbert wanted children. Linda remembered what being a child was like.

"Aw, you used me," Gilbert said. He laughed. "You're hurting my feelings."

Gilbert didn't look hurt, though. As far as Linda could tell, he was amused. He looked *happy*. How irritating. She looked up at the television: some guy from Phoenix got off a wobbly short punt.

Linda said, "I mean, it's not like I never thought that I

wasn't in *love* with you, you know, that you weren't the love of my goddamn life, or whatever."

Gilbert thought that over. He finally asked, "What?"

"Feelings!" Linda shakily lit the new cigarette and exhaled a tremendous cloud of smoke. "They're goddamned *complicated*!"

Gilbert laughed. "I know that's right!"

A waitress brought over two more bottles of beer. Linda sank back into her seat. The stupid meaningless game was reflected in the lenses of Gilbert's glasses.

"I really do need you at the East location," Gilbert said. "You know that."

"You're not listening to me."

Gilbert laughed again. "Of course I'm listening to you, Sunshine—I'm just not taking you seriously, you know?"

Linda filled her glass with beer, looking first at Gilbert, then at the football game. *COPS* was probably over by now, anyway. Goddamn.

Delia kept the car running, and the air conditioner blew out a thin stream of cool air, but it was not a comfort. She fidgeted behind the wheel, staring always at the townhouse complex across the street.

"You're doing the right thing," her friend Terrie said.

"I want to catch him," Delia said. "I just know he's with that bitch." Delia felt a growing fullness in her chest, almost as if her lungs were congested, as if her blood had suddenly solidified—tight, full, and at the same time distant and dreamlike. "He's not gonna get away with this."

"Huh-*uh*," Terrie said.

Two boys were playing basketball in the driveway across from the complex, and the ball got past one of them and rolled up to the car. The boy who retrieved it stared impassively at the two women before returning to the game.

"Hope they don't go and call the cops on us," Terrie said.

"Sitting out here in a car like this."

"I'll kill him," Delia said. "He can't do this to me."

"He—" Terrie began, but then she realized Delia was talking about Gilbert, not the boy with the basketball. "Well, you might not want to kill *him*," Terrie said. "I mean, it's *her* fault, isn't it?"

"Gilbert never did have any sense."

"Exactly!" Terrie was delighted. "That's why you need to confront the bitch!"

"I'll confront *both* of them," Delia said. Constructive Confrontation, she thought. It might be a good topic for her next Dating Do's and Dating Don'ts column. "Damn."

The two women sat quietly in the car. A man on a bicycle coasted around the corner and up the street.

As Paige predicted, Raul waited until she was fast asleep, and then had taken her new house key off to copy. Now, sweating from his ride back from Charlie's, Raul unlocked the door with his new key and went inside.

"Paige?" he called. No answer. He went upstairs and peered into the empty bedrooms and then came back down again. On the kitchen counter he found a business card: Judge Richard A. Cantu, Travis County Court-at-Law 6-B. Cantu—that fat bald guy at the bar. With the tattooed woman. Both drunk, a pair of bar rats. Paige, though—it was Saturday night and she was probably out somewhere being disrespectful. Or out somewhere in trouble—or on the verge of being in trouble. With the tattooed bitch? Or with the drunk fat bald guy? Or both?

Raul circled through the living room and back to the kitchen. There was nothing unusual except for an empty Diet Dr. Pepper bottle in the trash and the business card—Richard A. Cantu. What did that *A* stand for, anyway? Asshat, alcoholic, adulterer. An asshat alcoholic adulterer taking advantage of Paige.

"Paige?" Raul asked aloud, even though he knew she was gone.

Outside the courtyard was dark. Linda's house was dark. A slight light came from behind the broken slats of Tim's window blind. Raul went over and banged on the door.

"Have you seen Paige?"

"Uh." Tim stood in t-shirt and briefs, wiping his hand. He looked—uncomfortable. "Paige?"

"Where did she go?"

"Go?"

"It's Saturday night—she went somewhere."

"Uh, yeah, I think she said something about the Eastside."

Raul frowned. "The Eastside?" Trouble. Serious trouble.

"That's a nightclub, right? The Eastside Room or something?" Tim asked. "She was with that guy."

"That fat guy?" Raul asked. "That judge?"

"Yeah," Tim said. "I mean, I guess."

Raul turned and went out to the parking lot, to Paige's battered Jaguar. He had a key, of course.

🍸 🍺 🍷

Their room was on the second floor of the motel but still below the elevated express lanes of the highway. Richard peered out the window, looking up at the northbound traffic, and he noticed a billboard: a cheerful smiling blond girl grinning down at him. DAD ALWAYS KNEW YOU'D DO GOOD. Richard suddenly deflated with guilt.

Poor Dad. Richard had always been something of a momma's boy—hard not to be, when your Mom was Boss of the World—but he had fond memories of his father, an accountant, a quiet man who had not only endured the Boss of the World but had taken good care of Richard and his sisters, who had been proud of Richard, and had told him so. The smiling girl on the billboard, it was like she was saying, Boy howdy, have *you* fucked up! Here you are in this creepy motel—with drugs! With a crazy woman who *uses* drugs!

There had been a tall, erect Sikh at the front desk, dark and bearded with a pale blue turban. Paige was waiting out in the car. Richard, still in somewhat of a sweat after the drug deal, wrote *Richard Gutierrez* on the registration form the clerk gave him—the name he always used when getting a room for Giselle. The Sikh looked at it and asked Richard for identification.

"Identification?"

"Driving license," the Sikh said. "Passport?"

"Oh," Richard said. "You always ask for identification? Some other motels—they don't."

"We try to run a responsible and clean establishment."

"Oh, yeah. I see." Richard nervously brought out his drivers' license and handed it to the clerk. He glanced around the lobby. "It *is* very clean here."

After a moment the clerk shook his head. "This, the name, it says Cantu, and on the form you wrote Gutierrez. Those are not the same names."

"Oh, no!" Richard glanced out at the car, Paige sitting looking straight ahead. There are drugs in my car, he thought. Also this woman that I'm not married to. This woman who uses the drugs that are in my car. At least, I think she does. I guess she does. "Wow—no, I guess they're *not* the same names, huh?"

"No."

"Ah—I must've written down my uncle's name instead of mine," Richard said. "I do that sometimes, when I get confused."

The Sikh silently slid a new registration form across to Richard. He filled it out correctly. Dad always knew you'd do good. Right.

"Close those blinds," Paige said sharply.

"Oh, sure." Richard closed the blinds and turned to find Paige standing at the room's sink, in front of the mirror. He watched as she put a tiny white pebble on the end of a glass pipe and applied a lighter. She's smoking crack, he thought, she's smoking crack in a room registered to *my name*. He watched, almost hypnotized. Paige inhaled and dense white smoke shot down the pipe into her—dense smoke, thick, heavy, it seemed to have substance, weight—*life*, even. Damn. Paige kept inhaling. Richard was amazed—her lung capacity, all that white smoke. Where did it all go?

Finally Paige stood holding her breath. She looked at Richard, eyes watering, face flushed, and she sat the pipe gently into an ashtray. She nodded at Richard.

"You okay?" Richard asked. Crack—people *died* from that shit.

Paige exhaled, wisps of smoke trailing out of her mouth and nose—not so thick or heavy as the smoke from the pipe.

"Wow," Paige gasped. She leaned back against the wall and closed her eyes. "Whew!"

"Are you okay?" Richard took a step toward her.

Paige pushed by him and sat on the bed and fell backwards. "Wow," she said again. "You need to try this."

"I don't know," Richard said.

Paige closed her eyes. Richard felt uncomfortable just staring at her, so he went over to the television and turned it on. People were yelling at each other on Fox News. He looked at the TV while trying to concentrate on Paige. He wondered, What if she dies?

After a while Paige sat up. "You need to try this."

"Maybe some other time."

Paige got off the bed and stepped back to the sink. She lifted the lighter to the pipe and more smoke came out, not so thick this time but still impressive and startlingly white. All that smoke, he thought, from that little rock.

Paige gently placed the pipe back in the ashtray and took two quick steps over to Richard. Before he knew what was up she grabbed his face and placed her lips against his—not kissing, exactly, but blowing, breathing, passing smoke—

Paige pulled back. "Breathe," she said with clenched teeth. "*Inhale.*"

Again her mouth was on his. Richard tried to breath, tried to slowly inhale, but he was so conscious of Paige—wet soft lips, sweet scent, warm warm warm so warm—that he wasn't sure if any of the smoke was getting in. And what if it did? What if I become an addict? he wondered. What if I die? A dead addict in a motel, Jesus.

Richard took a step backward and sat on the bed. He sort of pulled Paige with him—her breasts just above eye-level, his hands still on her hips. His heart was racing. Paige, or the drug? Did it make a difference? Oh Lord! I am going to be an addict, he thought wildly. A dead addict. Dad always knew I'd do good.

🍺 🍸 🍷 🍷

Tim stood silently in the dark, smoking a joint, almost ashamed. He hadn't really meant to nark on Paige but yet—he had. He hadn't been able to come up with a good lie to tell Raul—the business about the Eastside had just sort of tumbled out of his mouth almost involuntarily. Raul tricked me, he thought. Poor Paige. Goddamn Raul. Tim had been around the night that Raul had thrown her bed down the embankment onto the expressway. Paige followed Raul out as far as the parking lot, half-naked, screaming at him to stop, and then the police arrived, then Raul's father—what a mess. Poor Paige. Tim thought that he had been in love with her a little bit, just after they had slept together for the third time. But Paige seemed unaware or unconcerned with his tender feelings and had always treated him like a friend. A good friend. Now Linda was in his life, maybe, and now he'd gotten Paige—her friend, his friend—in trouble. What the fuck.

A car pulled into the parking lot, a wide car with bright headlights. He heard a voice—Linda.

"Goddamn, Gilbert, you're still not listening to me!"

"Oh, I'm listening." A deep voice. That Gilbert guy. The adulterer. The greedy bastard, he probably had a huge penis, too. Why wasn't he at home using it on his wife? Tim hurried out to the parking lot.

"Well, you're still not taking me seriously."

"That's right."

They were looking at each other over the hood of the Cadillac. Tim walked up between them and looked from Linda to Gilbert and back to Linda.

"Listen," Tim said, "I think I might've done something wrong."

"You *think*," Linda said. She looked at him with distaste. It hurt, the way she looked at him. "Why should I care what you *think*?"

Gilbert laughed. "You don't care what anybody thinks."

"No, that's right, I don't! Not any more I don't!"

"No," Tim said, "I'm serious—"

"So am I." Linda headed up the sidewalk to the courtyard.

"No," Tim said. "It's about Paige."

Delia put her car in drive and was about to swoop down on them—like an angel, she thought, I am a powerful angry avenging angel—when she saw Gilbert and that bitch get back into the Cadillac. The fat car started and backed unsteadily out into the street.

"Where do you think they're going?" Delia asked.

Terrie shrugged. "We can follow, I guess."

Delia took her foot off the brake and sped down the narrow street until she was just behind Gilbert's car.

"Are you gonna pull 'em over?" Terrie asked.

"Let's see where they go."

"This is gonna be good!" Terrie said happily. Delia looked sharply at her and the smile faded. Terrie said, "No, really, you're doing the right thing."

Paige went into the bathroom and shut the door. Richard could hear water running. Paige, he thought. Damn. Richard stood next to the sink, looking down at the ashtray. There were still two—rocks—left. I am going to become a drug addict, he thought. Oh well! He picked up the pipe: there was a brownish resin in it. He lit the lighter and tried to inhale, but there was only the faintest wisp of smoke. Still, his heart raced. Drug addict!

"You're doing that all wrong," Paige said.

Concentrating on the crack he hadn't even heard her open the door. Paige looked fresh and lovely, her face a little red, maybe, and eyes dilated, but lovely. "The pipe has to cool down. You need to let it rest."

"Oh—okay." Richard felt a sudden pang of regret. No crack for now. He suddenly *wanted* some. "Okay."

Paige took the pipe from his hand and then—kissed him. No sharing smoke now—a kiss, deep, warm, wet. Like on the bed at that Tim kid's place—except that was play, sort of, Paige bouncing on the bed, grinning, and this was—serious. Real. A real kiss. His heart thumped harder. I am going to *die* tonight, he thought. Oh well!

"This is—like a fantasy," Richard gasped.

"Don't ruin it by talking," Paige said softly.

They stumbled toward the bed, Paige dropping her clothes to the floor but Richard—heart thumping—pausing to place his pants, shirt and underwear more or less neatly onto the desk by the television. Paige laughed at him—so nervous and yet so neat—and laughed again as she reached down to grab his cock.

"Good lord!" Paige said. "Your poor wife!"

Richard asked, "Who's talking now?"

🥃 🍸 🍺 🍷

"We'll just let her know about the Raul situation and then leave," Linda said.

"And have a drink," Gilbert added.

"No—I'm not hanging out there." Linda punched buttons on her cell phone, calling the motel again.

237

"They'll have a TV," Gilbert said. "You can watch *COPS*."

"*COPS* is over by now—we missed it," Linda said. The room phone was ringing but no one was answering. "It just *irks* me when people don't answer their damn phone."

"Yeah, me too." Gilbert glanced over at Linda: she was frowning, looking out at the baseball stadium, clutching the big cell phone. A few blocks ahead the motel's sign flashed yellow through the trees. "Cheer up, baby."

"And I'm *not* going to work at the Justice Store."

"Maybe get some sleep," Gilbert said. "You'll feel better in the morning and change your mind back again."

"*Morning*?" Linda asked. "What—"

Suddenly a silver car appeared to their left—horn honking, lights flashing.

"Drunks," Linda said. "Goddamn road-ragers."

Gilbert hit his brakes and the Lexus shot ahead. Gilbert pulled over to the side of the frontage road. The Lexus lurched to a stop and then reversed toward them.

"It's Delia," Gilbert said.

Delia got out of her car and stood tall with her hands on her hips, glaring.

"That's your *wife*?" Linda asked, impressed. Linda had never really seen Delia before and had always imagined her as some sort of gross fat woman. Now, standing in the headlights of her husband's car, Delia looked—majestic, and dramatic. "Damn!"

"Stay here," Gilbert said. He got out and shut the door. Delia—the big woman—his goddamn *wife*—stood motionless like a great patient she-bear while Gilbert approached. Linda could see Gilbert say something—Delia reply—arguing—but she couldn't hear anything. Damn! She punched the redial on her cell phone, calling Paige's room again, but there was still no answer. Irksome. Gilbert and Delia were waving their arms. It was like watching a muted television—no, Linda decided, it wasn't—watching a TV would be comfortable, and comforting, and she'd have a drink, and she wouldn't be watching Gilbert and his big wife argue, she'd be watching something good—*NYPD Blue, CSI, The Wire, Homicide, The Sopranos, COPS—*

A dark, sporty-looking car swerved by them, horn blasting. The left taillight was broken, covered with red plastic tape. Paige's Jaguar? Shit!

Linda dialed Quincy's number. When he answered, she said, "Hey, help! I really need some help here!"

🍶 🍷 🍺 🍸

Outside, Delia said, "I been following you all night."

"So?" Gilbert asked. He wondered how long all night meant. "I was just showing a new attorney the office."

"I bet you were showing her the office—yeah, and here's a motel just up the road?"

"Aw, fuck," Gilbert said. "There's always a lot of motels just up the road."

"Uh-huh, that's something you'd know about."

Gilbert was at a loss. Busted. And he really hadn't done anything wrong, either. At least, tonight he hadn't. Yet. He looked back at his car, at Linda. She was just sitting there, talking on the cell phone as if nothing was going on. Maybe she really *didn't* care about anything. Crazy girl.

"Out all night last night—at that motel, I suppose!"

Gilbert looked back at Delia, hurt. "Fuck no, I wasn't out all night last night—I was with you!"

Delia thought for a moment. "Well, the night before, then," she said. "Does it make a goddamn difference?"

"I—"

"Sleeping all day when you should be working—"

"Oh, hell, I've got something big goin' on."

"Yeah, I see that!" Delia pointed at Linda. "Something big keeping you up all night, keeping you from home, keeping you from working."

"I've *been* working."

"Working behind my back!"

Linda got out of the Cadillac.

"Bitch, you stay away from my husband!"

"I don't *want* your husband," Linda said. She could see the yellow lights of the motel sign seven or ten blocks up the frontage road. Quincy said he would look for her walking north. But first she had to get around Delia. Linda backed into the stadium parking lot, hoping to circle wide around.

"I said, stay away from my husband!"

"I don't want your goddamn husband—okay?"

Delia took a step toward Linda but Gilbert grabbed her arm. Delia broke away and slapped at him, knocking his glasses to the ground.

Linda hurried up the road. She said, "Y'all are *crazy!*"

🥃 🍸 🍺 🍷

There was a bang at the door. Richard sat up. Paige jumped for the bathroom.

"Police!" a voice from behind the door yelled. "Open up! Police!"

"Shit," Richard said.

"Hold 'em off," Paige said. "Don't let 'em in."

"Police! Open up!" More banging.

In the bathroom Paige flushed the remaining rock away. Then she tried to smash the glass pipe so that it would flush, but when it shattered it gashed the palm of her hand.

"Damn!"

Richard stood naked, slick with sweat, looking from Paige to the door and back again. "Are you okay?"

"No—talk to them! But don't open the door." Paige flushed the broken pieces of the crack pipe, leaving bloody handprints on the toilet.

Richard stepped over to the door. He cleared his throat. "Yes?"

"Police! Open up or I'll kick the fucking door in!"

Richard thought about it, then opened the door an inch. "Where's your warrant?"

Raul pushed past him into the room. "Where's Paige?"

"You're not the police."

"Get the fuck out of here!" Paige shouted.

Raul saw Paige—saw the blood—and spun around and punched Richard in the mouth. Richard sat on the bed. Paige leaped from the bathroom onto Raul's back, swatting him around the ears, but he easily tossed her over his shoulder onto the bed. She was screaming. Richard lurched up and pushed Raul away—Raul punched him on the forehead, knocking him back a step, but he shoved Raul again, shoved him into the television and the dresser. Paige was screaming, "Get out! Get out! Get the fuck out!" Raul spotted Richard's stuff on the desk—pants, underwear, shirt, billfold, keys—and grabbed it all and took off running.

🍸🍺🍷

Quincy's black cab pulled slowly into the motel's cramped parking lot.

"Room 218—I think," Linda said.

"Over there?" Quincy pointed toward the end of the building.

"Shit!" Linda spotted the green Jaguar parked next to the staircase. "Can you come with me?"

As they got out of the car a door above them burst open and Raul staggered out onto the walkway. He was running for the stairs. A naked fat man—Richard Cantu, Linda realized, damn!—ran up and hit Raul on the shoulders with both fists. Raul stumbled forward, banging against the railing, and two sets of keys fell from his hand, sparkling in the air before they hit the ground. Raul pounded down the stairs.

"Raul!" Linda yelled. "Stop!"

"Fuck you," Raul gasped.

Richard—my God, Linda thought, the Judge, naked, look at him!—came charging down the stairs after Raul but tripped on the next-to-last step and fell forward, banging against the hood of Quincy's cab.

"I'll kill you!" Richard gasped. "Motherfucker! I'll *kill*

your fucking ass!"

"Goddamn!" Quincy looked over at Linda, laughing. "He is naked, and we see his shame!"

Linda yelled, "Hey! Judge! Get in the car!"

But Richard ignored Linda. He pushed up from the cab and started off across the parking lot—barefoot, naked—chasing after Raul.

"Get those keys," Linda said to Quincy. She headed up the stairs two at a time and ran down the banging metal walkway to the room.

Paige was stumbling around naked apparently trying to find her clothes. She looked up and saw Linda. "It was Raul!" she said. "Did you see him? That son of a fucking bitch!"

"Let's get out of here before somebody calls the cops," Linda said. "You can get dressed in the car."

Paige was pulling a black thong over her hips. She asked, "Where are my shoes?"

"Forget the shoes," Linda said. "Is everything else gone? *Everything*?"

"Yeah—I think." Paige ran a bloody hand through her hair, distracted. "I guess."

"Then let's go!" Linda scooped up Paige's blouse and jeans and pushed her toward the door.

Outside Quincy stood by his cab. He took a long look at Paige, half-naked, but there was nothing shameful about the way *she* looked. He said, "We better go before the damn cops get here."

Paige saw the Jaguar. "My car!"

"Let it get towed," Linda said. "We'll get it later." She pushed Paige into the back seat of the taxi.

"I got those keys," Quincy said. He fastened his seatbelt, looking at Paige in the rearview mirror.

"Let's go!" Linda ordered.

"That son of a bitch Raul," Paige said. "I'm going to make him *pay* for this."

"Let's go find them," Linda said to Quincy. She leaned up over the front seat. "We need to go find those guys before the police do."

"That-son-of-a-bitch!" Paige smacked the seat behind Quincy's head with every word.

"Watch that goddamn blood," Quincy said.

"Find them!"

"Got goddamn blood all over the back of my car." Quincy turned the car around and pulled onto the frontage road. "I have to get this piece a shit inspected next week, you know?"

They drove north, slowly, past a porn shop and a topless bar. A pickup truck sped past them, honking, and Paige laughed.

"Human fucking drama!" She shook her head. "Did you *see* him?"

"Put your blouse on," Linda said. She looked over at Quincy. "And you—keep your eyes on the road."

"Shit," Quincy said. "I'm driving fine."

"There he is!" Linda leaned up over the seat and pointed. A naked fat man was stumbling past the pumps of a gas station—Richard. Quincy caught up to him and Linda leaned out the window.

"Get in the car!"

"Fucker's got my clothes," Richard wheezed.

"Forget your clothes—get in the car!"

"No—no, there he is!" Richard stumbled forward, belly bouncing, cock flopping, people at the gas station staring.

Quincy spotted Raul at the far side of a strip mall parking lot, next to a grocery store. He punched the gas and made it through a yellow light and on up to the store. Raul saw them and stuffed a bundle—Richard's clothes—into a blue mailbox and then took off running around the corner of the store. Quincy stopped by the mailbox.

Linda looked out the back of the cab. Richard was hobbling toward them. Even from a distance he looked horrible—fat bloody lip from Raul's punch, scraped shoulder from the cab's grill, feet cut and bleeding. And that belly— and that penis. Good Lord.

"Get in the car!"

"Fuck you," Richard said. He opened the mail slot and tried fitting his arm through it. "I want my clothes."

"C'mon, get in the goddamn car."

"They patrol this lot," Quincy said quietly. "Security guys, cops. They got cameras here, too."

"Fucking Raul!" Paige smacked the back of the seat again. "I'll kill him!"

"Judge, c'mon, get in the car."

Quincy, watching in the mirror, saw a police car pull into the lot. "Cops here," he said. "We goin."

"Get in the car," Linda ordered one last time. Richard didn't even look up: he was still fumbling with the mailbox, trying to somehow fit his arm into it. The cab pulled away and was on the far side of the parking lot when the police car's blue-and-red lights lit up.

Chapter Twenty

I Will Help You

Blind Drunk Justice? It's the Naked Truth

by Wes Leonard—This is a city that always enjoys nakedness and near-nakedness. We have happy half-naked swimmers at Barton Springs and full-naked swimmers at Hippy Hollow. We've seen topless joggers from time to time. We have topless clubs and bottomless clubs and naked bongo-playing movie stars. A few years ago we even had a naked football player running crazed through the streets.

But a naked judge?

Yep.

Judge Richard A. Cantu, of Travis County Court-at-Law 6-B, was arrested early last Sunday morning on charges of indecent exposure, public intoxication and resisting arrest. The cops nabbed the nude dude at, of all places, a Central Austin strip mall (yeah, strip mall, go ahead and make up your own joke).

"Judge Cantu is the victim of a cruel practical joke gone horribly wrong," says Judge Cantu's attorney, Gilbert Hardison. "We're going to clear everything up in a few days. Judge Cantu is the victim here and I will help him clear his name."

(Hardison of course is being investigated for his "acquisition" of historic Beitleman Ranch in southwest Travis County. Do we prefer our members of the bar naked or unethical? Unless they look like they've stepped out of a *Playboy* centerfold or off the cover of *Men's Fitness*, I vote for unethical).

Still, Hardison said that Cantu would resign this Friday.

"He needs to concentrate on getting his life back together," Hardison said.

That's no reason to end our fun, though. I used The Honorable Judge Naked as an excuse to drop in at the Rip Stop, a topless club out on Bastrop Highway, to see what some professional naked people had to say.

"You know, I bet he's naked all the time," dancer Candy Woolfolk says with admiration. "Under those robes? I bet he's naked, and I'll bet it makes him really, really happy."

Dancer Star Garcia said she once saw Judge Cantu in court. "He was kind of fat," she says, "and he kept staring at the tattoo on my chest. I don't know if I'd like to see him naked or not." Star wouldn't say why she was in court, but she did add, "It does makes me feel a lot better knowing he's some kind of freak."

Hey, it makes us all feel a lot better.

🍺🍸🍷🍶

Dusk on Sixth Street, and though the night was young, people were busy passing from one club to another in groups, music spilling from open doors, bands unloading equipment from station wagons and vans, beer trucks making deliveries, kids in cars cruising slowly along, looking, looking. Gilbert Hardsion noticed that the Judge was limping a little.

"Your feet still hurting?" Gilbert asked.

"I'm all right," Richard said.

"C'mon, Judge, let's go in here sit and sit down." Gilbert pulled Richard into a bar and they sat on stools near the door. "Give those dogs a break."

Gilbert watched closely as Richard pulled a University of Texas baseball cap down over his eyes and sipped listlessly at a glass of beer. He had seldom had a more depressed client; even men facing long prison terms could sometimes look at the brighter side of things, occasionally, or at least ignore or deny the negative trend of their lives, projecting an empty bravado. Richard Cantu just moped, though. He was depressed, and depressing. Gilbert had gone so far as to offer Richard Linda's position at the convenient location on East Seventh; it would give the poor guy something to do, and Gilbert could deduct Richard's legal bills from his salary. At any rate, Linda had not been returning his phone calls and might actually be serious about not wanting to work at The Justice Store—though if she changed her mind he could still fit her in somewhere else. Or maybe she could share an office with Richard. That might be good.

"A few years from now you'll be making more money than you ever figured on," Gilbert said. "Get rid of that Buick, get yourself a Lexus. Get yourself a house out in Justice Estates, maybe Circle C—"

Richard wasn't paying attention. He was staring glumly at his reflection in the mirror behind the bar. He took his baseball cap off and looked at it, then put it back on—backwards, like a college kid, the bill covering his neck—and nodded at himself.

"A great big fucking house," Gilbert said.

"I don't *want* a house out at Circle C," Richard said suddenly. What would he do with a house way out there on the edge of town? Kelly had taken the kids and gone back to Houston—maybe for good. Maybe for the best, too. Who needed a house? "Maybe I want a loft downtown."

"A loft!" Gilbert said. "Now, there you go—you'll be close

to the bars, you can go looking for chicks. Shit, you'll have it goin' on! You'll have the power!"

Richard looked a little happier thinking about his loft downtown. "Let's go," Gilbert said, finishing his beer. Outside he marveled at all the young girls, all the young flesh, firm bosoms, flat bellies, jeans riding low low low on swaying hips.

"Look!" Richard pointed at a girl with a tattoo on her butt, some sort of spastic Chinese dragon crawling out of her jeans and up her lumbar. "I want one of those."

Gilbert chuckled. "I know *that's* right."

"No," Richard said. "Not the girl. The tattoo."

"What?"

"A tattoo—it's time I got a tattoo." Richard looked around. There was a tattoo shop down the block and across the street, over a piano bar. Richard hobbled toward it. "I always wanted a tattoo," he said. He thought of Kelly and shook his head. "I just never did it."

Gilbert followed Richard up the stairs to the tattoo parlor. The walls were covered with intricate designs and several young people—tattooed, pierced—were standing around considering them.

"There's what I want," Richard said. "Right on my forearm." He pointed to an image of a blind justice. "Except I'd like the scales a little more tilted to one side." He looked at the guy behind the counter. "Can you do that?"

"Sure." The guy behind the counter had a pair of big stainless steel loops hanging from his nose and what looked like a ¾ inch piece of dowel rod stuck in his ear

"Jesus Christ," Gilbert said. "I'm not going to wait around this place while you get that thing put on your arm."

"Wait downstairs then." Richard looked up at Gilbert, and Gilbert was touched by the childlike look of trust in Richard's brown eyes. What happened to the depression?

"What the hell," Gilbert said. He went back down the stairs. More people were milling around—girls, boys, old folks looking lost, mounted police on big horses trotting by. A line of taxis stretched up the block at the cabstand. Music came from the piano bar beneath the tattoo parlor. Gilbert noticed one of the cab drivers—a familiar-looking black guy, wiry, with bloodshot eyes—staring at him. Staring. *Glaring.* The driver was pissed about something. Gilbert looked back at him, trying to place the face but failing. The driver opened his mouth and said something.

"—let not the rich man glory in his riches."

Gilbert couldn't quite hear him—traffic on the street and music from the bar rode over what the driver was saying. Gilbert took a step closer. He asked, "What?"

"He who oppresses the poor to increase his riches shall surely come to *want*."

Gilbert backed away from the cab, then quickly turned and headed toward the piano bar for a drink. He said, "Fucking nut."

The stitches in her hand kept Paige from playing tennis or lifting weights, so she ran. Raul had disappeared, and for several days Paige felt a pleasant sense of freedom. She ran, she read, she rested. She even printed out part of her long-neglected—abandoned—dissertation on the influence of Scottish Common-Sense philosophers on Thomas Jefferson and showed it to Roy Weston. While at the bar with Roy, Charlie Bessent and Linda came in and joined them. Neither one of them had heard from Raul. The feeling of freedom faded. Paige grew worried.

Then, coming home from a run, Paige found Raul sitting outside her door in the late afternoon shadow, smoking a cigarette.

"What do you want?" Paige asked.

"To see you," Raul said.

"Well, you've seen me—now go away."

Raul stood up. He was filthy—hair matted, face smeared with dirt. Maybe he had been gardening, Paige thought. That was the most positive possibility.

"Have you been hanging around the park?" she asked.

"I've been staying with my parents."

"Which is right next to the park." Paige stepped around him and fitted a key into her new lock. She opened the door. "Take off your shoes and then get in there and take a shower."

Hot and sweaty as she was, Paige didn't want filthy Raul to touch anything in her home. While he showered she sipped at a glass of chilled white wine and vacuumed the carpet where Raul had walked in his dirty socks. She just hoped that he would remember to use the guest towels.

🍺🍷🍸🍹

Linda looked out Madame Bustos's window and watched a tow truck driver in the parking lot across the street hitch up a car and prepare to take it away. That reminded her—the Suburban. She needed to get it. Those storage fees were steep and were getting steeper.

Madame Bustos shook her head. "I don't see anything different in your life."

"What?"

"No changes in your—situation."

"What the hell," Linda said. "That enemy I had sort of self-destructed, and—"

"No, the bad influence is still present."

"—and I made a whole shitload of decisions."

"No." Madame Bustos continued to shake her head. "No, the crucial decisions are yet to be made."

"Well, hell," Linda said. "I thought everything was all set up for the next forty years or so. I thought I could just relax and watch TV."

"No."

Linda sighed. The room was dim, lit only by a few flickering candles. Madame Bustos was gazing at the stones with a look of slight amusement on her face. How annoying. Outside the tow truck's yellow lights began flashing as it towed the car from the parking lot.

"I need to go get my truck," Linda said.

"That would be a positive decision," Madame Bustos said. "But it is not the *crucial* decision."

"Whatever," Linda grumbled. She sighed again. It was useless—the non-advice of Madame Bustos, her own life, everything. What a goddamn chore.

Outside Tim was sitting in his battered Monte Carlo under the grackle-filled trees. Linda got into the car and shut the door.

"Well, that was a waste of time."

"I'm sorry," Tim said.

Linda tried to avoid looking at Tim. So far she had managed to deflect his half-hearted, timid attempts at seduction, but the time seemed to be coming when she would have to decide—there was that damn word again, *decide*, goddamn, decide decide decide decide—whether clean dishes and a vacuumed floor was worth—*It*. With him. But, hell, maybe this was the damn decision that Madame Bustos was so excited about. Sex with Tim! Good lord.

"Is this all I have to look forward to?" she asked aloud.

"What?"

"I need to go get my truck," Linda said. "It's over off Slaughter Lane by the railroad tracks."

"It can wait, if you want," Tim said. "I kind of like driving you around."

"You're sweet." Linda stared straight ahead and sighed. "But no."

The complex was mostly dark when Linda got home. Tim's car was in the lot, and a glint of light came from behind his blinds. All the other windows were dark, though, even Paige's. Good. She didn't feel like talking to anyone, and had taken much longer than usual to get home, driving her dirty black Suburban up back streets and lingering at the grocery store, taking her time shopping, picking up two bottles of merlot, a big steak, and a can of peas, hoping that people would leave her alone to eat in peace. But as she walked up the path to her townhouse, she saw something glimmering on her doorstep—a birdcage. Another one of Tim's futile traps, she thought.

But when she got closer she found two little birds in the cage, two new monk parakeets, sleepy in the dark, swaying on their little swings. And an envelope.

"Gilbert," she said aloud.

Linda sat her groceries on the concrete and reached inside the cage. The birds—That One New Bird, Linda decided, and That Other New Bird—flopped around a little bit but she was able to grasp the envelope and pull it out. There was something chunky inside. She opened it.

Pearls.

"Goddamn," Linda said. "You son of a bitch."

A heavy string of lumpy natural pearls glistened under her porch light. There was a note, too.

> My Sunshine,
> We finished painting your office at the Justice Store and got the air conditioning put in. It's ready when you want it. I love you. I will help you!
> — G.

"You son of a bitch," Linda said again. *Love!* Good lord. How complicated. Just like Gilbert to complicate things. She looked at the pearls in her hand and wondered if there was some legal issue there, some sort of contract implied in accepting them, and quickly decided—No. *Hell* no.

Linda clasped the pearls around her neck and was satisfied with their weight. Finally, the damn pearls. Now

Gilbert needed to get her some chocolates, or some roses, or something. *Love,* after all. Help, too. She unlocked the door and picked up the groceries and then stood regarding the new birds. She felt half-temped to set them loose, to send them off to keep That One Bird company—That Original One Bird. They could start a new commune, maybe. But what the hell.

"You guys can come in if you don't die or anything," Linda said. "I've got enough messes as it is."

Epilogue

From the *Austin American-Statesman*:

> The Travis County Commissioners Court Wednesday selected Austin criminal-defense attorney Linda Smallwood to fill the vacant judgeship at Travis County Court-at-Law 6-B.
>
> Smallwood is a former associate at the law firm of Foster Moomaw. She replaces Richard A. Cantu, who resigned August 6th after being arrested and charged with public intoxication and indecent exposure....

About That Demon Life

I STARTED *THAT DEMON LIFE* IN THE FALL OF 1998, when I was the Dobie-Paisano Fellow. As part of the fellowship, I got to live at Paisano Ranch, the former property of old Texas writer J. Frank Dobie west of Austin, and it was beautiful and quiet and isolated—a good place to concentrate on my writing. Before I got the fellowship I'd been working as a cab driver, an exhausting and enervating way to make a living, and when the six-month fellowship was over I took my manuscript-in-progress and went back to the cab.

 Most of this book was actually written after the fellowship in the cab, between passengers. I drove nights most of the time, and I would start my shift out at the airport, waiting in the cab line. It would usually take about 45 minutes or so of waiting to get to the front of the line and get a passenger—plenty of time to do some writing. Later, when the airport shut down, I'd park in various parts of central or south Austin and wait for a call. More time to write. You can see the influence of the cab in the text of the novel itself—all those little short sub-chapters show where I had to stop writing and drive someone someplace and make some money. (I really fell in love with the pace of the short chapter-subchapter structure—you'll find them in all my subsequent books).

The novel took about three years to write, and about six years to find a publisher. (When I mention that to people, they are sometimes daunted by that vast-seeming expanse of time—nine whole years! But I tell them that if writing teaches you nothing else, it teaches you patience). *That Demon Life* was turned down by publishers and agents at least 60 times. But I believed in it and kept sending it out, and eventually the great John Domini, judging for the Gival Press Novel Prize, pulled it out of the stack and understood what I was trying to do. (Thanks, John and Robert!)

My main inspiration for this novel was/is Austin, Texas—the life I lived there, the lives I witnessed there. I wanted to write something that would reflect the craziness and ridiculousness and ongoing dislocation of the city and of the people who live in it. On a technical level, I had two literary models: *A Confederacy of Dunces,* by John Kennedy Toole, and "The Flea Circus," the opening novella in Billy Lee Brammer's *The Gay Place*. I've always loved Toole's ability to handle plot and setting, and to interrogate American society through the point of view of the magnificent Ignatius J. Reilly. "The Flea Circus" depicts Austin political and social life of the early 1960s, and when I first read it, in 1979, there were still echoes of that earlier time floating around—I could hang around and look at the buildings, the sky, listen to the people around me, and I could feel the rhythms of that book and that city and that time.

If you go back to the front pages of this book, you'll see the epigraphs. The first epigraph is from the Rolling Stones and is where the book's title comes from—"Sway," one of my all-time favorite songs. I remember back in 1977 or so when I was hanging with some ne'er-do-well friends and I pompously said that I wanted to write a book that sounded like "Sway." So—here it is, and I hope it does.

The second epigraph is by our old friend J. Frank Dobie, of the Dobie-Paisano Fellowship. The quote is his reaction to

Brammer's *The Gay Place*. I'm guessing that he didn't like it! When I came across the quote, I was living at Paisano, and I had just started on *That Demon Life*, and even though I was only in the first chapter or so, I knew where the book was heading, and I thought—yeah, okay, J. Frank, just you wait....

LMW

Acknowledgments

MANY FRIENDS HELPED MAKE THIS BOOK HAPPEN!
Thank you to Andrea Bates, Patricia Bjorklund, Pamela Booton, Abigail Bowers, Florence Davies, John Domini, Alan Gingras, Robert Giron, Jason Marc Harris, Alysa Hayes, Wende Hilsenrod, Kathryn Lane, Erika Liesman, Teri Sink, Chuck Taylor, Javier Booton, Diane Wilson. Also: Alex, Dakota, Rudy, Grady, Walter, and Vernon.

I'd especially like to thank the University of Texas at Austin and the Texas Institute of Letters for their support through the Dobie-Paisano Fellowship—and, of course, thanks to the late Dr. Audrey Slate for all her many kindnesses.

About Lowell Mick White

LOWELL MICK WHITE IS THE AUTHOR OF SEVEN BOOKS: *That Demon Life, Long Time Ago Good, Professed, Burnt House, The Messes We Make of Our Lives, Normal Schoo*l, and *Answers Without Questions*. A winner of the Dobie-Paisano Fellowship and a member of the Texas Institute of Letters, White received his PhD from Texas A&M University.

Contact Lowell Mick White at www.lowellmickwhite.com

Recent Books from

ALAMO BAY PRESS

To Those Born Later: Selected Poems, 2017-2020
by Ken Fontenot

Forty Years at Paisano: A Literary History
by Audrey Slate

Answers Without Questions: Conversations about Writing and Creativity
by Lowell Mick White

Broken to Mend: Poems
by Ricardo Tane Ward-Ramirez

For more information, contact Alamo Bay Press

www.alamobaypress.com

Printed in the USA
CPSIA information can be obtained
at www.ICGtesting.com
LVHW090045201024
794167LV00006B/557